ROMANOV

Also by Samaire Provost

Mad World: EPIDEMIC

Mad World: SANCTUARY

Mad World: DESPERATION

ROMANOV

Samaire Provost

Black Raven Books

This is a work of fiction. All of the characters, organizations, and events portrayed in this novel are either products of the author's imagination or are used fictitiously.

Black Raven Books

The text was set in 12-point Californian FB

www.BlackRavenBooks.net

ISBN-13: 978-1-948594-08-0
ISBN-10: 1-948594-08-0

First Edition: January 2018

10 9 8 7 6 5 4 3 2 1

For Tyrion, the inspiration for Jinx and Gypsy, and the best owner a person could ever have.

Special thanks to Eric Goldman, who lent me his name.

Yesterday upon the stair

I met a man who wasn't there

He wasn't there again today

I wish, I wish he'd go away

- William Hughes Mearns

"Dark thoughts are most comfortable in the company of dark deeds."

ROMANOV

AMBUSHED

Anna was trapped. Crouched up on the wall in the corner of the room, defying gravity, surrounded by a dozen vampires leering up at her, she considered her situation.

In the opposite corner of the room, her enemy sat in an ornate burgundy and gold velvet chair, crossed legs clad in elegant trousers, smiling as he drank deeply from his goblet. Thick crimson fluid, just recently drained from the catatonic socialite slumped on the bathroom floor, glinted off the rim of his cup, and at the corners of his mouth. He grinned at her, half-drunk with the heroin and alcohol content in the blood, and threw his head back, laughing.

"It will all be over soon. He'll be here in a minute, and then he will die. And then you will die, my sweet." He took another sip of the fluid and closed his eyes in ecstasy, head tilting back and hand holding the goblet drifting off to the side.

Narrowing her eyes at his henchmen, Anna jumped back and forth from wall to wall, at one point moving faster than the naked eye could follow. Dressed all in black leather in slim pants, laced-up knee-high boots, and jacket trimmed snug to her body to allow no margin for error when she wanted to move fast, Anna flitted from one corner to another like a trapped bird, trying to get to the door.

But every time, they jumped with her, blocking her. The one time she made it as far as the door, in the time it took to reach for the doorknob and open it; they were there, slamming her back with superhuman strength, grabbing her, manhandling her, forcing her back to the far corner. She made a noise of frustration bordering on panic as her mind raced.

"Give it up, Anna. I will not let you go, not now, not ever." Grigori drained the last of the blood from the cup and set it down, then stood. Shivering at the drugs flooding his system, a rapturous look in his eyes, he smiled at her.

"Look how good it is here in America," he said. He pronounced "America" with a thick eastern European accent, *Ah-mer-ee-ka*. "Back in Mother Russia, most addicts I tried were sick, dirty, and poor. Now in Manhattan, I find myself surrounded by wealthy socialites willing to do anything to climb the ladder." He threw his head back at the thought and laughed in delight.

Anna, crouching upside-down on the ceiling in the

corner of the room, silently agreed with him: It was a stupid system. Oh, it worked, when you were just dealing with humans, people who were playing the game with clearly defined rules. But add vampires to the mix and you had something entirely different. A game the humans had no idea they were playing. A game of intense manipulation and power. A game Grigori was winning.

"Anna, Anna, Anna. Why do you care so much for these animals?" He smirked at her. "They are nothing. Something to crush under our boots as we dominate them. Pretty pets, food we eat. Nothing else." His steps took him right up to her, nose to nose. She looked down at him from her perch up on the wall and scowled. His stooges laughed around them.

Anna spat at his feet and glared at him. Talking would do no good. Grigori had been insane for nearly a century.

Suddenly, the door flew open with a blast and a whirling dark cloak entered the room, almost too fast to see. Head swinging around, Grigori leapt up to meet the new threat, and caught him as he tried to strike.

"Nikolai, how good of you to join us." Grigori said with a hearty laugh.

Nick took one look at the scene and roared in anguish as he launched himself at his enemy. Grigori laughed and vanished, only to reappear in the opposite corner of the room. Nick followed him, and the chase began. Flitting from corner to corner, Grigori scampered like a demented cat playing with his prey. Nick followed, trying in vain to catch him, snarls of rage issuing forth from his mouth at regular intervals.

Anna tried to take advantage of Grigori's preoccupation with her father and jumped to the door, but vampire lackeys followed and pounced once again as she pulled it open. It slammed shut as the fastest one landed on it, appearing crouched on the upper portion. He bared his fangs and hissed. The others were there in an instant, grabbing and mauling her while her father and Grigori fought to the death behind her.

"Mmmmff! Get off! Arrgh!" Anna screamed and let loose a roar of her own as she fought them off. They toyed with her, teasing and laughing, grabbing and pinching and pressing, shoving hands and fingers at her body, trying to humiliate her.

Anna had had enough. Eyes glowing red with rage and energy, she began targeting the weaker vampires. She had been turned for a hundred years and had grown strong with the passage of time. These men had been vampires for maybe a year or two; they usually didn't last too long as Grigori's worker bees.

She leapt and landed on a surprised henchman, grabbing his head and, lightning fast, her mouth lowered and she bit hard, tearing half his throat out. Another fast chomp, and his head was off, blood shooting up, body slumping to the ground. She tossed the head aside and went for the next one.

Anna knew these vampires had strict orders from Grigori

not to harm her, just to hold her there. He wanted the kill for himself and had threatened eternal death to the vampires who harmed her. She, however, was operating under no such constraints, and it showed.

In a deadly dance, she darted from one to the other, tearing off heads left and right, bathing the room in blood; after a few minutes the coppery scent filled her flaring nostrils. Grigori and Nick fought around her, chasing each other, darting from wall to ceiling to corner, Grigori laughing, Nick raging, both ignoring Anna and the vampires who were dying around her.

Bloody stripes and wave patterns peppered the walls with an almost artistic flair as the vampire thugs died. Finally, Anna stopped, breathing hard. Her eyes fell on the two vampire lords locked in combat, and she decided to help her father.

As they flew by, she leapt at the first shadow flickering past and grabbed hold of Grigori's shoulders. With lightning speed, he shoved Nick against the far wall, momentarily stunning him, then whirled and caught Anna's head in his own tight grasp. Looking deep into her eyes with a piercing stare, he bared his teeth.

"Do not tempt me, little girl. You will be last, and I will take a long time to kill you." Grigori looked down at her breasts and then lower. Licking his lips, he slowly brought his gaze back up to stare at her again. "A long time." He smiled.

Anna reared back in disgust and brought her head down, teeth bared, aiming for his throat. In an instant, Grigori brought his own mouth to face hers, teeth bared, but it was a different face, a different mouth than a moment before.

Red skin covered his face, eyes glowed deep purple, and his teeth had grown to two inches long, too long to fit in his mouth. His grin was more grimace as his jaw opened wider, and Anna felt icy fear crawl down her back. Blood and saliva dripped from his teeth, and he winked at her. Growling low, he closed his arms around her torso, squeezing her closer, pressing his body against hers and grinding against her. She pushed against him, trying to keep those deadly teeth from her face.

"You will pleasure me for days before I let you die, my sweet. I will peel the flesh from your body until you scream for mercy." His smile curling into a sneer as he leered at her. "Call it a repayment for all the pain your family has caused me these last fifty years."

Anna saw her father approaching in her peripheral vision, but she betrayed nothing. Sneering at Grigori, she spat to the side. "You will never win, you sick monster."

She reared back as Nick sank his claws into Grigori's shoulders from the back. Inch-long nails as strong as steel bore into Grigori's flesh. Nick's own teeth, nearly as long as Grigori's, were an inch from Grigori's neck before he reacted.

With a roar, Grigori released Anna and swung around to

face Nick. They fought, locked together, tumbling to the ground.

Anna leapt to the door and was through it in an instant. As she raced away, her heart constricted as she heard a faint wet ripping sound followed by a scream of rage. Her heart pounded in her chest and tears streamed from her eyes. She fled as if the hounds of hell were after her, disappearing into the moonless night like smoke.

———⟫⟨———

In the dark shadows of some nearby bushes, pale, dead
eyes focused on Anna as she fled. Breath quickened and
heartbeat accelerated as the creature watched her leave. Its
attention was quickly drawn back to the building the girl
had fled as the ripping sound of death echoed from within.
When the howl of triumph that quickly turned into dismay
reached its ears, its head jerked sideways, keen eyes darting
toward the building, then back to Anna. Its milky white
eyes set into bloodshot rims sprayed tiny flecks of watery
blood onto its pale cheeks, and it brushed these away
impatiently. As Anna disappeared into the night, the eyes
narrowed.

MEETING AND FEEDING

Eric pulled up his hood, buried his hands deep in his coat pockets and hunched his shoulders against the wet fog. His backpack, bulging with textbooks and notebooks, thumped against his back as he walked. It was eleven at night, and the library had just closed: time to head back to his apartment on the other side of campus.

His sneakers made no sound on the damp grass as he crossed over to the sidewalk. The night was still, the street lights glowed in the fog, and every sound was dampened in the mist.

He went through the things he had to do before he went to bed: call Michael, text Julia, and send an email to his parents. Julia's birthday was coming up next week, and he'd be driving the fifty miles south to spend the day with his family. His little sister was pleasant and sweet, a talented artist who was beginning to make a decent living selling her paintings.

Eric's breath steamed slightly in the cold night as he walked, and he loved it. He felt at home in the mists of Seattle's cold, damp weather, and he loved the night. Checking his watch, he saw he was going to be able to sleep in the next morning; he didn't have to be in at his supermarket job until 10 o'clock.

He hummed as he walked, his pace quick and sure, and noticed a shape slowly emerging out of the mist a short distance ahead of him. A figure was walking in the same direction he was, and he was gradually overtaking it.

As he drew closer, Eric realized it was a girl from one of his classes. Dressed in a heavy brown coat, she wore an orange knit hat, her eyes focused on her phone as she walked. Squinting as he approached her, he saw the hat was topped with green and looked like a pumpkin.

He smiled as he drew alongside her, and she glanced at him with a distracted look. He saw then that she had dark eyes, and wavy chestnut brown hair, curling out from under her hat and flowing down past her shoulders. An old-fashioned leather satchel was slung over one shoulder. A purple knit scarf, blue jeans and black leather boots completed the ensemble. Glancing at her face, he felt his breath leave him momentarily. She was beautiful.

He slowed his step as he walked, keeping pace with her. "Hi," he said. "Anna isn't it?"

She nodded, slipping her phone into her pocket. He tried again. "Are you just coming from the library?" Classes had just started the week before, and a few other students were walking along the sidewalk from late classes or library study.

"Yeah."

He thought for a minute as they walked. Then: "Don't you love the fog?"

She smiled and nodded, "Hides a world of things."

That was a peculiar thing to say. Mentally shrugging, Eric pressed on. "You're in my art class, aren't you? Mr. Newcomb's class?" The night class ran from 9 to 10 at night Mondays, Wednesdays, and Fridays. It was the class he took to relieve the stress from the economics and business classes. His artistic revelations emerged in his sculptures and paintings, something he took great hope in.

"Yeah, I guess so," she said. Eric thought he detected a slight accent. She sniffed. Something told him to look closer. Her eyes looked red. Redder than what the weather was responsible for.

"Are you okay?"

"Not really." She kept looking at the ground as she walked. "My father died last month." Her voice was quiet.

"Oh. God, I'm sorry." He thought for a minute. "I'm so

sorry." After a long pause, he continued, "Would you like to get a coffee or something, comfort of strangers and all that?" There was an all-night coffee shop two blocks away called *Lestat's* he was fond of.

She sniffled again, then took out an old-fashioned cotton handkerchief and blew her nose loudly. Stopping and looking up at him, she studied his eyes.

"Okay," she said, giving a little sideways nod with her head that charmed him.

As they walked he said, "You're not from around here, are you?"

Anna cleared her throat. "What makes you say that?" She glanced around them before returning her eyes to study his face.

"I just thought I heard a slight accent, that's all."

"Um, well, actually, my family is from Europe. Demark and Germany mostly." She chuckled to herself, a grin peeking out the corner of her mouth.

"Yes, I think Denmark is funny, too," Eric said, smiling. "Hamlet was hilarious." At this, she looked up at him and burst out laughing. Eric smiled broadly, his plan to distract her from her tears a success. He hooked his arm around hers and turned to cross the street. "Come on, kid, let me show you the world."

Laughing, they both made their way to Lestat's Café. As they approached, the fog seemed to part for them, and the light through the windows glowed like magic. Decorations hung in the window; metallic star and moon cutouts hung on threads and twirled in the twinkling lights that framed the front window, and hanging curlicues rotated lazily as people moved about inside.

Several couples sat together, cupping steaming mugs of coffee or hot chocolate, leaning in close until their heads almost touched. Eric could see a couple kissing on the corner loveseat, mugs forgotten on the table beside them.

The door was black with a stained-glass center: a brilliant purple, green and gold leafy orchid design stood out against a starlight background. As Eric pushed it open, a bell jingled softly.

Holding the door open for Anna, Eric allowed his eyes to drink her in as she entered the coffee shop. He inhaled deeply as she moved past him, closing his eyes briefly as he detected a scent he could not place. She smelled like blackberries and oranges and trees and a primeval forest, and somehow none of these and yet all of these, all at the same time.

And then the moment was gone and he was following her through the door, pushing his hood back, a feeling of both loss and wonder growing in his heart.

"Eric! Buddy, how're you doing?" a friend hailed him from behind the counter.

"Not bad, not bad. What's new with you?"

"Mocha's on sale, and the turkey looks good."

He turned to Anna. "What would you like?"

"Just a small coffee, thanks." She looked around. "I've never been in here. It's nice," she smiled.

"Two coffees," Eric said and then turned to Anna. "Yeah, I love this place." Grabbing the coffee, he led her to a pair of chairs, and they were soon seated, steaming mugs held close.

"I don't remember you around campus last year, did you just move here?" he asked.

Smiling at him, she bent her head to her coffee cup, inhaled the fragrance wafting up from inside and nodded without speaking. Her hair was at least seven varied shades of brown, from dark gold graduating up to a rich mahogany, with touches of red in the strands.

He sat back and sipped his coffee, taking the opportunity to study her. He'd seen her at a distance in class last week but hadn't remembered her looking so striking.

"What are you looking at?" She chuckled, peeking at him over the rim of her mug.

His head dipped, caught in the act of studying her. He quickly recovered and changed the subject. "Is this your first art class?"

"No. I've taken lots of art classes before." He noticed she wasn't drinking her coffee, just inhaling the steam. "I'm also taking Government on Tuesday and Thursday nights. So far I'm enjoying it." She smiled, like sunlight shining down on him after a rain. "I'm really enjoying the climate here in Seattle, and I love the underground," Anna let her lips touch the hot liquid steaming up from her cup. "My little brother got lost in the tunnels the first week we were here." She chuckled, remembering.

"Oh no!" Eric laughed out loud, "The first month I was here, I went exploring down there and got turned around, too." His eyes glinted in the café's soft light as he smiled. His short brown hair had natural red highlights and was styled in a devil-may-care uplift often called "bedhead." Anna studied him over the rim of her cup, taking him in.

He grinned as he studied her right back. His jeans were faded and comfortable, and his dark coat opened to reveal a dark red t-shirt underneath. He was clean shaven, and his full lips smiled easily, crinkling the corners of his eyes merrily. Anna smiled too. "But you know," he said, "I've never felt more at home in the Seattle underground. I think I might've been a smuggler in another life." He laughed again.

Anna's smile turned into a laugh at this, and her eyes sparkled in the light from the window.

Eric noticed for the first time that when she laughed, dimples appeared on either cheek, deepening when her mouth opened in wider laughter. *Oh, this girl is delightful,* he thought, entranced. Her beauty seemed to glow from her like moonbeams, invisible, but just as energizing. He felt his heart constrict.

Anna rose, "I've got to go to the restroom." She tripped slightly, falling to one side and spilling half her coffee on the floor. "Oh!"

Eric jumped up and put his hand on her arm to help. "You okay?"

"Yes, it wasn't too hot anymore." She made motions of brushing off the wetness and then walked over to the counter. "I'm sorry; I spilled some of my coffee."

"No worries, ma'am." The young man grabbed a mop and came over to clean the mess.

Anna turned to Eric. "I've got to go now."

"Can I walk you to your car?"

"No, I don't have a car."

"The bus stop, then?"

Anna hesitated. She normally got home on her own, but he looked so determined to walk with her that she nodded. "Okay."

Eric held the door open for her, then wondered why he was acting so old-fashioned with Anna. Something about her seemed timeless, and he guessed he wanted every tiny thing he did to give him a better chance with her.

They walked out into the fog, which had grown thicker while they'd been inside the coffee shop. Anna walked fast, and he quickened his step to keep up with her.

"Are you just taking night classes or some during the day?" he asked.

"Just at night. I'm kind of a night owl." She smiled and continued walking.

Eric's breath came faster, and his left hand closed into a fist then relaxed again. This girl was amazing. Thinking quickly, he spoke.

"Hey, what are you planning on making for the second assignment? I'm thinking of doing something I can use, something practical." His breath gently fogged in the cool night air.

"I'm not sure. It's something I'll have to think about." She walked on, looking slightly pensive. "Maybe some kind of animal."

They had arrived at the bus stop. Two others sat waiting on the bench. Eric looked around and saw they'd arrived just in time. The bus was trundling up five blocks away, slowly approaching. He had to act now if he was to have any chance at all. He turned to her and looked into her eyes.

"Listen, would you like to go out to a late dinner on Friday night?"

She looked down at her shoes, then back up at him, her lip caught in her teeth. "Actually, I can't."

"Oh." He thought. "Well, what about Saturday?" She began to shake her head. He rushed on. "There's a new exhibit at the Museum of Modern Art."

Anna's face brightened. "I can come if it's at night." He looked puzzled. She went on. "I ... I have a job, I work during the days." She looked up at him, into his hazel eyes.

Eric said, "They're open until 10. We can go at night." Her face brightened, and he exhaled in a jumble of relief and excitement. She was so beautiful he almost forgot what he was saying. "Uh, maybe I could pick you up at seven? When do you get off?"

Anna smiled. "Seven will be fine, but why don't I meet you there?"

Eric was just happy he was going to see her again. "Yes. 7 p.m. on Saturday at the MOMA. You know where it is?"

"I'll find it. I'll be there." Anna assured him as the bus pulled up and stopped with a squeal of air brakes. She turned to get on after the other two people.

"Okay, sounds good." Eric wasn't sure what else to say, but he felt happy he had a date with Anna. Strangely happy.

Right before she got on, she turned and smiled at him again, and he grinned back and raised his hand to bid her goodbye. The bus doors shut, and it began to move off again.

Eric watched it go, then turned to walk back down the street. He felt like singing. It started to drizzle, and he pulled up his hood against the wetness.

Eric whistled as he walked away from the bus stop and back across the campus toward his apartment. He felt happy. Happier than he'd been since earlier that evening. Happier than he'd been for a long time, in fact.

He made plans for his next date with Anna as he walked. She seemed excited about going to the museum, and he smiled; he loved museums. He thought briefly of the museum docent job he was planning to apply for next year and he smiled again. He had a feeling about Anna: She was someone special. Not your run-of-the-mill college coed. No. There was definitely something different about this girl.

Anna waited until the bus had traveled down the road a mile, then got off on the corner and watched as it pulled away. The street was deserted; wet fog curled around the corners of the buildings, and the glow of the streetlamps pressed dimly against the heavy, wet air.

She looked around her at the quiet neighborhood and took a deep breath. Smiling at the thought of her Saturday date with Eric, she walked a block more, then turned down an alley between two stores. Walking to the end, she ducked between some dumpsters and was gone.

Five miles away, Anna coalesced from smoke into human form on the roof of a rundown apartment building and lowered herself into a crouch. She didn't have to wait long. Listening intently, she heard faint noises in the quiet night. Some banging, an angry voice, then a muffled scream.

Cocking her head to the side, she focused on which apartment the noises were coming from, and quickly zeroed in on the second floor, in the back. The corner apartment with the trash piled up outside the front door. Running silently across the rooftop, then dropping lightly to the second-floor landing, she paused again and listened.

Yes. This was the one. Anna knocked on the door. The voices fell silent, and there was nothing for a heartbeat or two. Then steps to the door, which opened to reveal an angry male, mid-30s, shirtless, holding a beer and scowling.

"What the fuck do you want?"

Without a word, Anna flew into motion. Quicker than the eye could follow, she leapt at the man and knocked him to the floor, her mouth instantly at his throat. She had landed on his chest, instantly reached around to the back of his neck and snapping his spine. He didn't even have time to scream.

As she drank, Anna lifted her eyes to the cowering woman and child in the corner who were staring at her, frozen in shock and fear. Focusing her eyes on them, she thought "sleep." They closed their eyes and crumpled to the floor.

Anna drank her fill of the abusive nightmare she'd just ambushed. This creep would harm these people no more. It took about three minutes to drain him completely. She was glad this one was not into drugs, but she did wrinkle her nose at the nicotine in his blood. No matter, she thought. Food is food, even if it was greasy, bad-for-you smoker blood.

Finishing, she rose to her feet like a cat, and surveyed the room. Sparse furnishings filled the dingy apartment. A soft light illuminated the woman and child asleep in the corner. Anna watched them sleep for a few minutes. Humanity would never change, they were the same, decade after decade.

She crouched once again and went through the pockets

of the dead man at her feet. Not a drop of blood had escaped her mouth; there was no trace of the attack in the apartment. She found a wad of bills in his back pocket. Rising and walking to the pair in the corner, she bent to one knee in front of them.

Anna studied the careworn face of the woman, then looked at the little face below. The little boy's cheeks were still round with baby fat. He couldn't have been more than two years old. Well, things would be better for them now, she thought. Her finger gently caressed the side of the woman's face as she murmured "awaken" in a soft voice.

The woman slowly opened her eyes. Below her, the little toddler opened his, too, and looked up at Anna, who smiled down at him.

"Forget," Anna whispered her last command. She tucked the wad of bills into the woman's hand, got up and walked over to the crumpled man, picked him up, and strode out the front door, closing it softly behind her.

She would dump the body into the nearby Pacific. The great whites were passing by right now, they would make short work of it.

Halfway across the city, a stray mongrel pawed at some food that had fallen out of a dumpster in an alley behind a greasy dive. Burrowing in with his snout, the skinny dog sniffed and then bit down, dragging some meatloaf out of the foam package, then began to delicately eat. His back was curved, and he shivered as he chewed. Thin ribs and sharp leg bones showed through his gaunt, mangy hide. A torn ear drooped over one eye, and blood was crusted over the wound. A sharp cry pierced the dank air as the dog's form crumpled under a sudden weight; sharp, wickedly long teeth in a mouth spread unnaturally wide reached around his neck and closed, snapping his spine like a cracker and silencing his yelp abruptly. The thing on the dying dog's back did not wait for him to die before settling down to a leisurely meal, moonlight glinting off a pale, hairless head as the thing slurped in relish.

HUNT

As Anna unlocked the door and stepped into the small home she shared with her family, a black cat ran in with her, twining her way through Anna's legs, curling her tail around Anna fondly. She closed and locked the door behind her with a happy sigh, picked up the cat, and walked into the kitchen, dropping her bag on the wooden settee on the way.

"Anya, darling, I just put your cat outside, she was interrupting me," a woman standing at the sink said, looking over her shoulder. "Oh, she's back in. Hello, Gypsy."

The black cat mreowed at her.

"Anya, I finished my painting," called a boy of about thirteen from the couch in the living room, where he was playing a computer game.

"Finally," Anna said. She walked over to her mother and gave her a kiss. "Mama, have you eaten yet?" She took off her coat as she talked, hanging it on the hook in the corner of the cluttered kitchen. Turning to the living room, she smiled. "Lexei, let me see the painting. Did you end up putting snow on the trees, as I suggested?"

Lexei jumped up from the couch. "Yes. I tried it on a couple in the corner, and it really worked." He smiled as he walked to the bedroom. His light brown hair curled around his ear as he smiled up at his sister. She was tall, as was their mother, and Lexei still had to look up a few inches.

His form was still boyish, although had begun to fill out and hint at the man he might have become, had he kept growing. As it was, his aging had been halted the day he'd been transformed, and so he remained a thirteen-year-old boy forever. A thirteen-year-old boy with a hundred years of living behind him.

"I knew it would," Anna called after him. Lexei emerged with the painting, turning it around to show his sister.

"Oh, little brother, it's marvelous." Anna clapped her hands together.

Lexei had used the new oils she'd brought home last week. He was really getting quite good. The scene depicted rural life in their homeland. She sighed with longing. Her mother came up behind her and put a hand around her shoulder.

"I know," Alix said. "It made me homesick, too." She bent and kissed the top of Lexei's head. "You are quite talented, my son. Your father would have loved to see this." She turned to Anna. "No, Anya, I have not eaten."

Anna turned to her mother and drew her aside to the couch. "Mama, are you all right?" she said. Alix had not hunted in the weeks since Nikolai's death. Anna worried her mother would never recover from the loss of her husband. Their flight from the East Coast had been frantic and hurried, and Alix had not spoken for two days.

"I'll be fine, Anya, really." She patted Anna's arm.

"Starvation is not 'fine,' Mama." Anna looked at her mother, noting the hollow, grey cheeks, the sunken eyes, the listless expression on her face. "Come." Anna rose, pulling her mother up and into the bedroom. Alix stumbled after her, her weakened state belying her words of assurance.

Anna laid her mother on the bed, tucking blankets around her, plumping the pillow and fussing over her. Alix closed her eyes, waiting. Anna closed her eyes as well, her face upturned, a look of concentration on her face. She opened her mouth slightly as her incisors began to extend, growing to more than an inch long. Razor-sharp and deadly, the teeth gleamed, luminescent in the dim light.

Anna opened her eyes and looked down at her mother. Lifting her right arm, Anna turned her head sideways and brought her upper right tooth down close to the elbow, and with a quick, practiced motion, swiped open the artery just beneath the skin. She quickly bent and pressed the arm to her mother's mouth, kneeling beside the bed.

Alix drank deeply from her daughter, gulping the

precious fluid, like a baby at her mother's breast. In her eagerness, she curled upward as she grasped Anna's arm, her thirst almost a passion. Her eyelids opened to show that her pupils had rolled back into her head in ecstasy; her cheeks began to fill out with a healthy pink color, and the dark circles under her eyes slowly faded.

Turned at age forty-three, she had looked to be around fifty-five when Anna had first come home that night, but now appeared as though she could pass for Anna's older sister. Alix glowed with the blood and the power of the vampire in full flesh, displaying an unearthly beauty, her whole body nearly as luminescent as Anna's fangs had been.

Alix had been in such dire straits that Anna let her mother drink her nearly dry. As Alix finished, she released the suction her mouth had made against Anna's arm. Her eyes opened normally as she fell back into bed, and she smiled, her teeth coated in the dark red fluid, her skin fresh and glowing, her health restored.

"Now, Mama, lie here and rest while I go out with Lexei," Anna said as she stood up. Being drained so thoroughly did not weaken her to anywhere near the point her mother had been, but Anna felt almost as weak as a human. She still had her vampire strength, and she could still hunt. Being a vampire for nearly a hundred years, she possessed a strength nearly unheard of in the younger vampire population.

As did Lexei and Alix. As did her sister Tati, gone these two weeks on a mission to the north. As had her recently murdered father Nikolai, and her murdered sisters, Maria and Olga had. They had died in battle nearly thirty years ago when the family had been taken by surprise during an ice storm in a small village in Maine that had been overrun by vampires.

The small town's infestation was known to all the Maine locals, but few knew of the feud two vampire lords had fought there that had consumed the town; nor how many vampires had fallen in the fight. The snow had been bloody red that night, as red as Gettysburg had been, Anna thought, remembering.

Tucking the blankets around her mother again, she sighed and smiled as she walked into the living room where Lexei was waiting. He was dressed in black, and pacing with impatience. On the ceiling.

Anna chuckled. "Sorry, Mama needed me."

Lexei hopped down to the floor and straightened. "Do you think she'll be better soon?"

"I hope so. I miss hunting with her." Anna put her arm around his shoulder and looked back at the bedroom, sighing. "Come on." She opened the door, and they left.

———————— ✕✖✕✖✕✖✕✖✕ ————————

Anna and her brother ran to the nearby trees that surrounded their home, trees so tall they reached over a hundred feet into the sky. At the base of the tallest one, they transformed themselves into rats and scampered up the trunk of the towering evergreen until they reached the top.

From there, they changed into bats and winged their way northeast toward the mainland and Bellevue. Landing in a secluded area of Wilburton Hill Park, they ran tirelessly for two miles and then quickly climbed to the roof of a five-story brownstone apartment house in a tree-lined neighborhood.

Lexei took a deep breath and looked out into the night, smiling. Anna stepped beside him and looked up at the midnight horizon. The fog had lifted, the sky was clear for a change, and the stars twinkled in the inky blackness. They could not see nearly as many stars as they had been able to in their native Russia so many years ago.

The recent loss of Nikolai had been nearly unbearable, Anna remembered. They had moved their base to the other side of the country, fleeing in a panic, filled with grief and loss, despondent. Alix, Anna and Lexei had established a new home in Seattle, and not even Grigori had found them in their secluded Mercer Island hideaway. As a rule, they hunted only on the mainland, far from home, so as not to risk discovery of their lair.

Anna sighed again and closed her eyes, breathing deeply of the night air. Beside her, Lexei flexed and stretched, hopping from place to place around her in anticipation. Anna smiled as she opened her eyes.

"Okay, eager beaver, come on." Eyeing an alley three

blocks away, she ran, jumping the twenty-foot gaps separating the buildings and was soon standing on the roof's edge, looking down. Anna spied a homeless man down below chewing on an old sandwich he had found in a trash can.

"I can smell him from here," Lexei said. Instead of wrinkling his nose at the ripe smell of vagrant human, he licked his lips. Anna smiled.

"Okay, you take this one," Anna said before lightly running down the side of the building. Lexei eagerly followed and zipped ahead of her, and as she landed on the asphalt, he was already at his meal.

Lexei had jumped on the vagrant directly from the wall, landing on the man's back and quickly biting his neck, crushing his spine and killing him instantly. His mouth was on the side of the corpse's throat, and his long incisors extended and reached to the still throbbing carotid artery pulsing less than half an inch under the surface.

With a practiced speed and movement he'd performed tens of thousands of times before, Lexei punctured his way down through tissue and was locked on to the side of the neck within seconds, drinking his fill. He instinctively released his aura, letting out waves of palpable fear as he ate, the vampire equivalent of a hawk hooding its prey, allowing him to feast at leisure.

Anna watched as her brother drank his fill. The alley was completely dark; nothing glowed from the nearby street corner. The streetlight had been broken for months, in fact. The vagrant had thought himself clever, holing up in this dark, secluded alley where no one ever ventured. Now, no one would find the vagrant's body for a long time back here.

Lexei rose, wiping his mouth and smiling. "Oh my god, that was good." He chuckled, feeling very merry indeed, as content as a human relaxing on the couch after a Thanksgiving meal, waistband button undone, toothpick in hand working away at the last strands of turkey caught between the teeth as they watched a holiday football game.

"I want to go farther in," Anna said, and walked to the side of the next building. Together, they ran up the wall on all fours, looking for all the world like a pair of ninjas.

———————————>≒≋≋≺————————————

Five blocks away, the pale thing crouched over the mostly eaten carcass of the dog, blood and fluids dripping out its mouth as it looked up from its meal and listened. Pale head raised, snout to the sky, the thing tilted its head in concentration. A shiver of fear ran through its body then, and the skin along its pale back and shoulders puckered up in goose bumps. After a moment, it scuttled to the other side of the narrow alley and under the eaves of the nearby restaurant, dragging the dog's body after it. Tearing at the grate it found there with long, razor-sharp claws, it tore off the old twisted metal and, squeezing its pale body through an impossibly small rectangular hole, dropped to the basement to hide.

JINX

"Okay, Michael, sounds good." Eric paced in his kitchen as he talked with his boss. Eric was the morning supervisor at the local market, one of the last small mom-and-pop stores to still carry fresh, local produce.

"I will. I won't. Yes, I promise." He paced some more. Michael was going to be gone for a week, leaving Eric and two other supervisors to hold down the fort. "Don't worry. Yes. I know. I promise, I'll call you if anything happens. Everything will be fine. Yes. Uh huh. Yes. Okay. Bye."

Eric sighed, walking into his kitchen and grabbed a banana, taking it to the small living room alcove where his computer was. Sitting down, he began to type out an email to his parents. He'd texted Julia when he got home, and she'd texted him back immediately. They'd gone back and forth a bit, as she'd told him all about her latest set of paintings.

Eric and his parents loved seeing her so alive and full of life and energy. Julia had suffered from a childhood illness. Long since recovered now at seventeen, she was expected to have a normal lifespan. She was the gem of her family and the apple of her brother's eye.

Eric sighed again, restless. He went into his bedroom, fell into bed, and clicked on the television to the national news.

"And coming up next, the newest rising star: Greg Ramsey! Is he the answer to all our problems?" the newscaster said.

A commercial came on as Eric peeled his banana and took a bite. Thinking a minute, he got up and walked into the kitchen and returned a few minutes later with a sandwich. Lying back down, he took a bite of the sandwich and focused on the newscast.

"Greg Ramsey is full of fire this month. After winning his state Senate seat last year, he seems unstoppable! Rumor has it he's going to make a run for the presidency, although his office denies those rumors. If you remember, Ramsey is the protégé of Calvin and Devon Kline, who head Kline Industries, the company they inherited from their father, Francis Kline.

Friends close to the Kline brothers say Ramsey has been closely groomed and his career guided nearly every step of the way by the two brothers, and although Kline Industries and Fox News interviews repeatedly deny this, sources have uncovered hefty donations the company has made to Ramsey's campaign."

Eric muted the television and muttered under his breath. "Great. Another bourgeoisie crook." After studying the silent talking heads another minute, he turned the television off.

A sleek, black form walked into the room and hopped up onto the bed.

"Well hello, Jinx," Eric said, petting the cat. "I missed you today."

Purring, the cat began to knead on his master's blanketed leg. Chuckling, Eric stroked the furry cat over and over. He had been lonely when he first moved north to attend college and had adopted the sweet black kitten to keep him company. He'd grown up with cats and loved the intelligent animals. He'd carried Jinx around the house whenever he was home, petting him and playing with him constantly. Nearly two years later, Jinx was the most affectionate cat he'd ever had, and Eric loved him deeply.

"I met a girl today, Jinx."

Jinx purred in response and kneaded harder.

"She's absolutely beautiful, and she goes to the college."

Jinx purred some more and looked up at his master with contented eyes.

"I love her style, too. I think she must knit or something."

Jinx began to lick Eric's arm.

"She's in my art class."

Jinx turned in a circle several times before plopping heavily down against Eric's side. Eric chuckled and stroked the cat several more times before picking up the thick novel by his bedside nightstand. With a happy sigh, he opened the book and began to read.

Jinx opened his eyes in the darkened room. Eric had read until his eyelids were drooping, then had put the book aside, turned off the bedside lamp, and turned over before falling asleep. Jinx had slept next to him to protect him.

Jinx sensed that dark forces had entered his realm, and he worried about his pet. He had adopted Eric and groomed him for years into the perfect companion, and they were fast friends. Jinx got up from his nap, arching his back and shivering before stealthily walking to the head of the bed and onto the nightstand.

He pushed his whiskered nose through the light yellow curtains and looked out the window. It was as black as 3 a.m. out there, and nary a soul in sight. Wait. No, Jinx could see three Kindred cats hunting in the night, through the grass and bushes, searching out some dinner. Huffing lightly, Jinx imagined himself out hunting with them, pouncing on every shadow, exploring every corner of the neighborhood, invisible in his black coat.

He saw one of the Kindred jump at some small prey and

capture it, batting it back and forth before chomping down and delivering a killing blow before trotting off to eat it. Jinx saw all these things from his perch on the windowsill, and his teeth chattered in excitement.

After a few minutes of this, the cat sighed and silently hopped down onto the thick carpet, and began to make his nightly rounds through the apartment. He first stopped in the hallway, where a faint moonbeam stretched across a soft throw rug. Jinx saw magic in light beams, dust motes dancing in them during the day, silvery half-imagined prey leaping through them in the quiet night.

He pounced and caught a small moth that dared to flutter across his field of vision. Picking up the murdered corpse, he chewed happily as he made his way into the living room.

Jinx patrolled the borders of the room, his nose sniffing for any change, his eyes glowing with concentration as he prowled. He then made his way into the kitchen, sniffing at his food bowl first, then hopping up onto the counter and lifting his nose to inhale the smells of different foods.

Finding a stray bit of chicken in the sink, he delicately picked it up in his mouth and began chewing it as he padded across the countertop. Hopping lightly onto the table nearby, then to the chair, he searched every corner of the dining room before padding back into the living room.

Starlight shone through big bay windows and across a comfortable loveseat and easy chair, and Jinx, finished with his snack, leapt up to the arm, then onto the back of the overstuffed chair, and settled down for a night of watching. He could see the whole hillside from this perch, and stayed there for hours every night, watching.

The watching was important. Jinx knew Eric wasn't aware of it, but cats could see things humans could not. At night, there was a world of magical escapades being played out across that hillside, and Jinx watched it all, every night.

Tonight was no different. From his high place in the dark living room, Jinx watched, undetected, as the creatures of the night came out to play. He didn't have long to wait.

The whole hillside spread out before him, dark and grassy with trees at the edges. Movement caught Jinx's attention, and his sharp eyes concentrated on the lower field to the right. This was new, he thought.

A shadow flitted from tree to tree, then swooped down and caught dinner. A great horned owl. As the owl grabbed its kill and swung back into the sky, another shadow, this one larger and darker, caught the owl mid-flight and they both dropped to the ground. Jinx perked up at this. He could not see what the larger shape was. His fur prickled with foreboding, and he dropped to the ground and hurried to the glass for a closer look.

<hr />

Out in the field, a newly turned vampire grasped the great owl in her hands, trying to subdue it. It scratched her with its long talons and drew blood. The vampire had been a thirteen-year-old runaway named Holly twenty-four hours earlier. She'd been sitting in an alley, shooting up with three older teens when they'd been attacked.

Straggly, dirty blonde hair curled slightly at the tips and hung past her shoulders; a ragged t-shirt, dirty canvas tennis shoes, and jeans with holes completed the picture. Holly counted herself lucky, because her companions' throats had been ripped out within seconds, while she had cowered in the shadows unnoticed.

Frozen in fear as she watched the scene play out, she had exuded such a strong smell of terror that the three vampires who'd been drinking from the other teens had scented her immediately. Immersed in the ecstasy of their meals, they didn't respond immediately, but they didn't need to. The aura the vampires emitted extended several dozen feet in every direction, effectively freezing any person or animal caught within its range. Holly was frozen to the spot.

"Emil, look what we've caught." A huge male vampire rose upright, his mouth dripping red with blood, his victim drained and growing cold on the ground below him. He grinned and closed his eyes in pleasure at the rush the heroin user's blood had given him. Face raised to the sky, he shivered in delight.

The other two vampires were still drinking, gulping blood like eager puppies at a bowl of cream, and didn't answer.

Holly knew she was in terrible danger. She expected them to kill her next, but she couldn't move. Her heartbeat thundered in her ears, and her breath came in quick pants. She felt like a cornered rabbit.

She had been the last to shoot up, and the needle was still in her arm, most of the fluid still in the syringe. She felt a slight buzz, but nothing like her companions had felt. Her eyes were wide with fright as she watched the predators eat.

"Claude, get up," the first vampire said in disgust. The other two rose hastily, and wiped their mouths.

"Triss," Emil shivered as he rose to his feet. Tristan looked at him and chuckled.

"What's the matter Emil, never drank your fill of a heroin user before?"

Claude kicked at the teen he'd drained. "So fragile." He said in disdain. "Such easy prey."

Tristan narrowed his eyes at the darkness where the girl was cornered. "Come out, pretty girl." He walked closer, the hard heels of his boots echoing in the alley, and she shrunk back farther into the corner.

Emil joined his brother and began taunting Holly. Crouching down on his haunches, he extended his hand as if she were a dog. "Come on, come out of there." He made kissing sounds to coax her out.

Claude joined them, laughing.

Holly nearly passed out in terror from the vampires' attention.

"BOO!" Tristan barked, and it somehow broke the spell. Holly leapt up and darted to the side, but she was too late. Tristan caught her in a tight grip, and leered down at her.

Emil burped. "I can't drink another drop."

"No wonder. The one you just drained was nearly twice your size," Claude laughed.

Tristan grinned down at the Holly and, with lightning speed, lunged and chomped down on her neck. A surge of fear overwhelmed her mind, and she nearly lost consciousness. She slumped, limp in his arms, her eyes half closed. He held her lightly, her small weight nothing to him.

"Triss, hurry up. We have to meet Mr. Ramsey across the water," Emil said, straightening his dark jacket.

Tristan bit down and drank a bit before stopping. Looking with regret at Holly, he said "Damn, this one isn't high." He dropped her to the ground and looked over at the others, now walking away. Looking back down at the girl in mischief, he grinned again, and then dropped to one knee.

"A gift for you, sweet child," He slit an inch-wide gap in his wrist, then held it over the semiconscious girl's mouth. "You will no longer be a frightened rabbit." The blood Tristan had drained from Holly not a minute before dripped from his wrist and into her mouth. "Join the courageous ones." He finished and licked his wrist wound, which immediately began to close and heal. Straightening his clothes, he walked away to join his comrades.

Twenty-four hours later, in a shadowy field under the cloak of midnight darkness, the owl scratched the young vampire girl on her first attempt at a kill. Frustration surged in her, and she grasped the owl's head in one hand and yanked, hoping to break its neck.

The whole thing came off, and she blinked in surprise; blood spurted out of the owl's neck. Holly quickly caught the stream in her mouth, drinking eagerly. Three minutes later, she tossed the owl on the ground and looked around, still hungry. Running off into the trees, she hunted in search of heartier prey.

Jinx sat, transfixed by the scene that had just played out before him. This new hunter was now in his forest, and he would have to protect Eric if it came near. He was about to return to his place on Eric's bed when he saw the young vampire run out of the trees and up the hill.

Jinx's eyes glowed in the moonlight as he watched the girl approach. Then he saw the deer, it was at the edge of the hill, halfway out of the trees, nibbling at the grass. Didn't it see it was being stalked? Jinx wanted to get out and join the fight so much he paced in front of the glass doors, his teeth chattering softly.

As Holly leapt onto the deer, clumsily biting down on its neck, Jinx stood still, transfixed, unblinking, as he watched the huntress take down her prey. Within seconds Holly was down on the ground with the motionless deer, drinking her fill. As she finished, she stood up, wiped her mouth, and turned to look directly at Jinx.

Jinx stood absolutely still. His eyes glowed in the darkness, the moon reflected in them. He locked eyes with this fellow predator that had invaded the land near his territory. Holly stared back at Jinx, her eyes unblinking, thick blood, black in the faint moonlight, dripping slowly down her chin.

Suddenly, she dropped to all fours, and in an elegant scramble across the grass, moving faster than the eye could see, she was immediately fifty feet closer. Jinx's neck craned up and his mouth opened in a soft hiss. Then suddenly, she moved again, faster than Jinx could follow, and was suddenly up against the glass, a foot away from Jinx, her eyes glowing with a supernatural light.

Jinx leapt fifteen inches straight up and back, and landed against the chair. He let out a loud hiss and a moaning growl.

"Wha...? Jinx?" Eric said.

Jinx hissed again and slowly approached the glass, his back arched and his fur standing straight up, his tail puffed out. Holly crouched there on the other side, unmoving except for her nose, which twitched and tried to catch his scent.

Jinx's ear twitched backward and forward again focusing back on the girl.

He ran up to the glass door and slapped his paw against it hard, just where the vampire's face was. She jumped back, and then like lightning, came forward again and pressed her face up against the glass, making it shudder loudly, and again looked down at Jinx. Dirty smudges mixed with smears of blood on her face as she cocked her head to the side, watching the cat.

Jinx slam his paw again and again against the glass, hissing and growling as Eric came into the living room. "What the hell...?" Eric looked out the glass door into the moonlit open back patio and stopped in his tracks.

A cold streak of fear made Jinx shiver as Eric rubbed his eyes and stared. The girl looked like a ravaged waif, dirty blonde hair a mess, clothes filthy and torn, no shoes, green depthless irises glowing in the whites of her eyes now turned red, blood from the deer smeared on her chin and mouth.

"What the ...?"

Eric walked closer to the door, and Jinx glanced back and twitched his tail. The vampire girl glanced up at Eric, but stayed where she was, looking into the apartment at the two of them. For a minute time froze, Eric and Jinx looking out at Holly and she looking back up at them. Then Eric reached over and switched the porch light on, and she turned and vanished.

Jinx went straight up to the glass and looked out with Eric. They searched the whole patio, but nothing was there. Eric snapped off the light so the hillside became visible again, and together, Jinx and his pet scanned the land, hoping to see the girl again. They stayed searching for ten minutes. But the hillside was empty except for the dead deer and the owl corpse farther down. She was gone.

Down in the dank restaurant basement, the pale creature held the dog's half-eaten corpse close, like a treasured teddy bear, and slept a restless sleep. It dreamt, and seemed to be in a nightmare, whimpering in terror from time to time. After a while, it woke again, and began gnawing at its meal.

RAMSEY

Greg Ramsey paced across the plush white carpeting that blanketed his huge office in a downtown Seattle skyscraper, speaking rapidly in Russian on his cellphone. He pursed his lips, his breath coming short and shallow as he talked, his voice rising to a yell before he slammed the phone down in disgust. Turning, he hollered at the door, "Gretchen!"

Gretchen Svenborg had been with the company for years, and had been transferred from the Ramsey Stockholm offices to the new U.S. center of operations in New York just last month. Mr. Ramsey had insisted she travel with him to this Seattle satellite office he had just opened, to assist him in settling some West Coast business deals.

"Yes, Mr. Ramsey?" Gretchen said, hurrying into the room with her tablet.

He swung toward her voice. "Get me Charles on the

phone, immediately!"

"Yes, sir." She hurried out of the room.

Ramsey began pacing again. His dark hair was cut in a short, perfect businessman's style, not a strand was out of place. His dark grey suit cost more than most midsize sedans. The tie resting against his crisp white dress shirt was a dark solid red, the color of blood. His Italian loafers had cost more than the suit. Even with his vampire aura suppressed, his mere presence exuded power and intimidation.

With quiet efficiency, Gretchen had Calvin Kline on the line for Greg Ramsey within minutes.

"Charles is on line one for you, Mr. Ramsey," she said on the intercom.

He picked up the phone and began his conversation.

Ten minutes later, Greg Ramsey stormed out of his office and made long strides to the elevator. Glancing back at her, he barked, "I need that finished by 5 p.m. tomorrow, Gretchen."

"Yes, sir. I should be done by 3 p.m. You can count on me."

Downstairs, Ramsey walked with quick strides into the parking garage on the first floor of the building. Instinctively, he unblocked his vampire aura. It felt like stretching his wings after being in tight quarters. Beeping the alarm on his black SLS GT Roadster Mercedes, he was about to open the door when three young men approached him.

"Mr. Ramsey, sir," said Tristan.

Emil and Claude stood nervously behind him, waiting. The vampire aura Ramsey exuded did not affect the three in the same way it did humans, but the vampire who had turned them still had the strength to take their heads off with a casual swipe. They respected Ramsey in the same way a human would respect a huge yellow jacket nest in front of their face. Ramsey grinned, inwardly thrilled at the fear he caused in them.

"Ah, Tristan, good." Ramsey opened his car and reached in, pulling out a large black sack. "Take this."

Tristan took the black bag; something inside was squirming. "What is this?" He looked up into Ramsey's face.

Ramsey's steely gaze met Tristan's, and the young man lowered his eyes again.

"It's your lunch." Ramsey got into his car and shut the door on them, then rolled down the window. "Take it into the woods and release it; see what you three make of it."

The thing in the bag bucked against the sides, and Tristan almost dropped it. "Here," he handed it to Claude. "You hold it." Claude took hold of the handles and winced as the thing inside let out an otherworldly hiss.

"Tristan, be sure you go deep into the park before you release it, and wait until midnight, right now it's still very groggy from its flight." Ramsey looked unblinkingly into Tristan's eyes and held his gaze for a minute. The command was very apparent and direct.

"Yes sir, Mr. Ramsey.

The expensive sports car roared off, leaving the three to perform their assigned task.

Ramsey drove his Mercedes to the High Tower High Rise five miles away and pulled into the private underground garage. A minute later, he was in the high-speed elevator zipping up to the penthouse luxury apartment he was leasing. The elevator ran along the outside of the building, and the winking lights of the city stretched out in a panorama.

Lights from watercraft moored in the bay and inlet glistened off the water in the wavering moonlight. The view was extraordinary, even at midnight, yet Ramsey paid little attention to it, studying his smartphone as he ascended.

Up at the penthouse on the thirty-third floor, he quickly showered and changed into a black designer tuxedo and overcoat. Flipping his collar up and wrinkling his nose at the mist outside the window, he felt a rush of excitement. He'd been turned for nearly 200 years now, one of the last to be made before Dracula went into thousand-year hibernation.

Stepping out onto the patio and closing the doors behind

him, he inhaled deeply, then crouched and jumped straight into the air with a force that would have made a jet pilot blush. His flight took him in an arc over the city, past several other high-rise buildings, and into the clouds. What descended was not a body, but smoke: dark smoke that billowed quickly outward with a purpose and disappeared into the city below.

The exclusive nightclub was a hotbed of action. Seattle nightlife never really stopped, and this club in particular had a strong reputation for its exclusive clientele. Millionaires rubbed elbows with socialites, and the cocaine flowed freely, with the owners looking the other way.

Out back in the alley, a thick black column of smoke descended, nearly invisible in the dark midnight air, and settled behind a dumpster, next to a rat. A minute later, Ramsey walked out and down the alley, rat squeezed in one hand, nose inhaling the stagnant, stinking air, not one hair out of place. He lifted the squealing rodent to his mouth and bit the head off, crunching it with relish as he walked.

Ramsey was hit with a green laser strobe light as he entered the darkness. Tiny spots of reflected light bounced off the many-faceted glass ball hanging from the ceiling, and back onto Ramsey's face and shoulders. Loud music reverberated off the walls and into his ears as he wound his way through the mass of bodies that danced to a bassed-up version of the latest Top 40 hit.

One socialite in particular stood out from the rest, her tall, lithe form bobbing up and down in time to the music. Long blonde hair swung from her head, the pulsing lights picking up glittering sparkles in the strands. Ramsey strode up to her and began dancing alongside her.

"What took you?" her half-drugged eyes, somewhat glazed over, but still alert, studied him. Bodies danced around them.

"Business. Not your concern." Ramsey grabbed her arm hard and pulled her into his embrace. Crushing his lips against hers and inhaling her scent, he began to drool. His fangs grew out a quarter inch before he could stop them. Lust and gluttony shone from his eyes as the loud, pulsating music echoed around them.

She pulled back from his lips and leaned into his ear. "Baby, let's go in the back." She took his hand and led him through the crowd of sweaty dancers and through a nearly invisible black door in a black wall. Entering a small room on the side, they could see several people crowded around a low table, snorting lines.

She walked on, to the back and through another door. The room beyond was smaller even than the first, and containing nothing more than a twin bed and a small table. As soon as the door was closed, the girl turned on Ramsey and began kissing him hard. His breath came faster as she worked her way down and unzipped his pants.

After she was done, they settled on the bed with cigarettes.

"Baby, you think you can get me in on it?"

He looked down at her with half-lidded eyes and remained silent.

"I would be able to assist you wherever you went." She pressed her naked torso against him and began nibbling on his ear.

He just stared at her, her eyes red-rimmed from the cocaine she'd snorted earlier, her lipstick smeared from their exchange.

"What makes you think you're any different than the last debutante to cross my path?" he smirked.

She sat up. "Daddy said he'd be working with your partners, and I have resources those other bitches don't." Standing, she began pulling her dress on. "I mean, do you have any idea who he is? Who I am?" She pulled on her stiletto heels and stood there in front of him, dressed; she drew a small brush out of her purse and quickly pulled it through her hair in a huff, then stopped and stared at him. "Well, do you?"

Abruptly he stood, grabbed her arm again, kissed her roughly and stormed out of the room, practically dragging her behind him. They left the club and walked several blocks in silence. Ramsey walked briskly, and soon turned down another dark alley. Mist swirled around their feet as they walked on in the darkness.

She was practically running in her heels to keep up with his long strides. Moonlight broke through the clouds and briefly illuminated the pair as they walked to the end of an alley. They were brought up short by a filthy brick wall and trash at their feet.

He abruptly swung her arm around and, with lightning speed, brought his mouth down to her throat. She never had a chance to scream as he drained her dry, so ferocious that by the time he was finished her head hung on by a thin thread of muscle. Her surprised eyes, blank and dead, stared up at him as he rose to his feet.

"What makes you think I care?" He grabbed his coat and swung it around him in a swirl, disappearing into thin air.

Fifteen miles away at the edge of an old, forgotten graveyard, Ramsey coalesced out of thin air, mist rolling off his black trench coat as he stepped into the dark, dank overgrowth. A crooked tree grew nearby and, as he passed it, an old raven startled in the branches and silently flew away in the opposite direction, perhaps sensing that, despite appearances, the newcomer was plainly not a man at all, but something far more deadly. Ramsey's eyes lifted at the movement, and nodded his head slightly, agreeing with the bird.

Dress shoes landed among dead leaves, and manicured hands straightened the tuxedo underneath as his long strides carried him farther in, through half fallen over headstones crumbling with age. The graveyard stood on a hill overlooking a highway to the right, and a marshy lake to the left. Straight ahead lay a brooding forest. Ramsey's steps took him deep into the graveyard, to the oldest part, at the top of the hill. A mist swirled over the graves, thick and rank, and puddled around his ankles as he walked.

As he approached the top of the hill, he looked down onto the highway below. A police car idled, and blue and red strobe lights blinked in the dark night air. He concentrated and pursed his eyes, and cocked his head at the scene below, focusing his attention and listening. Inside the cruiser an officer sat inside just finishing a traffic stop. The vehicle he'd pulled over, a rusty old pickup of indeterminate color but closely approximating muddy brown, started up and rejoined the flow of traffic, taillights slowly disappearing down the highway.

Ramsey's keen vampire hearing could hear the driver cursing under his breath and crinkling the ticket the officer had just issued him.

"Broken headlight, my ass. It just flickers. And I was not going seventy, it was sixty-five if it was anything." An old dog whined softly on the seat beside the driver, then huffed out a sigh as the truck rumbled away.

Ramsey glanced back at the police officer still below him.

He saw the man glance out his side window, up toward the hill where the vampire stood watching. Too late, he realized the city lights were behind his left side, providing a silhouette in the mist for the officer to see. With a sigh, he watched the officer exit his cruiser and make his way toward the cemetery, flipping his flashlight on and shining the beam up the hill toward where Ramsey stood. He watched the cop cross the highway and begin climbing the steep hillside, through the overgrown brambles and up to the cemetery fence. He watched him climb over the low wooden beams and he saw him stumble, catching himself with his hands as he scrambled up toward the vampire.

Ramsey let out a small sound of annoyance at this, and looked back toward the rear of the old graveyard, just at the top, where the old trees grew thickest. He'd come to this old cemetery to find something, something important to his rise to power back east. He'd smelled the artifact the minute he'd arrived in Seattle. They existed in many old graveyards, all over the world, and were usually hidden in dark places mortal men would never think, or dare, to look.

Glancing back at where the officer was just coming up into sight, the vampire shimmered in the cold, dank mist, the northern mist, the breeze that blows 'round the feet of the dead, the mist that smelled of nasty rotting things. He loved this mist; it felt like home. He sighed and turned, then threw a shadow around himself and disappeared.

He reappeared high overhead, flying weightlessly over

the treetops, smirking as his acute hearing brought wind of the police officer's exclamation of disbelief at being inexplicably robbed of his prize. He glanced ahead as he flew, grinned nastily, and made a decision. Pushing on and altering his direction to the right, he caught up with the old pickup truck. He landed in a column of smoke in the middle of the road, square in its path. His wings and fangs appeared in a ghostly, monstrous image illuminated by the truck's headlights.

With relish he took in the old driver's look of surprise and exclamation of "Holy shit!" He saw the old dog raise his head in mild surprise. He watched as the driver jerked at the wheel, brakes squealing, and run his vehicle into the ditch at 60 miles per hour. The front of the pickup crumpled immediately as it hit a telephone pole just on the other side of the ditch straight on, pushing the hot engine into the cab of the truck.

The dog was killed instantly. The man, impaled by the steering column, hot metal burning his old patched jeans and searing the flesh of his legs, screamed weakly before his cries ended as blood bubbled out of his mouth. His eyes turned toward the vampire as he died, and his last sight was of a clawed hand reaching for him. Smirking, Ramsey chuckled, looking down at the man's death grimace, mouth opened in a silent scream. Then the amusement vanished, and he folded into smoke and rose again into the air as mist, and headed back for the graveyard to see if the cop was gone.

Returning to the graveyard, he saw it was again deserted and he coalesced among the weeds at the far end, where the oldest tombstones stood, some crooked and slowly sinking into the damp Washington soil.

He closed his eyes and concentrated, sending out waves of fear-inducing power that rolled out like a tangible force over the hill. Several owls hurriedly flew away over his head, and under his feet, half a dozen ground squirrels fled through their tunnels. Even the spiders quickly scurried away. He did not want to be disturbed again. Closing his eyes, he let his senses zero in on the artifact and located it. He walked forward, following the smell of power the artifact exuded.

He opened his eyes and spotted the entrance to a crypt next to a dead tree. The rotted wooden door was wedged closed against the stone walls, which had begun to topple over. Weeds crowded the entrance, obscuring the lower half of the small building. It was built into the hillside, the interior extending about five feet into the earth. In all, it was roughly a dozen feet long and half again as wide. He pulled the rotted wood door open and flung it aside within seconds, then poked his head into the small room, smelling the three coffins there. Dust greeted his nostrils and clung to his eyes, and spider webs reached from ceiling to wall to floor. No one had entered this crypt in a very, very long time.

He focused on the coffins. The two on either side did not matter at all; it was the one farthest from the door that held the prize he sought. Reaching for the lid, he pried it up, ripping out nails that had for centuries secured the contents of the coffin. There was no light in the crypt, but the vampire's eyes glowed with an unearthly light all their own.

He shivered in restrained excitement as he beheld the rotted corpse within. The skin was blackened and moldy, the oily strands of hair grey and sparse, reaching down across shoulders clad in an old, rotting knight's garb. Spiders crawled across empty eye sockets, and a centipede slowly made its way out of the corpse's mouth, having been stirred by the slight wafting air the rising coffin lid had produced.

The corpse remained silent and still for a moment longer, then its armor began to move slightly, the insects that made their home within stirring as well. Ramsey had to be quick. He studied the corpse for any hint of animation and saw none. Clutched in the hands that lay across its chest was the object of his quest. Sneering, he grabbed the circular disc, yanked it out of the corpse's clutches, and took a step back, watching the body as he went. He took another step backward, then another. The corpse began to rumble softly, and out of a dozen places, insects of every morbid kind began to boil out of it.

Narrowing his eyes, Ramsey softly spoke a single word, and the creatures settled down. A few twitches later, and the corpse suddenly collapsed in on itself, its task finished. As a final movement, the coffin lid slammed shut on the whole thing, small clouds of rancid dust billowing out and settling around Ramsey's feet. He grasped the disc tightly in his hands, took one last look back, then turned and walked away. The crypt's rotted wooden door closed behind him by itself, wedging back into position under the stonework, and the dust settled, as though it had never been disturbed at all.

Down in the city, something white and rotten discarded a stinking corpse of what used to be a dog and climbed through the sewer system. It was drawn to the dank watery depths, where it feasted on rats when it wasn't lucky enough to kill a stray dog. There had been whispers of things best avoided, and the word was passed through the homeless community that lived in Seattle Below like lightning: stay away from the tunnels.

THE MUSEUM

"What do you think, Mama?" Anna held a black lace top up to her shoulders and twirled in front of the mirror as Alix and Lexei looked on in bemusement. A small pile of clothes lay on the bed, discarded.

"Oh, I like that one, Anya. I like it a lot," Alix sighed and smiled, remembering what is was like to be freshly in love and excited about a date.

"Anya, I think you should wear the blue shoes, not the black ones," Lexei grabbed a pair of glossy midnight blue pump boots with filigree work going up to the knee. They were gorgeous. Anna had had them custom made in Paris in 1933 by a leather worker who had made the most intricate shoes for the French elite of the time. She had a black leather filigree corset made to match; it lay on the bed, waiting to go over the top. Deep blue accented the edges of the corset, it was striking. Sure to melt hearts. A weapon that could subdue any soul. Anna loved it.

"Yes, I decided the blue ones would be better than the black." Anna tossed the black lace top onto the corset, reached for a shimmery black skirt and held it up to her waist, swishing her hips back and forth to make the fabric move.

"This boy, Anya, he is special?"

"Yes, Mama. He goes to the college; we have a class together. He is so handsome."

Alix made a sound through her teeth. "Handsome is everywhere. Tell me about *him*."

"Well, he's a bit taller than me, and he has brown hair with these gold highlights that catch the light," Anna paused, a dreamy look on her face. "His eyes are green, Mama. Green!" Alix smiled at her daughter's enthusiasm.

"What kind of boy is he? How did he talk to you?"

"He is very respectful. He held the door open for me; he bought me coffee."

"Coffee?" Alix looked amused.

"He was concerned about my tears, Mama. I was walking and thinking of Papa." Anna paused. "He reached out to a stranger who looked sad."

"I like him already," Alix smiled, tears in her own eyes. She hugged Anna tightly.

"And Mama: he *saw* me. I had a shadow wrapped around me, but he saw me."

Alix sat up straight. "What? Are you sure?"

Anna looked at her mother. "Very sure. And later, when we went into the coffee shop, he was so affected I thought I'd energized my aura, but it was tamped down, not active at all, completely off. There was another boy in the shop, I was within several feet of him and he was not affected at all. It was the strangest thing."

"Anna, I don't know what to make of this."

Lexei piped up. "Maybe he's your true love." He giggled.

"That's just a myth." Anna smiled.

"You never know. I heard somewhere that all myths have a basis in fact."

"Oh you," Anna threw a sock at her brother. It fluttered to the floor.

Alix looked pensive. "Anya, go on this date with this boy and see if he is still affected. In fact, wrap a shadow around yourself at some point, see if he still sees you."

"Maybe," Anna swirled the skirt around some more, thinking. "I may just forget myself. He's a total dream," she sighed.

"This dream sounds very different. He sounds like he may indeed be your true love. Does he live with one of the Kindred?"

"I don't know, I just met him. I don't even know where he lives. But he's something special. He made me smile," Anna smiled, remembering. "He made me laugh." Anna tossed the shimmery black skirt to the discard pile and reached for another, this one black with brilliant navy tulle accents. She held it up to her waist and twirled in a circle, letting the lights catch the shimmers in the skirt.

"Oh!" Alix put her hand to her mouth.

"That's the one!" Lexei jumped up with a WOOP!

"Yes." Anna's eyes gleamed, and her smile broadened. "This is the one."

Eric straightened his jacket nervously and looked at his cellphone. He was twenty minutes early, standing at the bottom of the low staircase in front of the museum, and there were major butterflies in his stomach. He inhaled slowly, closing his eyes, trying to relax.

Dressed in dark grey slacks and a crisp dress shirt with tie, he felt formal, but right. This girl was really something special, and he wanted to make the evening memorable. He didn't own a tuxedo, but this was close. Smart dark brown leather dress shoes clicked on the pavement as he took a few steps, running his hands through his freshly cut hair.

Eric wondered if he should have worn his overcoat, then decided he was fine, unless it should rain. *If I have to run or fight, the coat would just be a hindrance.* He chuckled to himself, thinking of what little chance there would be to do such things, in this very crime-free part of town. But that's what he felt with this girl. *I want to be her hero,* he thought, then shook his head, wondering where these thoughts were coming from.

He'd dated other girls in the past, but none of the short relationships had ever gone anywhere, and after a few weeks of dating he'd grown apart from them all. He'd never felt that certain spark from any girl until he'd met Anna. Spark, he chuckled inwardly. Yeah, it was a spark all right. From his eyes drinking her in, down to his throat, swallowing nervously, right down his spine like a zap of lightning and settling into the core of his being.

He paced now, remembering his reaction to her. Remembering her smell, the way she'd smiled at him over the lid of her coffee cup. The two dimples that only appeared when she laughed.

Swallowing again, Eric continued pacing, shaking his head to clear his mind. It would not do to greet the prettiest girl in Seattle in such a state. He glanced around him. With a careful pull, he tugged the jacket lower over the top of his slacks and buttoned the middle, then turned to scan the street again. Well, he *was* early. He sighed again.

"Hi," Anna said behind him. Eric startled, then turned with a smile and fell speechless.

Anna stood before him in the outfit she'd put together. Her hair curled softly out of a purple knit cap, framing her face and spilling down her shoulders. Rosy brown eyes sparkled above cheeks ruddy from the cold weather. Her lips curled into a friendly smile as he took her all in.

She wore a short leather jacket, open at the front and revealing the black lace blouse under the black and blue leather filigree corset. An inch of belly showed before the skirt began, its material floating lightly about her waist, black and blue, ending just above her knees. Blue filigree boots completed the picture, reaching from her knees down to the ground, where spiked heels raised her several inches above her normal height. My god. Eric had to work to catch his breath.

"Hi," he gulped as he saw her. He grinned nervously. "How are you?"

Anna studied him as a soft breeze blew past her hair, gently lifting the soft curls. It moved on to ruffle his hair slightly, drawing her attention to his head from where her gaze had previously rested, somewhere near his jawline. She was the one to swallow nervously this time. A small smile played on his lips, and she gave an answering grin. His smile grew larger.

"I'm great," she smiled. "Shall we go in?

Once inside the museum, they strolled through, looking at different works of art and talking.

"How was your week?" Eric's hand hovered near her back, guiding her through the front hall of the museum. Huge statues rose twenty feet above them in the center of the foyer, with a dual marble staircase curling around and up on both sides.

"Oh, good, good. Kind of slow and steady; things getting back to normal." She glanced at him, smiling, "the way I like things, actually."

"I know what you mean. Sometimes having a lot of stuff happening in your life can be really stressful," He slowed his walk to match hers, his hands now locked behind his back. They wandered around the first floor, looking at each exquisite painting and sculpture in turn, each trying very hard to concentrate on the beautiful works of art. Each failing miserably. Finally, they reached the front, where they'd begun their tour. Eric took her hand lightly. It was soft and small, but he felt a strength beneath the ladylike exterior. He turned and faced her, gazing into her eyes for a long moment without speaking. He smiled softly, and was rewarded with an answering grin from her. He gently squeezed her hand.

Eric's heart was swelling with quiet emotion, and as he looked out the window at the starry night sky, his full concentration was on the incredible young lady beside him. He sensed her contentment and felt a growing wonder at his own emotions.

"Let's go up to the top floor. I think they've got a special exhibition going on right now." He led her to the stairs. As they ascended the broad, curving staircase, they could see the first-floor foyer, and the statues at the entrance, from a different perspective.

Anna turned and stopped halfway up. "Oh, they're really beautiful from this angle."

"You can really see them from up here." Eric agreed. They both stood there for several minutes, appreciating the beauty of the huge marble artwork, then continued their climb up the shallow stairway.

The second floor of the museum was dedicated to statuary and there was a curving glass atrium that reached up ten feet above their heads. At night, with the city lights glowing in the distance, it was striking. Off to the side, they could see the water twinkling in the nearby bay. Anna was drawn to the view and stood there, not talking; Eric stood behind her and to her side, just barely touching her hair with his chest.

They stayed together like that for some minutes, not speaking, just enjoying the view of Seattle and the bay. Anna sighed with contentment and gently leaned back into Eric, enjoying what was for her a rare, perfect evening. He lowered his lips to her head and opened his mouth slightly, inhaling her scent. She smiled.

Anna's vampire aura was completely tamped down; she felt relaxed, perfectly at ease in this young man's arms, something she had never felt before, not in more than a century of living. Warmth began to spread in her heart for Eric, and although their courtship was still young, she felt a growing sensation that she could only describe as destiny. After some time, they turned to go up to the top floor and the new exhibit.

The top level was only accessible by the rear stairway, and separated from the rest of the museum by heavy black curtains for the exhibition. Parting the drapes, Eric led Anna through and up into the darkness. Eric kept Anna's hand in his as they slowly ascended the shallow stairs, lit only by twinkling lights set in the wall and glowing lights at their feet.

"Watch your step," he said.

"Oh look!" She had spied the landing they were approaching.

Spread out in front of them as they reached the top step was a panorama. Everything was in dark colors, with only backlit midnight blue touches here and there. The banner across the top far wall read, "The Vampire Across the Ages."

Anna kept her face straight. What were the odds? Did he know? No, he couldn't. Could he? No ...

"Oh, this is fascinating," he marveled as he let go of her hand and moved to examine the first piece in the exhibit.

Spread across the spacious top floor, the exhibit showed both the literary figure of the vampire, beginning with the most famous, Count Dracula, throughout the ages; and the historical figure of the vampire. A huge corner was dedicated to Bram Stoker's novel. Anna moved to study the many artifacts and panels explaining it all.

Eric moved to the next piece, which was a large display of the historical Vlad the Impaler, and the history of his time.

"I had no idea Count Dracula was a real historical hero," he said, half to himself. Coming up behind him, Anna looked over his shoulder at the presentation.

"Fascinating," was all she said.

Eric lingered for several minutes reading the background on Vlad the Impaler; the Prince of Wallachia, he learned, was still hailed as a folk hero in Romania and Europe for defending the population against the Ottomans. The exhibit also featured some artifacts from Eastern Europe, including a painting of the prince against the backdrop of the Danube. It was beautiful.

Eric and Anna moved to examine all the artifacts near the front of the exhibit, then they walked to the side to examine depictions of vampires in various cultures. It explained how myth and fact merged, and how both were clouded in the mists of history. One display focused on African legends of creatures called shetani, primitive vampire-like animal spirits whose bodies were pitch black, distorted and shaped in unnatural ways, as if evolution had gone mad.

The back wall of the exhibit was cloaked in shadows. A diorama stretching back to half the length of the building and reaching up over twenty feet high had been set up as a huge European forest. Majestic great horned owls perched on high branches, hunched over, glowering down at the forest floor.

Back in the dark outer reaches of the forest, just visible from behind the trees, wolves and foxes with glowing eyes could be seen. Eric's steps brought him toe to toe with the edge of the 'forest' and he peered into the dark shadows. Several silhouettes were suggestive of vampires lurking deep in the forest, peering out from behind the trees in this almost surreal woodland, which stretched back farther than they could see in the dim light.

A trail had been built, suggesting that patrons walk the winding path through the forest. If they looked hard, the suggestion of a black painted wall could be seen on the edges of the diorama, but otherwise, the illusion of a spooky forest reaching back a hundred miles was convincing. Eric stood at the head of the trail, not wanting to appear nervous, but feeling uncertain nevertheless.

"Do you want to go in?" he asked quietly.

Anna knew she could handle anything in a real forest, and this was a very good facsimile of one, so she smiled and made her voice sound lighthearted. "Sure."

Eric took her hand and led the way onto the path.

As soon as they stepped three paces into the diorama, darkness closed in around them, completing the illusion. Motion sensors had detected their bodies entering the mockup and had dimmed the lights in the outer exhibit they'd just left to a low backlighting sepia. Anna smiled at the elaborate setup. A few more steps into the forest and the path turned to carry them up and over a low hill, then behind a tree before curling back into the center of the exhibit.

Eric held Anna's hand and led the way as they slowly walked up the narrow path. He stopped still as he saw the first vampire come into view. A black hood covered the head of an old man, skin paper white, eyes glowing with an unnatural light, mouth half open and canine teeth extended past his lips. Eric studied the mockup closely. It was fascinating. Behind him, Anna was about to roll her eyes, then stopped as she sensed something she couldn't quite put her finger on.

"Eric, do you...?"

"This is incredible..."

They both spoke at the same time.

The vampire wore a long trench coat and black boots under black slacks. Its arms were extended, half raised, its fingers curling into the suggestion of claws, ready to grab its victim.

Eric studied the figure for a minute, then started walking again. As they passed the vampire, Anna looked it up and down closely, then closed her eyes, trying to sense the new energy she'd felt. She couldn't put her finger on it.

They walked on, farther into the diorama. The light from the outside world had faded completely, leaving the lights in the forest to illuminate the way for them. Purple and grey glowed from behind bushes and trees, and the creators of the exhibit had even provided a dark sky over their heads. As Eric and Anna peered up through the trees, they caught their breath. The moon shown, partially obscured by dark clouds that scuttled across it.

"They must have some kind of projection," Eric mused.

Anna shifted uneasily. Eric brought her hand closer, and they walked on.

An owl that suddenly screeched directly in front of them, making them both jump and look up.

"Looks a bit fake. Look: it's not moving at all, no owl would sit so still with people this close," Eric said.

They walked on.

The path curled to the other side and forward, bringing them to a particularly dark cluster of trees. A rumbling of uneasiness clutched at Eric's chest, but he kept walking. A low growl made them start as they rounded the cluster. Rotting moss hung from the trees, and a dripping sound reached their ears. At the other side of the copse, a strong smell hit their nostrils, bringing them up short. Another owl screeched an ululating cry. Eric's heart beat faster.

Anna had stopped. "Eric, I'm not sure..." This was no longer a mockup. She could sense movement in the trees above them, and before them a swamp glowed with a sickly green light. Water, thick and slick with some kind of oily scum, rolled lazily as something under the water swam past. Moss curled around the trees and dripped from the branches, Louisiana style. They walked farther in.

Anna sensed several deadly creatures coming toward them. Their origin? Anna's mind raced at the only logical conclusion: A tesseract, or time portal, existed at what should have been the back of the "exhibit," which stretched far beyond the back wall of the building and should not have existed where they were now standing. The air glowed purple, and glittery fragments swirled in a soft wind that also should not have been there, inside a building.

They looked up and saw the real night sky, no longer a dark ceiling with a projection of clouds but the real moon, with clouds scuttling across it and stars twinkling in the distance. Their eyes traced the path of an owl across the sky, flying in a high arc, then dropping closer to the ground as some animal screeched nearby. Eric swallowed and whispered, "This can't be real."

Anna squeezed his hand, her heart beating faster. "It's real, and I think there're several things in this forest we do *not* want to meet."

A form blacker than night itself scurried across the side of the path a couple of feet off the ground, running sideways along the trunks of the trees growing along the way. Recoiling in horror, Eric gripped Anna's hand and positioned himself between her and this living nightmare. They heard a second growl as another jet-black creature joined the first. This one leered at them, its head too big for its thin neck to support, yet supporting it nonetheless. Its mouth, filled with jagged teeth, took up most of its nightmarish face. It scuttled behind the first, and both giggled madly in anticipation of an easy meal before rushing to attack Eric and Anna.

Eric bent and grabbed a nearby branch off the ground, the only thing at hand. Straightening, he swallowed, and tensed himself for their attack.

Anna, recognizing the creatures that were attacking them as shetani, closed her eyes and glowed up her power. Long canine teeth grew rapidly out of her mouth, claws grew out of her fingers, and her eyes glowed. She could feel the surge in her body's energy and ferocity swelled in her chest as she opened her eyes. She felt a rush of protectiveness for Eric. He stood beside her, holding her hand and pulling her behind him protectively as his other hand wielded the branch that was his only defense against these nightmarish creatures from hell.

She felt a warmth in her chest, incredibly strong, for this mortal. He could never hope to win a fight against these shetani, but he was determined to try.

Anna whispered, "Sleep," and Eric softly crumpled to the ground, unconscious. Looking beyond him to the chittering creatures rushing to attack them, Anna narrowed her eyes. This was something she understood, something she knew she could handle. Rushing to meet them, lest they harm the human with her, she screamed a furious challenge, her voice deafening and nearly ultrasonic.

The two shetani screamed back and paused in their headlong rush. They had not anticipated one of the People being here to challenge them. They hesitated, and before they could get any closer, Anna rushed past Eric and, screaming in fury, set on the first shetani.

It never had a chance. In a second, she had the thing's head in her arms and was ripping it in two. It screamed, black claws clutching at her in an almost intimate embrace, then abruptly went limp, its cry cut off in a gurgle as its throat was forcibly split. Its head went rolling off to the side, and Anna held its torso away from her as black blood shot out and splattered against a nearby tree, where it smoked and peeled off the bark.

Dropping the body to the ground, its blood still spouting, Anna turned her attention to the second creature, which had begun to turn and flee. Screaming another challenge, she jumped, launching herself ten feet through the air and landing on the oversized head of the nightmare that had come to feast. It shrieked and turned, trying to bite Anna, but she was far too quick for it. Moving with unnatural speed, she quickly dispatched this second shetani, throwing its body to the side as well.

Anna drew her arm across her mouth as she turned to Eric's form. He had remained asleep, oblivious to the carnage that had taken place mere feet from him. As she walked back to where he lay, Anna concentrated and her teeth shrunk back into her jaws; her claws were once again fingers.

Turning to look back at the fallen shetani, Anna watched as their bodies, smoking and melting, dissolved into two wet, black smudges, tendrils of smoke curling up from the ground where they'd fallen. She narrowed her eyes, staring into the black reaches of the false forest become real.

Looking back down at Eric, she whispered, "Awaken." Eric slowly opened his eyes and sat up, shaking his head to clear the fog he felt.

"What happened?" He looked at the wet smudges, not realizing the shetani had fallen there. He looked around everywhere, trying to locate the nightmarish creatures that had just seemed poised to attack.

"They are gone, but I think ..."

An owl screeched quite close to them, and they both looked up at the same time at the huge brown and white bird perched on the branch above the path. Its head swiveled back and forth, its eyes studying them. It seemed almost accusing, as if it were part of the forest and resented them for killing its nightmares instead of succumbing to them.

"We need to get out of here. More can come," Anna said in a low voice. Feeling shaky, Eric nodded mutely and took her hand again, a bemused expression on his face. He turned to the left to go down the path, but now there were three paths going off to the left. Two more were heading off to the right.

"Which way is out?" he said.

"I think it may be creating more paths just to confuse us," Anna said, taking a few steps forward. Palm fronds seemed to move, encouraging her to go forward, as if they were herding them in a specific direction. "We're not safe here."

Eric shuddered. "The forest is creating paths?" he whispered.

"This place isn't just real. It's ... alive."

Anna took Eric's hand firmly and, sniffing the air, moved away from the breeze blowing in from the night sky above them.

"We need to move back toward the door, away from this." She stepped backward, then turned and began walking quickly, pulling Eric along. The forest did not want them to leave. Huge trees appeared to block their path, and they heard a high-pitched scream of a cheetah off to their left. Something scurried through the bushes alongside them, and they jumped.

"Come on." Anna led Eric back away from the wild breeze, skirting trees and bushes that appeared to block their path. Squeezing around two trees, they had to duck as branches caught their hair and tried to pull them back in.

Fifty feet later, diving through a thick, black wall of diseased palms and bushes, Anna pushed her hand out and felt nothing but air. Squeezing through, she saw the fake forest path on the other side; the sight of its straight lines of manicured redwood mulch flooded her with feelings of relief.

"Finally," she said, pulling Eric through behind her. As they stumbled onto the museum floor, leaving the exhibit behind them, they turned to look at the forest they'd escaped. Something screamed quite close, from beyond the wall of bushes they'd just come through.

Turning, Anna and Eric ran to the dark staircase, and down it; then down the wide center staircase of the large museum foyer, and out the door of the now-deserted museum. They saw no one, anywhere, and they wondered where the other visitors and museum docents had gone.

The thing had waited for so long, alert, smelling, listening, that when it finally sensed the disturbance, it fainted. A minute later, it came to, and began frothing at the mouth. Chittering away in the dark, talking to itself, it scrambled blindly toward the disturbance, crawling on all fours through the water in the tunnel. As it approached its target, it moved to the side wall and, using its razor-sharp talons, began to crawl up the black stone, slick with grime and muck and slime growth. Soon, it was on the ceiling, moving forward upside-down, breathing fast in excitement through its sharp black teeth, which were so long it could not entirely close its mouth.

INVESTIGATIONS

Eric and Anna hurried down the street, away from the museum. A block away, Eric turned and looked up at the building, rising up several stories, multicolored spotlights playing on the outside, it looked like it had always looked, whenever he had passed this way before, except ... Eric gazed up to the top-floor windows on the side of the building. He could see forms flickering across, shadows flitting past, moving faster than any human or animal should. Shivering, he kept staring, unable to tear his eyes from what seemed impossible. Something hit the window full-on, and a crack appeared in the glass.

"Come on," Anna pulled Eric along and hurried down the sidewalk toward a city bus a couple of blocks ahead. They ran for it and jumped on at the last minute. Eric remained silent and allowed himself to be pulled along. She led them both to the back of the nearly empty bus, where they stared out the rear window as it pulled away, their eyes searching the night to see if anything had followed them in the dark, sleepy city.

They leaned forward and pulled their coats together against the chill. They sat that way, in silence, looking out at the passing city, for a good ten minutes. But Eric could not keep quite forever.

"Anna..."

Anna lowered her eyes, knowing what was coming.

"What just happened?"

"I don't know," she said honestly. She had no idea why a tesseract had been opened at the back of a museum exhibit, in a building in downtown Seattle. She looked out the window. It had begun to rain. Droplets of water ran down the glass, reflecting the lights and colors of the vibrant yet slumbering city.

"I saw those creatures. I know I didn't imagine them. Then, the next thing I knew, I'd blacked out. I have no idea why. What happened?"

Anna was silent.

"Can you tell me how long I was out?" Eric asked in a low voice.

"Only a few minutes," she said quietly, still looking out the window.

Eric remained silent.

After a while, she continued, "I saw them, too." She

looked down at her lap.

"Do you know what happened, Anna? Because I feel clueless, and I don't like feeling clueless."

Anna looked into Eric's eyes. They were so earnest, an honest pleading for some explanation of what had just happened. She knew she could fix this in a second, erase his memory and go on her way. But she didn't want either of them to forget the experience that just happened, even though it hurt, even though it made her feel horrible.

"Sometimes I just wish I could have a normal life, even a normal day, just once." Horrified at the feeling of tears gathering at the corners of her eyes, she quickly wiped them away.

"What do you mean?"

Anna sniffed and looked out the window. "Things like what happened tonight? Things like that happen to me on a regular basis."

"What??"

"What I mean is, for my whole life, I've never been able to have anything normal, like a date, or a romance, or any relationship, that wasn't..." Anna searched for the right words. "...interrupted in some way."

"Interrupted in what way?"

Anna looked at him. "I..." she looked down at her lap, struck mute.

Eric waited.

"I just wish that for once I could have a normal day." Anna

sniffed quietly. Eric remained silent. "My life, don't get me wrong, I'm not bitter or anything, I am just ... My life is very ... complicated." A tear rolled down her cheek.

"Here," Eric handed her a handkerchief. As Anna blew her nose he continued. "Well, I will help as much as I can." He studied her face, then leaned forward and softly kissed her cheek.

The bus was nearing the campus. "Do you want to grab a coffee?"

Anna blew her nose again and smiled. "Yeah. Doing ordinary things is wonderful. What happened back there ..."

"I know. Weirded me out. I mean, what were those things? I don't think they were part of the museum exhibit at all."

Anna laughed, "No, I don't think so, either."

Anna burst through the door to her home, her eyes searching for her mother. Alix looked up from her book, and her eyes met her daughter's. She knew right away something had happened. Lexie was there, too, working on a painting.

"What is it?" she asked.

Words tumbled out of her mouth in rapid succession and she rushed to recount the story of all that had happened at the museum.

"A doorway, opened here, in Seattle?" Lexei said, pausing

in mid-brushstroke.

"That means one of the People has come into possession of a runestone, somewhere nearby. I wasn't aware there were many on this coast." Alix looked worried.

"I haven't felt any disturbances lately." Lexei continued painting.

"Anya, we must try to seal it."

"How, Mama? We'd have to use the runestone that was used to open it." Anna paced in the small central room.

"Well then, we search for the runestone. But first, maybe an exploration of this museum's exhibit is in order."

"A hunt?" Lexei looked interested.

"I'm not sure ... " Anna stopped, looking pensive. "Mama, Eric saw them, the shetani. There were two of them, and they attacked. When they jumped out at us all of a sudden, I couldn't put him to sleep before he saw them." She began pacing again.

"And you didn't wipe his short-term memory? Anya, why not? You know what's at stake." Alix's brow furrowed.

"Mama, I couldn't bear to." Anna looked at the ground. "I ... I feel close to him. I don't know. Maybe I'm falling in love with him. For sure I at least want something real with him."

"It's too dangerous, Anya."

"What if I trust him, Mama?"

"Anya, you place us all in danger if you trust this boy with your secret. Our secret."

"Mama ..." Anna fell silent, tears at the corners of her eyes.

"Oh, Anya, my sweet Anya," Alix came and embraced her daughter, who turned and buried her face in her mother's bosom. Anna's back began to shake as tears came. Alix ran her hand down Anna's hair. "Anya ..." Alix kissed her daughter's head and laid her cheek on top of Anna's head.

Since being turned so many years ago, life had become desperate and surreal for all of them. The ache for normalcy was palpable in the room. Lexei came and patted her sister on the back as his mother held her. "Anna," Lexei spoke quietly. "I trust your instincts. They have always kept us safe and alive." Lexei turned his face to his mother's. "Perhaps we should trust this boy as well."

Alix looked pensive. Anna lifted her head to look at her brother, who handed her some tissue. She blew her nose and wiped her eyes, which were red and wet.

"He has a pure heart; I sensed it immediately," Anna said quietly. "I trust him, Mama."

"You'd trust him with your life, Anya?" Alix looked into her daughter's face.

"Mama, I trust my own instincts to keep me alive. I mean, if I did not feel I could keep myself safe, I'd never leave this house." Anna stood up straight. "Eric could become a real ally, not just a friend, but someone that we could trust for years to come."

Anna could almost see the thoughts flit across her mother's mind, the instinctive desire to keep her family safe, to protect her children, warring with the realization she couldn't possibly keep them safe all the time. She could not keep them locked away from the world completely, with no life at all. They'd all lived for decades in secret at the castle in Russia, and while it had been necessary at the time, and it had been torture.

"I think we must wait longer, see how this boy grows in this relationship. Anya, are you going to see him soon?"

"Yes, he made another date for next week. His sister has a small exhibition; she's a painter." Anna looked over at Lexei.

At this, Lexei looked sharply at his sister in interest and smiled. "A painter?"

"Yes, apparently she is quite the natural talent." Anna looked up at her mother again. "So, I will take it slow, get to know him better, Mama. Then we will see."

"Yes. A person's character shows itself, eventually. Usually when you least expect it." Alix cupped her daughter's face.

"Well then, you'll be happy to know that when the shetani first appeared, Eric grabbed a nearby branch and was prepared to fight to keep me safe."

Alix looked intrigued. "This is interesting. It may mean more than a good character, Anya."

"What do you mean, Mama?"

"He may be falling in love with you. Did you keep your aura tightly clamped down?"

"Yes, I was sure to. But it was odd. At first I thought I was slipping."

"Why, Anya?"

"He seemed affected by it. But I checked, I knew I'd kept it tight down." Anna looked pensive. "Even after tightening it down, I saw him. His reactions, they were..."

"Hmmm..."

"Well, we have more immediate concerns." Alix looked at her two children. "Fly with me?"

"Absolutely," Anna smiled, happy to see Alix ready to hunt once again.

"Let's go!" Lexei jumped up with excitement.

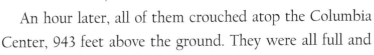

An hour later, all of them crouched atop the Columbia Center, 943 feet above the ground. They were all full and happy, contented and energized. The sky above them was solid with clouds so dark grey as to be nearly black.

Anna stood, stretching her arms to the heavens. As she focused, an impressive set of black wings sprouted from her back. Sleek and dark as midnight, they resembled a raven's wings, but more curved. Black iridescent feathers, long enough to drag the ground when she walked, curled around and crossed in front of her feet, soft and warm. Lexei and Alix stood up as well; soon, their own enormous wings appeared behind them.

All three vampiric auras were fully extended, so no

mortal could see them. Invisible to the naked eye, they blended perfectly with the night around them. Soon they were in flight above the city, winging their way over downtown skyscrapers to the Museum of Modern Art.

Anna, Alix and Lexei rose ever higher in the sky, up through the clouds until their silent flight carried them above the billowing formations and gave them a clear view of the crescent moon. As each emerged from the mist, they twirled tightly, spraying droplets in every direction, then rose higher still and, wings flashing out, glided onward.

Lexei flew out in front. Swinging up and around and twirling about, he played in the warm autumn night's breeze and danced with his family in the pale moonlight. They all laughed in delight at their freedom in the air.

After a while, their flight brought them close to the museum, and they slowly descended in lazy circles to street level. Standing there in front of the museum entrance, they all looked up and studied the building. It was silent and dark and shut tight for the night.

"When we left, there was no one inside, even though it had been packed less than an hour earlier when we went in," Anna said. "It seemed abandoned then, but lit up inside; now it's dark." Anna pointed toward the highest windows. "The vampire exhibit was on the top floor."

"Well, then, let's go have a look." Lexei leapt into the air, and, flapping hard, winged his way up to the roof; Anna and Alix followed. Upon reaching the top, all three shook their heads slightly, and their wings disappeared.

They again wore dark street clothes, looking like ordinary humans, although their auras remained strong. Alix approached the door on the roof that led down into the museum. She gripped the doorknob and turned it sharply, breaking the lock and sending pieces of metal falling to the floor. They entered and descended the short, dark staircase in seconds.

They stepped silently into the room that held the vampire exhibit and the diorama on the right; the area, the whole building in fact, was quiet as a grave. Anna stood before the artificial forest path she'd stumbled out of only hours before; Alix and Lexei stood behind her. Anna closed her eyes, stretching her senses, reaching out.

Her ears became slightly pointed, further enhancing the vampire's acute sense of hearing, making her look like the oddest Vulcan that might ever be seen aboard a starship. She lifted her face and sniffed the air like a cat, her mouth opening slightly, tongue extended, inhaling the air for any hint of disturbance. Beside her, Alix and Lexei extended their senses into the room as well, trying to detect whatever might be there. All remained silent.

Anna took a few steps closer to the edge of the diorama, pausing, listening, smelling. Nothing. Sighing, she took five more steps and set foot on the fake path, her hand touching a frond that extended from a potted palm, the pot mostly covered by the fake moss that lay everywhere. She stilled again, sniffing the air, ears straining for any noise, any movement in the fake forest which she knew hid a real forest within. A minute passed. Then another.

Without warning, the piercing scream of a jaguar assailed her ears from off to the right, and almost immediately, the deafening growl of a large wolf answered from the left, very close by. Anna turned back to her mother and brother, nodded, and returned her attention to the forest. Eyes closing, they each took a deep breath and pushed, allowing their vampire energy to glow.

Long fangs appeared in their mouths, extending their canines; claws emerged from their fingertips, and each of the three grew in height. Their eyes opened again to reveal pupils that glowed an ethereal, unnatural red. Anna squinted, focusing on the forest, feeling energy surge through her body. She was strong, fast, and deadly. As were the two vampires behind her. Having just eaten, all three were at the height of their power. There was not much on this earth that could threaten them.

As a hunting unit, they sprang into the forest, tearing through the plants that reached out in vain to halt their progress. Giant palm fronds were tossed aside, bouncing back into place behind them as they passed. Within a few seconds, the exhibit room and diorama held no trace of the three vampires. It was as if they'd never been there.

In his high-rise office downtown, Greg Ramsey paused from his work, thinking. He had been focused on the paperwork in front of him: a contract. One that, when fulfilled, would bring him another step closer to his political goals. But something tickled at the back of his mind. What had that been? He'd felt something, something ... He glanced up at the ceiling, then suddenly realized what had flown overhead.

"Oh my god."

Within a minute, his office was locked tight, and he was on the roof of the building. His brow furrowed in concentration as dark wings practically exploded out of his back. Their feathers were like midnight, a flat black that disappeared in the night's shadows.

Silhouetted against the night sky, he closed his eyes and inhaled deeply, trying to discern the direction of the air's disturbance. He concentrated until it seemed as though he would sweat blood from his forehead. But it was no use; it had been too long. The trail had gone cold. Launching himself off the building, he winged his way higher and higher, then leveled off. He decided to go check on the doorway he'd opened with the runestone he'd stolen from the knight's tomb.

———————————<≪♦≫———————————

Deep in the dark forest, Anna, Alix and Lexei realized they were no longer inside the museum. Looking up, they no longer saw the its shadowy ceiling; in its place was a sky that went on forever. Stars could be seen that had not been seen since the invention of the electric light. Since the discovery of fire. Since before man was more ape than human, and still screamed at the night and huddled in the trees for comfort.

This was forest from a long-ago epoch, when what was now the Western Hemisphere had been covered almost completely with wild forest. It was from a time, hundreds of thousands of years before they'd been born, indeed, many millions of years in the past. The trees went on forever, in all directions, and reached up hundreds of feet into the sky. Ancient redwoods, spruce, and trees that had never been named crowded together and fought for light, straining to reach a sun that, given the nature of this magical place, would never again appear.

Anna, looking about the trees and giant ferns, and noticed that the fake diorama path transformed itself almost immediately into a path worn by predatory animals chasing their quarry. It was wider than normal, and the plants were cleared for at least ten feet over it.

Lexei came to stand close to his sister, and Alix bent to whisper in their ears. "This path ..."

A loud, ear-splitting roar sounded off in front of them, and a large creature covered in dark brown feathery fur appeared on the path, supported by four powerful legs that ended in razor-sharp claws. As it spotted them, it let out another scream.

Its head was a nightmare, teeth extending so far out it would have impossible for the creature to entirely close its mouth. It stood at least eight feet tall at the shoulder, and its neck extended down from there to meet prey six feet off the ground. Powerful muscles rippled under the hide, which was half fur and half feathers, close to its massive paws. The thing was at least fifteen feet long, not including its tail, which extended another nine feet. It looked like a dinosaur version of an oversized saber-toothed tiger. It was utterly deadly. Eyeing the vampires again, it screamed a challenge.

Alix screamed back an answering roar, sounding just as ferocious as the creature before them. Anna and Lexei screamed with her. The sound was deafening, and partially supersonic. Induced fear, palpable and nearly visible, rolled out from all directions from the vampires. As it hit the creature, it reared up, screamed again, then backed off. Before it could disappear in the direction it had come, a dozen pitch-black shetani appeared to block its path.

Some were low to the ground, a mere two feet high, yet deadly, with mouths full of slashing teeth, claws extending far out in front of them, poison dripping from their fangs. Others were tall and slim, with leathery wings tipped with sharp hooked claws that sprang forth from their backs.

Still others rode astride what appeared to be small,

feathered velociraptor-like dinosaurs. They held on by grasping fistfuls of feathers on the sides of the dinosaurs' necks, and straddling four longs legs on the sides, with heels cocked against the velociraptors' flanks, needle-sharp claws digging into the sensitive flesh. The dinosaurs screamed, and the nightmarish shetani let out insane giggling sounds from atop their mounts. Behind them, a twenty-foot-tall shetani poked its head through the tree branches and made a low rumble, its mouth sporting foot-long sharp, jagged teeth.

The dinosaur-tiger screamed in frustration and took a huge bounding leap to the side, disappearing through the ferns to escape. Six of the smaller shetani ran after it, in pursuit. After a minute, the chase carried them beyond hearing.

The vampires kept their eyes on the remaining shetani, staring them down, unblinking, as they hissed through their fangs, claws extended. The vampire fear hung thick in the air, oppressive, and the shetani, nightmarish entities though they were, were nonetheless imbued with an instinct for survival. Because of this, they hesitated. And that hesitation gave the three vampires all the time they needed.

Anna, Alix and Lexei leapt forward, so fast the shetani only saw blurs of movement. The creatures in front went first. Where one shetani stood, suddenly there was just dark blood, and a blacker-than-black nightmarish head flipped up through the giant ferns and palm fronds, into the air in an almost elegant arc, off to the side of the fight.

Other animals saw the head spinning lazily, spraying black blood in a delicate splatter against leaves, branches and the trunks of several trees before its path turned downward, and it plunged into the thick forest undergrowth, out of sight.

The observers fled in terror. The few screams the remaining shetani managed to let out cut off abruptly, and although the fern and undergrowth thrashed about for a moment or two, the forest was soon plunged into deadly silence once again.

Anna stood up straight and turned to look at her brother. He grinned at her, his claws covered in black blood as his arm wiped it from his face. "Gross." He spat out a bit of it that had managed to get in his mouth.

"Pah!" Anna smiled, then looked beyond him to their mother.

Alix stood, panting slightly, face glowing with a big smile. "God, that felt good." She took a deep breath, turning her face up to the moon and letting out a "Woot!" in exuberance. Anna's smiled broadened. It was good to see her mother feeling better. Alix was a deadly creature when in full power, and she was nearing that again.

"Let's get a better look at how far this forest extends," Lexei turned to one of the larger trees, which reached more than a hundred feet into the sky, and began to run up its huge trunk.

Ramsey dipped his wings and dove down into the dark city, entering a familiar alley and ducking down behind a dumpster. Wings gone, and overcoat in their place, he soon strode quickly to the dark little metal door in the side of the building. He wrinkled his nose at the filthy alley and, with one leather gloved covered hand, wrenched the door open, breaking the lock in the process. Entering the small storeroom, he stepped around the cans of paint and litter to the back, where Tristan lay against a metal door.

"Get up, fool." Ramsey kicked him hard. Tristan jumped and opened his eyes. "You should have been awake hours ago; it's past midnight."

"Sorry." Tristan rubbed his eyes. He tried to stand and failed, falling back against the wall. He made it on the second try, though, and stood in front of Ramsey, swaying slightly.

"You're drunk," Ramsey spat off to the side and refrained from knocking the other vampire to the ground. He needed Tristan and the other two tonight. Looking around, kicking through the rubbish, he asked, "Where are Claude and Emil?"

"Uh," Tristan took a deep breath and began to retch off to the side, trying not to hit Ramsey's shoes, which were polished to a mirror shine. Finishing, he wiped his mouth and turned to the small door he'd been lying against.

"There."

Ramsey grabbed the handle of the door to the enclosure, which looked like it had once been used to store coal. Pulling so hard the door came off in his hand, he reached in and grabbed a leg, pulling hard.

"AH!" Claude was wrenched out of the coal closet hard, his head knocking against the floor repeatedly. He scrambled to his feet, also rubbing his eyes, and tried to pull his coat down to appear neater. Behind him Emil, wakened by Claude's scream, scurried out into the open and stood next to the others.

"I need you all to follow me." Ramsey looked at the three with deep disgust. "Can you do that?"

All three brushed at their clothing, straightening it, and nodded, deciding it was probably safest to remain silent and do as they were told. Ramsey snorted and stepped back out into the alleyway again. The others followed.

Soon, all four were winging their way toward the museum.

Anna, Lexei and Alix crouched in the forest's treetops, swaying on the upmost branches as they gazed out over the land that stretched away beneath them. The crescent moon hung in the sky, a curving sliver of silver-white light that did nothing to illuminate the land. The millions of stars scattered across the sky were intense and amazing, but what caught the vampires' eyes was the purple glow emanating from a large cave in the side of a hill about a mile away. The light drew their attention even more so because it was flickering irregularly.

"What is that?" Lexei squinted his eyes to see better.

"Nothing natural to this world, I think." Alix was grim. "Although..."

"What Mama?"

"It almost feels ... ancient. But of our line. I feel the blood draw... Something in this land calls to me."

"Do you feel anything?" Anna felt a slight pull coming from the direction of the cave; it was so slight it might have been her imagination. She shifted on her branch.

"Come." Anna couldn't wait another minute. Curiosity may have killed the cat, but it was a boon to vampires, and it kept them alive. Ignorance could kill. She concentrated, her wings appeared, and she launched herself into the air. Alix and Lexei followed.

Winging their way across the short distance to the cave, they studied the land as they flew over it. The forest was huge and dense, and they could see a large lake off in the distance. The air felt incredibly clean; a wet mist rose from the trees and scented the air above the forest with a smell that hadn't been present on modern day Earth for over a million years.

Off in the distance, a smallish pterodactyl-like dinosaur

winged lazily through the air, then dove suddenly down near the lake, silent and deadly. It rose again moments later, a small animal trapped in its large beak. Toward the cave, something leapt out of the treetops, another, larger creature flying after it in pursuit. This was a dangerous, tragic land; wild, clean and feral, but utterly deadly. Anna felt no fear, but took careful note of all she witnessed and filed it away for later use.

Arriving at the cave, she landed silently and delicately among the ferns and palms, neither breaking nor disturbing leaf or stem. She folded her wings tightly against her back as Alix and Lexei landed next to her; then, nodding to them, she approached the cave entrance.

***

Ramsey entered the museum with his three companions through the back entrance. He had procured a key, so they hadn't been detected. They sensed nothing amiss as they made their way up the stairs to the top of the building; everything was as expected. The museum had been placed under a huge enchantment when Ramsey had hidden the runestone through the tesseract he'd created at the back wall of the vampire exhibit's diorama.

As his steps took him to the top and across the exhibit floor to the diorama, he was almost smiling.

Ramsey stepped onto the diorama path, with Tristan,

Claude and Emil behind him, and they swiftly made their way through to the back of the false forest, through the tesseract and into the real forest. The primeval forest. The forest inhabited with the nightmarish creatures, both real and imagined, that would quickly attack and consume any museum visitor that happened to wander through, Ramsey thought with a smile.

They were soon through and running down the path as it cut through the forest. It was a trail carved out by huge, primitive creatures that had haunted the forests of North America when it was still a part of Pangea, the mother continent.

It was here that vampires had first appeared, born of a branch in the odd family tree from which the shetani also sprang; which had given rise to all the weirdly malignant, predatory, nightmarish animals native to Earth. As they traveled, Ramsey wondered how only the vampire had survived throughout the epochs and millennia to reach the modern age.

Outside the museum, crawling up the side of the building like an alabaster cockroach crawling up the wall of a filthy kitchen, the creature stuck its nose up in the air, sniffing excitedly. Reaching a third-story window, it hit the glass impatiently with its fist, shattering it; then, looking about momentarily at the sleeping city, it crawled inside. It found a dark corner of the museum staircase, where a forgotten vent cover was loose, detached from the rusted screws that had held it in place. Pushing the grate aside, it crawled in to hide and to wait. Light from a nearby streetlamp streamed in through a grate in the side of the building and hit the side of the creature, revealing filthy, tattered clothes it had stolen decades ago lying against pale, mottled, shivering skin.

A DISCOVERY

Anna and her family approached the cave cautiously, not knowing what to expect. The light coming out of it now looked closer to indigo, and as they watched, it deepened to a navy blue. She shivered in anticipation. She just had a feeling.

Anna sensed something inside the cave, something alive. Glancing over at Lexei, she could see in his face that he felt it, too. The cave thrummed with life, in noise, vibrations, and smells. Anna, being the bravest, or, as her mother would put it, the most brash, took the lead and stepped inside.

The cave was set into a large hillside, and as she put her foot down, she felt moisture, slippery on the stone surface. Turning to the others, she put her finger to her lips. They all stepped in, as carefully as cats, and felt wet, packed mud under their boots, slippery and slanting downward. The walls were covered in moss and ivy, growing in from the outside hill. Anna sniffed the air, smelling ... something ... she couldn't place it.

Lexei put his hand out to examine the cave wall. They proceeded in about ten to fifteen feet, where small creatures crawled and slithered up the glowing the walls of the cave, which were bathed in bioluminescence. There also, a rivulet of water ran downward, past their feet, disappearing into the depths of the cave.

Alix breathed in deeply. Whispering, she said, "Anya, Lexei, I don't know if ..." she never got any further. A deep, throaty, impossibly loud rumble sounded through the cave, resonating from deep inside. The vampires had never heard anything like it. From the sound, they could tell the creature that had made it was enormous. They looked at each other, then smiled. More than curious, they felt confident in their strength and were eager to explore.

Making their way downward through the ever-widening cave-turned-tunnel, they kept to the sides, picking their steps carefully, all but lost in eager curiosity. About fifty yards in the tunnel widened into a proper cavern, and they saw the far side opened onto the lake they'd seen from above. The yawning mouth of the cave at the lakeside reached more than two hundred feet high.

Vines, ivy, grasses and other vegetation grew over the large opening, hanging several dozen feet down. Off to their right they saw, high up, a massive ledge, the source of the faint blue glow that had drawn their attention. On this ledge were several shetani, crouched, watching them but unmoving. Beyond these creatures, the vampires could see the top of something massive, mostly out of sight beyond the ledge. They stood there mutely for several seconds, watching it.

As a unit, they all moved back into the tunnel a bit, until they were out of sight of the large cavern and the ledge with the thing on it. They carried on their conversation in a whisper.

"What do you think is up there?"

"What is making that light? And why did it change from purple to blue?"

"Do you want to go up there to look?"

"Of course."

"We have to go look."

"Well, no, we don't have to go look."

"Mama, really? You could go back without looking?" Lexei looked at his mother, disbelieving.

Alix looked back at him, her deep curiosity warring with her protectiveness toward her children. In the end, especially after a hundred years as a vampire, curiosity won out.

"Okay, let's go look."

Another loud rumble sounded as they made their way toward the huge cavern. Their wings were still out, held tight against their backs as they moved forward, ready to lift them into the air should the need arise. It was only when they reached the cavern that, in unspoken agreement, they opened their wings and launched themselves into the air.

They flew silent as owls, silent as bats emerging after a day's sleep to venture forth into the night in search of an evening meal. But although their flight was noiseless, their wings, spanning twenty feet across in flight, disturbed the air around them for a good distance. Anna glanced back and saw the creatures on the ledge lifting their noses and breath in the scent of the vampires. The thing that slept behind them awoke, and one very large eyelid lifted lazily. Nostrils many feet in diameter flared as the thing took a deep breath to rouse its slumbering brain. Anna smiled.

Anna, Alix, and Lexei rose high to the top of the cavern and, flying close to the far ledge, found a rocky outcropping on which to perch. They grabbed hold with their claws and settled in, crouched upside-down on the ceiling, about fifty yards from the ledge. They hung there, like three huge bats, and looked down onto the ledge and what was there.

What was there was a huge black shetani, bigger than any other they'd seen. In fact, this shetani was so huge, so deadly, and had made such an impression on the world, that it had, along with its cousins and descendants, down through the ages, been known by the name of "dragon." Their kind had survived into the time of the saber-toothed tiger and the massive mammoths that had served as its main food. Anna remembered the stories, and was amazed at seeing the legend in real life.

The dragon was utterly massive, easily the biggest shetani they had ever seen. In fact, he looked several times bigger than their Mercer Island house.

Anna and her family, perched in the near-pitch darkness on the ceiling, looked down on this creature, this dragon. The dragon looked up at them with his opened eye. He looked curious, but sleepy. After a few minutes, he rose on the ledge, arching his back, stretching after a long sleep, looking for all things like a cat.

He was midnight black all over his back hide, across his tail, and up his long neck. Sharp spines ran the length of the dragon, from tip of nose, to tip of tail. His head was an elegant nightmare of sharp teeth, eyes that glowed green and gold, and his nose, from which tendrils of smoke curled up to the ceiling.

As he stretched, and then stretched some more, reaching his legs out one by one, again like a cat; the vampires could see that his underbelly had produced the softly glowing light they'd seen from afar. A rainbow of colors, from deepest indigo, moving through purple, and then to crimson toward his hindquarters, glowed from his underside, from his throat and belly, down to the tip of his tail. The light seemed to be coming from inside him, glowing through a semi-translucent underhide.

The dragon walked leisurely to the edge of the small (if it could be called small) inlet on which he had slumbered inside the large cavern. Eyeing the intruders on the ceiling, he spread his coal black wings, stretching them and airing them out, before launching himself off the ledge and gliding lazily down across the cavern and through the far opening to the lake.

Anna and the others looked at one another. Shrugging, they took to wing and followed the dragon out, staying high above the lake, and flew in circles for a few minutes before settling down in a tall tree to watch the creature drink his fill of water and snap up a few midsize animals for his lunch.

Both the massive forest and the huge lake were teeming with animals of all sizes, and the dragon spent the next hour winging circles in the sky and dropping low to snap up easy prey here and there. As he ate, he began to play with his food. Looping down again and again, at one point he dove into the lake, emerging with a fat, ten-foot-long aquatic dinosaur in his jaws, and flipped it up in the air before quickly catching it by its fat belly.

He crunched the thing and ate it alive, relishing every bite. He continued to eat for a long time, devouring dozens of creatures that had no chance against the massive, deadly dragon. He moved faster than a creature of his size should, and it was obvious that magic played a large part in his biological make-up, much as it did with the vampires.

Anna, Alix and Lexei watched from the top of some tall trees nearby, as though they were watching a live play at an open-air theatre. After a while, the dragon slowed down, becoming more selective in what he caught to eat. Several smaller flying creatures made it into his belly, along with some large eggs from an unfortunate nest that had been unwisely built under a tree near the lakeshore.

The dragon eventually settled next to the lake's edge, a large pile of smaller animals next to him, their necks broken. Paralyzed but in some cases still alive, some of them squeaked weakly in protest. The dragon smacked his mouth in obvious relish, slowly eating them at his leisure as he looked out across the beautiful moonlit waters of the lake.

"Looks deadly," Alix said.

"Just like us," Lexei said.

"Let's go say hello," said Anna, smiling.

They winged their way down to the dragon, landing next to him, about ten yards away. They could see he was intelligent, and Anna thought she should put her best foot forward. Walking closer, her beautiful wings dragging the ground behind her, she spoke to the dragon in the ancient tongue native to all magical creatures from the beginning of time.

"Namaste," Anna bowed.

The dragon turned his head to her, swallowed the morsel he'd been chewing on, and blinked. "Greetings, young one." He dipped his head.

Alix and Lexei approached behind Anna.

Alix spoke next. "We are new in your land, great one. This is surely a marvelous realm you guard."

"It is indeed, Madam Vampire," the dragon answered. "I am very proud of it." He reached for another animal from the pile and began eating. He ate the belly first, slurping up the blood and soft organs with relish as they dripped from the dying creature.

Anna, Alix and Lexei stood respectfully nearby for some long minutes (it's not wise to hurry the conversation when talking with so ancient a creature as a dragon) and after a while, sat on some nearby boulders. The dragon continued to eat for some minutes. He appeared to be deep in thought. After a time, he began to talk again.

"Tell me, Mistress Vampire, how is it that three such as you come to be in my kingdom? A land where no vampire should be for at least a few million years hence?" He looked directly at them. The dragon's gaze was direct and formidable. His eyes pierced through to their souls. He would immediately know if they were lying.

Anna spoke first. "We discovered a tesseract into your forest, likely created by an ancient relic: a runestone. We did not create this doorway; and we do not know who did, but it is creating problems in our land. We were curious, so we followed the path through and found ourselves here."

At this the dragon's chest rumbled unhappily. "While I am always happy to entertain visitors, I am troubled by your smell. Do you come from the time of man?"

"Yes, we do. A very dangerous time," Alix answered.

The dragon shook his head, upset. He exhaled roughly

through his nostrils, throwing flame several dozen feet into the night sky. "This is not good, Madam Vampire. I will not allow man here. I have heard the legends. We all know the prophecies."

Lexei could not help himself, "Sir Dragon," his high voice piped up, "How is it that here, in our distant past, you have heard of man, who resides only in your distant future?"

At this the dragon made a strange rippled-rumbly sound deep in his chest, for a long time, and eventually they realized he was laughing.

"How is it that one of the People does not know the Rules of Time?" The dragon asked. "They are written in the stars, in the land, in the air, and in the waters. Everyone knows these things."

Lexei shifted uncomfortably. "My apologies, great one."

"Oh, do not apologize, you have given me my first belly laugh after waking." The dragon laughed again. "I thank you, young one. Now, explain how you do not know what all things here" (at this he spreads his huge arms to encompass every plant, every animal, every drop of water in the land) "seem to know."

They didn't know how to answer him.

"Has man corrupted the world so much that the land, the waters, the trees themselves do not hold the knowledge anymore? They do not speak to you? Surely this cannot be true."

Alix spoke quietly, "Lord Dragon, I think they cannot.

But perhaps we have not listened lately. Being our present, we did not think it had much to tell."

"Oh, it has much to tell. Tell me, is there no more wild land? Is there no place where the earth still has memory?" The dragon leaned toward them, staring directly at Lexei. "Little one, I will tell you this much. The wild land, the wild water, the wild trees, the air and the stars, they hold all the knowledge you need."

"In our time, the stars are seldom seen." Anna stared up at the night sky, at the immense number of stars clearly visible, and the spray of stars and gasses that made up the brilliant cluster of the Pleiades, then she turned to face the dragon again. "Man has so corrupted nature that we only see a few stars at night, if we are lucky enough to be able to see the night sky at all."

A tear appeared at the corner of the dragon's eye, and he looked very troubled. "Then the legends are true. This blight will come. I hope I am gone long before man arrives." He seemed to gather itself, then turned again to address Lexei.

"Young one, as to your question of how I know of man and its blight on my planet: everyone knows. The knowledge is in the land itself, and the waters, and the very air we breathe." The dragon inhaled deeply, his eyes half-closed.

"We are all intertwined in a great spiral of quantum entanglement, all of us, including all the stars. For the future can affect the past, just as the past affects the future, just as you, from the future have traveled here, and as you are here, for this time, you can affect the past, for that is our present." He took another animal from his pile and ate it, smacking his mouth in sheer pleasure.

Anna and the others sat back and thought of what the dragon had said. They were silent and stared up at the gorgeous night sky.

After a few minutes more, the dragon paused again in his snacking, "This unnatural magic, it has frozen my land. The sun is not returning."

He was right. It was pitch black, and the sky showed no signs of even pinking with dawn, though they had been there for many hours.

"I feel it is the relic that has done this. The runestone." He looked over at them. "You said you did not bring it here?"

"No, Dragon Lord, we did not. We would very much like it if it were no longer here, and no longer creating the doorway," Anna spoke quietly.

The dragon grunted in agreement. "I would like that as well, Mistress Vampire. I think it has caused much mischief in my land. It has been here for a few days, keeping the doorway open, stopping the sun from returning. The forest cannot survive without the sun's illumination."

They all looked around at the magnificent, massive forest, each of them deep in thought.

The dragon stood up, stretching his back in an arch again, drank a few more dozen gallons of water, and then took himself just into the edge of the forest to urinate. Small animals scuttled to drink it, and the dragon chuckled at their antics. "Idiots." He returned to the three vampires. "Let us be rid of this runestone. If I take it from where it was placed, will you return with it to your own land and so swallow up the tesseract with your passing?"

The three vampires nodded. Yes, they would.

Once through the doorway, Ramsey, Tristan, Claude and Emil had traveled in the opposite direction Anna, Alix and Lexei had taken, eventually nearing the glade where the runestone was buried. Clearing the forest of the small shetani they encountered as they traveled, Ramsey and his vampire henchmen soon had the grass running slick with black blood. Laughing, Claude ripped off the arm of one, and, chewing on it, found it to his liking. He continued to carry it along with him, eating a bit of it every now and then.

Ramsey glanced at Claude and smiled. "Did you ever let that thing I gave you loose?"

Emil nearly gagged at the sight of Claude ripping a chunk out of the black arm and chewing it, blood dripping down the side of his face as he walked. "Claude?" Tristan turned to look and laughed.

"Yes, Mr. Ramsey, we did. And we had a fine time chasing it down." Tristan patted Claude on the back. "Although

Claude was the fastest, it took all three of us to eventually track it down and kill it. It fought well. It took almost a half hour to subdue it."

Emil looked curious and reached out to have a taste.

Ramsey looked around them. "The shetani are fierce." A loud cry echoed through the trees. "And they come in all sizes." He looked at all three of them. "Don't forget that."

Trampling through the forest, Tristan and his friends didn't even try to remain quiet. Ramsey stopped and looked at them. Staring them down, he shook his head and held a finger to his lips.

"Do you want every predator in this forest drawn to us?"

"Sure," Emil laughed. "Bring it on." He slapped Claude on the back, and they both giggled. Tristan smirked, looking down at them. Ramsey frowned and shook his head. When dragon listening to them just beyond their sight snorted, it sounded like an explosion. The three young vampires each jumped several feet into the air. Ramsey unfurled his wings in a flash and was a hundred feet up within seconds, his eyes searching for and immediately locking on the dragon. Eyes widening, he rose another dozen feet, making sure the giant shetani nightmare was far enough away.

Tristan, Claude and Emil scrambled in fear, but soon had their wings out and were rising in the air to meet Ramsey. As they rose, flapping furiously, the Dragon Lord slapped Emil out of the air like someone would swat at a mosquito. He then caught the spinning, tumbling vampire at the last second before he could hit the ground. Holding him up to eye level, the dragon peered at him suspiciously. "What are you? You smell like..."

Ramsey flew in closer. "Drop him, dragon! He is my servant, and I am the great Rasputin!" Ramsey beat his wings as fast as he could, creating a wind that buffeted the surrounding trees with near hurricane-force winds, trying to intimidate the huge creature in front of him. "Let him go!"

The dragon felt the strong winds as if they were soft summer breezes, and ignored Ramsey. Staring at Emil in his grasp, the dragon squinted again suspiciously. "You smell a bit like man. How long ago were you turned, vampire? You seem like a newly hatched thing." He opened his mouth, showing dozens of razor-sharp teeth, and gave a snort. Flames shot out of his nose, missing Emil by several feet but mildly scorching him nonetheless. Emil felt his bladder release. Urine dripped down his legs and into the forest. The dragon wrinkled his nose in disgust.

Ramsey, with Tristan and Claude behind him, flew closer to the dragon. "I command you to release my minion. I have recently turned him, and he is mine to do with as I please. Now, release him before I..."

The dragon rumbled deep in his throat. "Before you what?" If a dragon could raise an eyebrow, this one did, in surprise. "You 'command' me?" He looked at Ramsey, pulling his head back in surprise. "Really? Bit arrogant, aren't you?" Turning back to study Emil, he continued.

"Newly turned is it? Well, little egg, you stink of man. I hate man." The dragon narrowed his eyes.

At this point, Emil was nearly frantic with fear. He closed his eyes and tried to collect his wits. The dragon waited. Ramsey was screaming threats again from off to the side, but Emil and the dragon focused only on themselves and tuned out the world. The dragon brought Emil closer to one of his eyes, waiting. Emil swallowed and tried to calm his rapidly beating heart. He took another deep, shaky breath and opened his eyes. The dragon tilted his head to the side, staring at Emil, curious as to what this newly hatched vampire would say.

"I ... If you will, please..." Emil stuttered to a stop and swallowed again.

"Yes...?" The dragon said softly, though it was a loud roar in the ear of the vampire, who was held not five feet from the dragon's teeth.

Emil felt his bowels release. He closed his eyes again, almost paralyzed with fear. He knew his life was but moments from its end. He opened his eyes again. "Pl ... please. Please do not hurt me ... l-l-let ... let me live ..." He swallowed in fear again.

"And if I 'let you live' as you say, little egg, what is in it for me?"

Emil shuddered. He could not think. All he could speak was the bald, honest truth; raw and untouched by any guile or subterfuge. "If you ... if you let me go, I p-p-promise to leave you ... you in p-p-p-peace, I pro-promise to leave here and ... and ... ne-never return. Ever. I promise." Emil closed his eyes and waited to be eaten.

The dragon chuckled and gently set Emil down. "It's a deal." He smiled in amusement.

Emil, upon being set down back on the forest floor, unharmed, unscathed, and best of all, uneaten; promptly fainted.

———————————— >≈✥✦✥≈< ————————————

Anna, Lexei and Alix had set about exploring the cave, up on the dragon's ledge, where he'd told them to wait. They came across a large nest toward the back, thankfully vacant, and covered in the most interesting things.

"Lexei, look at this," Alix pointed at the walls at the back of the cave. He indicated a huge mural, painted in what looked like sprayed wet powders. It depicted a sunrise, with the lake in the foreground, and dozens of animals jumping out of the water, drinking at the water's edge, and sunning themselves on the shore. The right edge of the painting showed the view was from the back of a dragon as it sailed out from the cave. The wings spread out on either side, and the neck and head rose from the perspective of the painter. It was magnificent.

"Look at this," Anna was at the back of the nest, looking at something half buried in the strands of dried grasses. She squatted on her heels, looking down at the nest. Lexei and Alix were still staring up at the mural, amazed at the intricacies. They finally glanced back at Anna and made their way over to her to see what she had found.

"Oh wow," Lexei bent to examine the objects too.

"What are they?"

Half buried in the massive dragon nest, hidden under old grass and leaves, were maybe a dozen varying pieces, each glittering, sparkling in the dim lights, shimmering even. Lexei dug his hands farther in the soft nest, retrieving another piece. He lifted it up out of the nest to get a better look at it. What he held was maybe a square foot in area, one side covered in iridescent gold, yellow and orange, merging at one point into a pinkish-purple-indigo color.

Turning it over in his hands, he saw the other side was dark peacock colors, blue, purple, even some glittery emerald green. Lexei gasped. It was breathtaking. He set the piece back down among the others, and spread some of the dried grass back over it. It seemed wrong to disturb such beautiful objects, and he had heard in the legends that dragons were very particular about their belongings. He rose and turned to look at the large mural, leaving Anna and Alix to examine the colorful shards buried in the nest.

Looking at the mural from farther back than the others had, he could see the whole picture better, and felt his chest constrict with feeling. Tears gathered at the corners of his eyes as he studied the painting.

He followed the natural line of motion, from the corner on the right, where the rider/artist was on the back of a dragon, along the line of the rising sun's rays spreading across the valley, to the shore below, then all the way to the other corner of the painting, the shore of the lake, teeming with life. His gaze rose again to follow the treetops depicted along the shore of the lake, and the way the artist had painted how the bright morning sun brought out the vivid colors of the forest.

"Do you like it?" A quiet voice behind Lexei asked. Swinging around, he saw the dragon. He has flown up to the ledge without a sound, and was perched just inside, looking at the mural over Lexei's shoulder. Lexei wondered how such a massive creature could move so silently. He looked back at the mural, and swallowed to regain his voice.

"I like it very much. Did you paint it?"

"No," the dragon answered. He studied it with her. "My mother painted it. She's quite talented, don't you think?" He tilted his massive head to the side. "She told me it was her aboard her own mother's back, right at the top of the descent as you glide down to the lake."

"It makes me feel so many things. The beauty. But also, a sense of loss. I can't explain it," Lexei's voice trailed off.

"She painted it with memories, and emotion mixed it," the dragon explained. "She painted it right before her own mother left, to remember her by. Her own feelings of both loss and joy are in the painting."

"I think I understand."

"Then of course, after her mother left, she stayed behind for a long, long time, and I grew up here in this cave." The dragon looked out over the huge cavern, remembering. "I have many fond memories of this place, and it is my home. But she, in time, left as well, to find other caverns and build other nests. I stayed behind, and will forever nest here on this ledge."

He looked over at Anna and Alix at the back of the nest. Seeing what they were studying and so mesmerized with, he chuckled. "Ah, you are entranced by the remnants of my shell casings."

They could now see how the large, glittering pieces were indeed, massive broken shards of an eggshell. "Wow," Lexei said. "Your shell must have been ... huge!" He gaped at the dragon.

Chuckling some more, the dragon smiled. "Little one, when I was born, the egg was as wide as you are tall, and newly hatched, I was no bigger than my tongue." At this the dragon opened his cavernous maw and waggled his great tongue at Lexei.

It was a good twenty feet long and half again as wide. Spittle flew off it at Lexei, spraying him with a light shower "Oh, sorry." The dragon closed his mouth, dipping his snout behind one massive paw. Lexei wiped himself off. Looking at his hands, he was surprised to see the dragon's spittle was iridescent and beautiful, like a fine spray of liquid glitter.

Bringing his hands to his face, Lexei inhaled. It smelled like a magic wind bearing the scent of a thousand wildflowers in a meadow.

Gazing up at the dragon, he saw the giant creature looking back at him from behind his paws. "You, why, you smell so good!" Lexei walked forward, right up to the dragon's snout. The dragon looked back at him with a smile and an amused expression on his face.

Lexei tapped on the dragon's mouth, and tried to wriggle his hand through the dragon's lips and inside. After a second or two, the dragon opened his mouth, and Lexei began to climb inside. He stepped carefully over the deadly sharp teeth and onto the tongue, which was spongy and wet, and smelled of elderberries and flowers.

"Your mother will worry ..." The dragon chuckled, trying to keep it quiet so the little vampire in his mouth wouldn't have his eardrums blasted. He heard Lexei laughing from inside.

"This is huge! Okay, okay, I'm coming out now." Emerging from the dragon's mouth, Lexei wiped his hands, and his eyes returned to where his sister and mother were still looking at the mural.

"Okay, my friends," the dragon said. Anna and Alix drew closer. "Here is the runestone." He placed the small stone disc on the ground. "Can you take it out through the doorway?"

Alix picked up the stone, which was thrumming with

power and warm to the touch. She held it with just her thumb and forefinger, out away from her body. It was very dark, nearly black, and very, very old, weighing only about a pound or two. Anna touched it with her finger, and then examined her finger.

Lexei held his hands locked together behind his back and just leaned over to look.

"Can you take it out of my lands?" The Dragon Lord asked again.

Alix looked up at the dragon and nodded. "Most assuredly, my Lord. Thank you for retrieving it."

The vampires prepared to go.

"Wait," the dragon said. They turned back to him. "If you like, you may each take a piece of my birth casing. It might bring you luck." Smiling, they each selected a piece of the iridescent shell.

"Thank you," Anna came close to the dragon and kissed him on his massive cheek. Lexei ran up to him and hugged him, his arms spread wide, trying to reaching around the dragon's neck.

Alix bowed very deeply. "It has been a true honor, Lord Dragon."

The dragon bowed his head in return, "For me as well, Madam. Farewell."

Grigori Rasputin was furious. Tristan and Claude remained silent as they carried Emil's still, unconscious body between them. Rasputin kicked at everything that crossed his path, periodically ascending like a shot to grab flying animals that tried to flee from his path. The dragon had taken the runestone, which had been quite a lot of trouble for him to procure, and had made off with it. Rasputin had tried to follow him, but the dragon had doubled back, threatening to eat Rasputin if he didn't leave his land, and Rasputin had backed off.

When they arrived at the doorway, the dragon was nowhere in sight. Dropping Emil on the path, they flew upward and had a good look around. Rasputin landed and kicked at Emil. "Wake up, idiot." Emil stirred. Three shetani entered the clearing next to the pathway and chittered to themselves.

"Oh, let's just get out of here," Claude said.

They passed through the doorway and back to their own world.

Several miles away, Anna, Lexei and Alix said their goodbyes to their new friend. Tucking the dragon's gift of shell fragments carefully away, they departed and were soon winging their way back through the cavern, through the cave, and back across the forest to the path that would take them back through to the museum.

Landing there, one at a time, they tucked their wings tight and began walking single file on the enchanted forest path. The land was strangely quiet; not a bird sounded, not a creature screeched. The very air held still, its shimmering halted for this one moment. It was as if the forest was holding its breath and watching as the vampires passed out of its realm.

The creature had fallen into an uneasy half-sleep in its hiding place and was startled awake by the scream of several rats. They'd come to investigate the new denizen of the building and had piled up one upon the other in the vent system directly above the pale, mottled creature. Too curious for their own good, their living tower had tipped over, and several of them had dropped onto the creature's back as it dozed. Like a whip, it came fully awake and, turning its head, fast as lightning, snapped up the first rat in its jaws. Squealing in agony, the rat scrambled, turned, and bit at the creature, fighting it as the creature ate the rat alive. Rat blood ran warm down its chin, black in the moonlight, as the other rats scrambled away in terror.

SMITTEN

The next week passed as usual, and Anna saw Eric in art class Monday, Wednesday, and Friday. They had taken to sitting next to each other.

Some impressive paintings and sculptures were coming together in their group, but there were times they barely noticed. The first time they'd sat together, they'd spent half the class time focused on each other, chatting softly until the professor had stood next to them and raised an eyebrow, clearing his throat several times to get their attention. Embarrassed, they'd gotten to work.

Eric found his clay sculpture improving after Anna made suggestions, and Anna remarked to him that she found her stone carving improving based on Eric's input.

Eric had been looking forward to his sister Julia's upcoming exhibition, the perfect opportunity to spend more time with Anna outside of class. He was proud of his sister and wanted to share her work with this enchanting woman who seemed to enjoy his company almost as much as he enjoyed hers. Truth to tell, he also wanted to introduce Anna to Julia. He was proud to have her on his arm, and he wanted his sister to get to know her.

The Saturday of Julia's gallery exhibition, Eric had suggested that Anna meet him at Lestat's at 6:45 p.m., nearly an hour after sunset, and at 6:43 she entered the coffee shop, making the little bell on the door dingle. She wore an emerald green outfit and her black jacket on, and Eric rose to meet her as she entered. Smiling broadly, he took her hand.

"Hello, Anna." He smiled and leaned forward, kissing her cheek softly and squeezing her hand.

"Eric." Anna gently squeezed his hand back. She smiled broadly at seeing him.

"You look wonderful." Eric's smile broadened. "Although you look great in the art smock you wear in class, too." He laughed and Anna chuckled, her cheeks warming.

"Oh my. You're blushing." She looked even more beautiful, if that were possible. "Well, let's get going. The exhibit should be open by the time we get there."

They walked down the street, and the old-fashioned

lights and little shops along the town made the walk very pleasant. Old maple trees planted decades ago were still full of leaves barely pinked by the autumn weather, and they fluttered in the breeze as the two walked by. Others were taking walks as well, and Eric even saw a couple sitting together on a park bench staring dreamily into each other's eyes. On a whim, he stopped Anna and, swinging her around to face him, cupped her cheek and gently kissed her lips.

"I've wanted to do that all week." Now it was his turn to blush. She smiled, and they continued walking.

The art gallery was packed with people. It was dark inside; backlighting illuminated the corners, each painting enhanced by a spotlight. Softly lit globes hung from the ceiling, sparkling with glitter. The effect was magical. They entered, and Anna inhaled with closed eyes, soaking in the atmosphere of the gallery. Eric's sister Julia was at the back of the exhibit, and their parents stood chatting nearby. As Eric led Anna through the crowd to introduce her to his family, she glanced at Julia's paintings. Most were of trees, but oh, what trees! Each picture looked like Julia had painted the trees and forests out of Alice in Wonderland. Anna was enchanted.

As Eric and Anna walked up to them, Julia and her parents smiled warmly. Eric kissed his mother and Julia on the cheek and shook hands with his father. Turning to Anna, he made introductions, and everyone shook hands.

"Julia, your paintings are enchanting," Anna said,

131

chatting with the young artist. "My brother also paints. I told him of your gallery opening, and he seemed quite interested in knowing more about you."

Julia smiled warmly and took Anna by the hand. "Eric has told me a lot about you," her eyes danced. "He's smitten."

"Well, I'm very fond of your brother, too," Anna replied, smiling.

Julia led her on a tour of the small gallery, explaining each painting and the inspiration behind it. Anna loved each one, and commented so at every turn. They stopped in front of a dark painting of the midnight woods, alight with faerie magic.

Moonlight illuminated an enchanted glade where all kinds of creatures danced and played. Anna was amazed to see one creature depicted off to the side was the spitting image of one of the shetani she'd recently seen in the dragon's land. It had four black shimmering wings and was shown diving for a fish in a small lake. She stared at the painting, and all the details shown in it. Julia remained silent while her new friend studied it.

"How ... I mean, what kind of ideas did you have when you painted this one?" Anna tried to sound casual.

"It's funny you ask. I'd been having strange dreams the month before, and one night they were particularly vivid. I found myself in a strange, beautiful land. The colors were bright, and the creatures were fantastic, and I remembered everything with such clarity, unlike most of my dreams. I tried to capture what I remembered in the painting." Julia indicated the painting's name on the small plaque next to it: "*Captured Dream.*"

"Well, I think it's fabulous. You have a wonderful talent." Anna lingered a bit more, made a mental note, and then moved on. "How long will your exhibit be here in town?"

"Just tonight, I'm afraid." Julia answered.

"Oh, I wish my brother could see your work." Just as Anna spoke these words, her eyes spotted her mother coming through the gallery door, followed by Lexei. Anna smiled and waved them over.

"Julia, Eric, I'd like you to meet my mother Alix and my brother Lexei." Everyone shook hands, and soon Eric and Julia's parents came over and every acquaintance was made. Lexei soon drifted over to look at the paintings, and he and Julia were soon talking quietly together, studying each painting, heads close, discussing techniques.

Anna drew Alix aside and whispered in her ear, "Mama, look at the painting in the corner." They both moved to take in the painting Julia had done depicting the forest scene with the shetani in the corner.

"Oh my," Alix stood staring, soaking in every detail in the scene. "This is extraordinary."

"She says she dreamed of this scene."

"This young lady is amazing," Alix was rooted to the spot, mesmerized. "Do you sense the magic in this creation?"

Anna nodded.

"I am going to buy it, before anyone else gets it. Wait here," Anna moved to the back table where a young man was sitting at a small desk. Julia's parents were standing nearby, and Anna smiled at them warmly, "Your daughter has an extraordinary talent."

"I'd like to purchase *"Captured Dream"* please," Anna smiled down at the young man at the table.

"Certainly, Miss." He looked up the painting in his book. "That painting is $12,500."

Anna opened her wallet and handed the man a gold American Express card. "Here you go," she said, smiling.

After processing the transaction, Anna smiled happily as the young man told her the painting would be delivered later that week, and went and placed a "sold" marker next to the it. Lexei looked over at his sister and gave a happy nod. The painting had real magic in it, which they'd all investigate later, when they had possession of it.

Eric's parents came to shake Anna's hand. "That's the third painting she's sold this evening, and the most expensive." They both beamed.

"It was a bargain," Anna smiled back. "I cannot wait to see what she comes up with next."

Julia came up to them and took Anna's hand. "Thank you for buying *"Captured Dream,"* Anna. That one is very special to me; I hope you'll enjoy it for many years to come."

"I know I will," Anna squeezed Julia's hand gently.

Eric joined them just then. "I think I will steal Anna and

take her for a walk now, if you will all excuse me." He put his arm around Anna's waist and gently led her away from the crowd and out the door.

<hr/>

Eric held Anna's hand as they walked out of the gallery into the night air. The crowds had thinned a bit, and Eric led the way down the street. They walked without speaking, just enjoying each other's company. After a few blocks, they found a street vendor near the city park selling roses, and Eric bought one for Anna that she held up to her nose as they walked. Their steps took them into the park, and they were soon swallowed by trees.

"Eric?" Anna kept walking but looked over at Eric, eyes glowing. Eric looked over at her and smiled.

"Anna."

"Eric, ..." Anna stopped and faced Eric. "I really like you." She smiled.

"I really like you, too. And I like your family." He smiled and stepped closer.

"I like your family too," Anna laughed. "My goodness, your sister..."

"I know." Eric smiled with pride. "She's really talented, isn't she?"

"She's more than talented. Really, I can't believe her paintings, especially the one I bought."

"Speaking of buying, Anna, that painting was more than twelve grand, and you bought it without blinking. That was amazing. You really made her day."

"That painting is incredible. I was glad to be able to buy it."

"How do I ask this. ... Anna, are you wealthy?"

"No. Well, maybe. No, not really. Well, yes, but I don't live wealthy." Anna looked at her toes peeking out from emerald green snakeskin pumps. "That came out wrong." She looked up at Eric and smiled. "Let's just say money isn't a problem, but I don't live lavishly," she looked down again. "I hope you don't treat me any differently because of it." She finished and leaned forward, kissing Eric on the cheek.

"Of course not." Eric smiled. "You are so different from anyone I've ever known, Anna. Even your family is different. I can't put my finger on it, but ..."

Anna knew then that Eric would be her one and only love. A love that would last the ages. She didn't know how she knew, except that she was tired of not knowing what was going to happen with Eric and herself, and she decided to take matters into her own hands and direct the relationship, instead of letting things progress blindly. She looked into Eric's eyes and saw his soul there, waiting, wanting, craving the same thing she craved.

Anna stepped forward and kissed Eric, deeply, on the mouth. She continued kissing him for several minutes, wrapping her arms around his neck, moving her lips sensuously against his. Warm pink colors flickered in front of her closed eyes, and she felt herself falling, falling the rest of the way in love.

Eric responded, his lips moving in concert with Anna's as his arms encircled her back possessively. Pressing his chest against her, spreading his legs to give himself better balance, he moved his mouth from her lips, across her cheek and to her neck, kissing all along the way.

"Mmmm, Anna..."

Anna exhaled a sigh of happiness, her closed eyes smiling with her face, her lips parting to better breathe in his scent.

They were alone in this part of the park, there was no sound except their own breathing, their own voices. Then suddenly, they were not alone.

A loud hiss sounded, followed by a rapid clacking sound. Surprised, Anna startled and looked up. Eric grabbed her tighter and looked around at the noise.

The park was dark except for a few lights along the walkway. Anna could see nothing in plain view, but noticed the bushes trembling. Her heart fell as a shetani emerged from behind the bush, black as night, jagged teeth exposed as it hissed again. This one was shaped like a small reptilian cat, with a tail like a scorpion stinger. It was this that made the rapid clacking sound, and Anna could see it meant to attack them.

It jumped suddenly, and they both backed up. Eric held on to Anna and looked at the creature, disbelieving. "That looks like the things I remember from the museum. I thought I'd imagined them. This is no rabid dog." He went silent.

Anna's heart sank at the thought that her relationship with this lovely man was once again being affected by the presence of these infernal shetani.

Then she decided she had had enough.

She stepped behind Eric and concentrated, and within seconds had sprouted her fangs, long claws and wings. She simultaneously wrapped a shadow around her so that she was completely cloaked. Launching herself into the air, she dove at the creature with supernatural speed, slamming it into the ground in an instant and crushing it like a frog under a tire. Hissing in disgust, she made quick rounds of the entire park, half running, half flying, looking everywhere for any other shetani in the surrounding area.

She found a second, circling them about thirty yards away, halfway up a tree. Making quick work of it, she watched as its body smoked and turned into a black liquid that rapidly soaked into the ground. Satisfied that no more of the creatures were lurking about, she leaned against the back of the tree trunk, her fangs, wings and claws disappearing, her heart sinking as she allowed herself to become visible again, sure that this episode had doomed her budding relationship with Eric. Eyes closed, head back against the tree, a single tear ran down her face as her heart constricted.

She felt a finger catch the tear as it made its way down her cheek. Opening her eyes, she saw Eric in front of her, face pale as a ghost, eyes wet and worried.

"Hey, you okay?"

She swallowed and shuddered at his touch. Closing her eyes again, she sent off a wish that this man not flee from her. "Yeah, I'm okay."

Eric looked down at the wet black liquid that had almost completely disappeared into the ground. "These were the same things that attacked us in the museum, aren't they?"

"Yes." Anna kept looking at him, hoping.

He looked back up and into her face. "Anna, you ...?" Eric fell silent.

Anna waited.

Eric tried again. "You ... uh..." he went silent again and just looked at her for a few seconds before speaking again.

"For a second back there, I could have sworn I saw wings on your back. Then you disappeared."

"Yes."

Anna decided then and there that she loved Eric. She closed her eyes and shuddered as she decided to trust her instincts and tell Eric her secret. She would not erase his memory, she wanted him to know and decide for himself. Anna opened her eyes as she felt Eric put his hands on her arms in concern. "Eric, I love you."

"Oh, Anna," Eric embraced her. "I love you, too. Whatever else is going on, of that I am sure."

"Eric, do you trust me?"

"Yes."

"Then let's continue our walk," she leaned over and kissed him again. Stepping off into the dewy night, they joined the stillness of late-night Seattle. Then she took his hand and they walked back to the center of town, and back to Lestat's. On the way, it started raining.

"Oh no," Anna put her purse over her head, laughing. Eric had come prepared with an umbrella and held it over their heads; they ran along, giggling together, until they reached the doors of the coffee shop. Purple, green and blue twinkling lights surrounded the shop, and they were especially beautiful in the rain. The two practically tumbled through the doorway, holding on to each other, damp but exhilarated by their run through the rain.

"Two coffees, please," said Eric at the counter.

"Oh, no. Just hot water with lemon for me please," said Anna beside him. "Oh, my hair got all wet," she laughed, wringing out water from her hair. Red highlights showed up when it was wet, and it began to curl up.

"It's getting curly," Eric chuckled, running his fingers through her hair. He was charmed by the curls forming there.

She looked at him with smiling, dancing eyes. "Wait until it dries, it will get positively frizzy."

"Well, I think it's beautiful." He smiled back at her, kissing her cheek.

They took their hot cups into a secluded alcove by the window and sat in the loveseat there, watching the water run down the window in rivulets. The lights playing on the glass, combined with the rainwater running down, were enchanting, mesmerizing even, and they spent some minutes looking out through the window in silence.

The creature sensed that the magic it sought had moved once again, and it made its way to the top of the museum. As it crouched there in the pale fog, it closed its eyes and concentrated for a moment in the silence. It had been a long, long time since it had last metamorphosed. Pale, almost skeletal wings finally sprouted from its back. As they stretched out in the fog, slowly flapping back and forth, blood from the rat and dog the creature had consumed gradually filled the wings, inflating them like some ghostly kite. And slowly, like a demon awakening from a long slumber, the pale creature focused its red-rimmed dead eyes on the horizon and flew off into the night.

MAGIC

After a while, Eric looked over and realized tears were running down Anna's cheek.

He reached out and touched her chin with his finger, gently raising her eyes to meet his. "Anna, you can tell me. I'll try to help in any way I can."

"I ... this," she gestured between them to indicate their blossoming relationship. "It means so much to me." Anna fell into speechlessness, unable to continue.

Unshed tears sparkled in her eyes, catching the light coming through the rain-soaked window. She looked beautiful, like some tragic figure out of history. He slowly leaned forward and kissed her lips, gently, tentatively at first. She trembled. Shifting forward, his lips moved and the kiss deepened as his arms encircled her, holding her against him. It all came so naturally.

Anna's lips warmed as Eric shifted again and pressed his chest against hers, his arms holding her gently but firmly. Her head tilted back, and she gave in to the feelings flooding her mind. She felt her heart melt and open, and her body relaxed further. Anna brought her arm up around his neck, and the kiss slowly deepened, until she felt her mind go blank and her heart reach out to entwine with his.

Eric's face flushed and his cheeks grew very red. Anna felt the rush of blood to his face. Her body responded, but not in the way she worried it would. Instead of a surge of hunger for blood, she felt her heart warm and rush that warmth to her own face. They kissed for a long, long time.

They were brought back to the present by the sound of another coffee shop patron laughing at something someone else had said. Conversations were getting louder in the shop.

Eric pulled his face back from Anna's and looked into her eyes. Love shone from him, and she smiled. "I want to hear everything, all of it. And I want to be lost in you again."

Eric picked up his coffee mug and drank from it, and Anna held up her mug of lemon and hot water and touched her lips to it.

Holding the hot mug close, Anna let the fragrant steam curl up and around her face. Her eyes were closed, and as Eric sat across from her, leaning forward, he studied her eyelids. They were delicate, the skin almost translucent, long mahogany lashes curling against her cheek, which seemed to almost glow from within. Anna slowly opened her eyes, caught him looking, and smiled. Eric ducked his head, trying to hide his smile. He took a sip of coffee and then lifted his eyes to look at her again.

Under the table, their feet intertwined, as if their bodies were unwilling to lose contact for any length of time. Their eyes communicated silently, and she felt understanding flow between them. Eric sipped his coffee a few more times, then set the mug down and, rising to his feet, took Anna's hand and walked out the door. She followed him, stepping lightly, her heart warm. She felt as if she were lost in a dream, the sweetest dream anyone had ever known.

Eric led her to his apartment across campus. Key inserted in the lock, he soon had them inside, and the door closed behind them, locked tight against anything that might be out there. A few steps in, Anna swung around and grabbed Eric, and they began kissing passionately. Her hands reached up and her fingers ran through his hair as her palms caressed the sides of his head. Her knee came up slowly and rubbed against his thighs as her mouth opened slightly in the kiss. He groaned and his tongue darted in, past her lips and back out again. She melted against him and, picking her up, he carried her, still kissing, into his bedroom.

Eric bent and laid Anna on the bed, following her down. Kissing her lips, his mouth began to wander around her face, kissing softly, smelling her, licking her cheek. Anna moaned and lifted her own tongue to his scratchy cheek, nibbling at his ear. Their hands roamed across each other, and they were soon divested of their clothing.

Eric lowered his mouth to Anna and began nuzzling her with his lips. She felt a surge of excitement as he kissed her and nibbled at her skin, moving his hands to caress her.

She threw her head back at the sensations she was experiencing, moaning in pleasure. Eric brought his hands to her face, cupping it while he kissed her deeply. Anna gasped, feeling tingles and delight as she writhed in ecstasy. After a few minutes, the sensations in her body threw her into such a feral state that her legs, now divested of clothing, spread wide of their own accord, as if inviting his touch there as well. Eric needed no further encouragement.

He lowered his mouth to the young woman before him. Eric's hands and mouth told Anna all she wanted to know, and she gasped as he kissed her again and again all over her body. She lost herself in the sensations, and with this losing, all her control was gone as well.

The vampire aura, that part of Anna's soul she kept so tamped down much of the time, that powerful part of her that could subdue an enemy in a matter of seconds, that could force the mind to obey her every command, that could wipe memories clear at a whim, was no longer suppressed. As Anna the woman's heart was lost to this man, as her body was lost to the sensations he was creating in her, Anna the vampire's control fled, entirely.

Anna felt a warm rush as her power was completely released and instinct as primal as the seas dashing against the new earth's shore took over. Eric's eyes flew wide open. Anna secretly reveled as her vampiric power extended over Eric and allowed them to each feel what the other felt.

She sensed everything Eric was experiencing; it flooded her brain. She felt him as he entered her, she felt his thrill and eagerness, she felt his ecstasy. This was her favorite part of making love as a vampire. She could not hold back and a happy chuckle escaped her lips.

She looked down at Eric and saw that he was completely lost in what they were feeling; his eyes were rolled back, and beads of sweat dotted his forehead.

Gasping, Eric moved faster, eagerly caressing and loving Anna with his entire body. His tongue moved as his hands found her tender flesh, and now it was Anna who groaned, as Eric completed what she needed so much, and a huge thrill of passion shuddered through her body. Eric kept touching, licking, kissing, caressing; moving his tongue's path to continue the rise of ecstasy after each of her shudders. Anna felt the rolling pleasure, over and over, each rise and peak followed by an ever-so-slight dip lasting only a few seconds, before rising again in a sweet rush of feeling: rising, rising, then peaking, she felt each swell of pleasure.

After nearly a dozen swells and lulls, Anna was gasping, her legs were trembling, and her hands pushed against him, stilling Eric's actions for a time. Rising up, his mouth and face wet, he rose over her, his arm muscles bulging. Anna opened her eyes and grabbed his face, bringing it down to her mouth and kissing him passionately as she simultaneously brought her hips up to meet his. Her long legs reaching up to grasp him, pulling him down to her. Eric, smiled as she grabbed him and pulled him to her hips, and he joined with Anna, trembling as the connection was made.

She felt so warm. He settled himself atop her, and began moving, kissing her as he did. She gripped him tightly and he gasped. Lowering his head to her again, he smothered her with kisses. She felt she was drowning in pleasure and love for him. Her legs locked behind his hips and locked him onto her. She reached up and began caressing him, and he gasped again, throwing his head back, then forward again.

Shifting his legs, he lifted her hips to meet his. Gasping, he opened his eyes briefly and looked down in amazement. Under him, Anna lay, her head thrown back in the sensations, her sable brown tresses laid out on his pillows in waves, glorious in the diffused moonlight shining through the window. Eric gasped again and again. Eric grinned in devilish delight as Anna's legs tightened again around his hips, urging him forward, thrilled at their bodies' union. She watched him closely, feeling triumphant in their lovemaking.

He began moving again, his body bathed in sweat in the moonlight. His mouth let forth an involuntary gasp as feelings as old as time filled him.

They continued this way for half the night, Eric melting into her again and again, Anna joining him in his ecstasy, both of them moving with pleasure and delight, until, finally, they both fell to the bed, exhausted, minds buzzing, bodies perspiring, tired, yet electric in their shared experience. And they slept.

In the living room, Jinx sat looking out the bay windows at the meadow, his eyes searching for any movement of Kindred, or other creature of the night. He'd heard Eric's return to their lair, with someone in tow. The second they entered the apartment and shut the door behind them, Jinx could smell the difference in the companion Eric had brought with him. Jinx knew she was one of the People, and the cat's interest grew with every minute that passed. He'd not ever encountered a vampire face to face, only faintly smelled them from afar; the last had been when the young vampire had been on the other side of the glass, crouched on the patio looking in with curious eyes.

Jinx had smelled the lust in the room. It was heavy in the air, like a thick fog in a low-lying valley, and after a while it was overwhelming. The coupling had gone on for quite some time, and the entire apartment had smelt of their rutting. Jinx had chosen to stay away, waiting them out in the living room. Let them do their dance in private, he thought, he'd investigate this newcomer soon enough. Jinx was patient; he could wait. At some point, the cat had fallen asleep waiting, and had just woken ten minutes earlier, as the two had fallen to the bed, their coupling subsiding, their bodies entering slumber.

The cat's eyes glowed in the moonlight, his fur, sleek and washed clean and black as the midnight sky. He got up slowly and stretched, arching his back and shivering, then silently padded across the floor and entered the bedroom. Sniffing at the interesting smells there for a minute, he then hopped onto the bed and investigated the female thoroughly. As the cat's examination of the newcomer arrived at her face, Anna opened her eyes briefly and focused on him.

"Greetings, brother," Anna murmured, making a soft purring trill of the tongue as she finished the last word. Jinx responded by purring and curling up against her, content as to her identity. She was one of the same as Jinx, and he could sense it. It wasn't often one found such a creature, and so benign in companionship with his pet Eric. Jinx began to knead his paws against her. Anna's hand moved to rest against Jinx's side and, contented he was watched over by one of the People, Jinx curled into a ball beside her and slept.

———————————>≍≍≍≍≍≍≍≍<———————————

The night watchman was late for work, and so sped in his truck down Interstate 90 faster than he should have. Gulping hot coffee as he drove, he did not see the huge, ghostly pale giant bat-thing fly in front of him until it had almost passed by. Out the corner of his eye, the old man saw the impossibly large creature pass yards in front of his truck at the last minute, and his subconscious reaction was to swerve. Tires screeching, his truck swung sideways and hit the edge of the railing, bounced off, and tore sideways on bald tires. As his truck flipped over the side of the bridge and into the water, the old man's wide, surprised eyes closed in pain as the scalding coffee spilled on him. At 3 a.m., the accident went unseen in the thick, ghostly marine layer, and the truck plunged into Lake Washington and quickly sank to the bottom, with only the fog as a witness.

DECISIONS

Sunday afternoon found Anna back in her home with her mother and brother. Julia's painting had just arrived by courier, and they were unwrapping it from its brown paper. It was raining again, and the drops pounded on the windows, peppered now and then by the sound of thunder. As the last of the paper fell off the painting, they all sat back and studied it.

Anna sighed and smiled. "This girl, she has painted it perfectly. It is almost like she was there."

"Amazing," Alix murmured, lost in the intricacies of the work.

Lexei fell silent, studying the painting, seeing how Julia had worked the brush to achieve the effects that made it so extraordinary.

Alix got up to kneel before the canvas to study it better, and Lexei came to sit next to her.

"Mama, do you think she is a clairvoyant?"

"I think it is clear she is, Lexei. I would very much like to watch her painting." Alix turned to Anna. "Do you think you could arrange it?"

"I don't know, Mama. I can ask. But Mama, I must tell you…" Anna stopped to think, and Lexei and Alix both looked at her, their attention drawn from the painting to Anna's face.

"Anna?

"Mama, yesterday, after Eric and I left the gallery we went for a walk in the park, and…" Anna paused here.

"What, Anna?"

"You know, I think I'm being followed." Anna looked worried.

"Followed?" Lexei asked.

"Well, tracked." Anna looked up again. "Eric and I were attacked again, by a shetani that was probably loosed before the doorway was sealed."

"Oh no."

"It jumped out at us. This one resembled a cat but had a stinger on its tale. I dispatched it immediately, but I think… I think Eric saw my wings, just before I went invisible."

"Oh Anna. Did you…?"

"No, Mama. He remembers everything. He doesn't know what's going on, but I can feel he trusts me. I think that is the only reason he does not freak out more."

"Maybe he saw your wings for a split second before you disappeared because he was so focused on you, so tuned in to you," Lexei suggested.

"Maybe," Anna looked worried.

"Anna, do you think the shetani are tracking you?"

"Well, yes, I do. After I killed the first one, the one that jumped out at us, I searched and found a second one tracking us. Tracking me. It was circling and preparing to attack. I killed it." Anna was breathing hard just thinking of the scene.

"And Eric saw the whole thing? Everything?" Alix leaned forward.

"Yes." Anna looked back into her mother's eyes. "Everything."

Alix looked troubled. Lexei went over to his sister and hugged her.

"Oh," Anna spoke again. "And then, well, we walked some more, and ... well, we spent the night together."

Alix smiled. "Oh, Anna. Oh." Alix's smile broadened. Lexei looked bemused.

"It was wonderful. We shared the connection." Anna smiled, remembering.

At this Alix looked up sharply, her smile all but gone. "Really?"

"Yes, Mama."

"Well." Alix looked pensive. "Well, this changes things."

"Yes." Anna looked down. "I want to tell him my true nature, but I am afraid of losing him."

"Well, but you say he's seen your wings and the shetani and has stayed by your side at the attack," Alix said.

Lexei, who had been silent up to this point, spoke up. "Anna, if you truly love him, if you share a connection, I think you must tell him, and let him decide for himself."

"I agree, Anna," Alix touched her daughter's arm. "It has already gone so far, it cannot be denied; unless you would break it off entirely, and even then, who knows the effect on this man? Anna, I once loved a mortal man, and that love almost destroyed any happiness we ever had."

"Father?"

"Yes, my daughter. Your father. In the end I had to turn him. He insisted. But before I did, it almost killed us both."

"But Mama, those were the times we lived in. The world is different now." Anna looked worried.

"Anna, I like this boy. I give you both my full blessing. But be careful. Try and remain in control of the situation. I would hate for anything to happen to him," Alix cautioned.

"Anna, if you tell him, he will become a target, as you are. If you are being tracked, this knowledge you give him could be deadly to him," Lexei sounded concerned.

"I know. I will tell him, and let him decide if he wants to continue the relationship. I have a very good feeling about it, though. I think he could be my soulmate," Anna smiled dreamily.

"You know, I am worried about you being tracked. I think we should do something about this," said Alix.

"I agree. I'm getting very tired of it, to be honest."

"A hunt then?" Lexei grinned broadly.

"A hunt." Alix smiled grimly back at her son. "Tonight."

"Oh, I almost forgot to mention: Eric lives with one of the Kindred. He greeted me last night, I think he recognized me as one of the People." Anna smiled.

"Now that might come in handy," Alix looked thoughtful.

The fat seagull squawked in midflight as the huge, pale creature flew past it, bumping it out of the air for a dozen feet. Gathering its wits, the gull flapped its wings and righted itself and was soon gliding along again, its eyes peeled for the predator that had brushed against it. Another 30 feet farther, however, the creature dove out of the sky and hit the gull straight on. It clamped down on the bird's fat middle with razor-sharp teeth, crunching with relish as it continued flying over the water. Bloody feathers dropped out of the sky into the lake below.

NIGHT HUNT

Humans who work during the night will tell you, when it is past midnight and all is silent, with the earth wet after a rain, and the moon looking down on the dark land, things move about. Things that are not there during the day.

The night watchman at the bank sees things scuttle across the corners of his vision as he makes his rounds, both inside buildings and out. The night clerk of the local convenience store looks out the windows and sees things flit across his vision in the air, things that move far too fast for the eye to really focus on. The suggestion of flight.

The night delivery driver making his rounds to drop off newspapers will see things cross the path of his truck in the night, a quick movement across headlight-illuminated pavement. Things zip across the highway in front of him, some coming so close it seems sure they will be hit, but never are. He slows down in a panic at first, but after months on the job, gets used to it, swallowing his fear now when it happens, and very wary when he gets out of his truck to place his deliveries. He looks back and forth, is careful to stay in the limited pools of light around the truck, and walks rapidly to place the papers at each doorway. He hurries back to the safety of his truck cab, secretly relieved he has completed one more night of work without encountering anything out of a nightmare.

Psychologists will tell you that children who have night terrors are imagining the creatures they fear; that the monsters in the closet and under the bed aren't real, but figments of the child's imagination. They will tell you that children who wake up screaming, insisting they saw SOMETHING at their window, something out of a nightmare, something LOOKING IN at them, are just having bad dreams. They tell parents and caregivers to just comfort the children and tell them that such things are not real. To assure them that they are safe in their bedrooms, and safe in their beds.

This is a lie.

Children, unlike adults, are not weighed down by the mundane world, by heavy responsibilities and obligations, and because of this freedom, they can sense much more than adults can. The younger children especially can sense every paranormal creature near them as well as the effects the creatures have on their environment. And they know. The monster in the closet? Real. The things lurking under the bed? Real. Every nightmare a child dreams has the ability to make itself real in that child's mind and therefore in that child's world. If kindergarten were held at midnight, oh the things they'd see.

The night hides a world most people never see, a world necessary to certain life forms for their very existence. An existence that is necessary to their survival, and in turn to the survival of the entire world. Just as normal animals are intrinsic to the ecosystem, so are paranormal creatures essential as well. And just as the lioness culls the weak and sick from the herd of antelope, so do the vampire and other paranormal creatures cull the weak. The stray small dog left out by accident? It was no coyote that got it, it was something else. The weak and sick homeless that lay on the sidewalk, half dead? Dead by morning, dead and cold, and ready to be picked up by the police and taken to the city morgue and thence to the Potter's Fields. No in-depth autopsy is performed on the homeless who died overnight. No one realizes death did not take them by natural causes. And if they did see a careless job done by some paranormal creature, vampire or otherwise: a ripped-out neck, or blood-soaked raggedy clothing? They assume coyotes or rats had done it.

They have no idea.

At precisely midnight, Alix, Lexei and Anna ventured out into the city. Walking into the park, three abreast, they looked very intimidating. Dressed head to toe all in black, their wings, fangs and claws were out and they were invisible to mortals. But not to anything paranormal out and about. Not to shetani. Not to other vampires. Not to anything else otherworldly out there.

The moon was at three-quarters waning and seemed to follow them as they walked. They heard owls hooting from every direction; some seemed to be greeting the People who ventured out into the night. Their night. No matter how civilized man may have thought he tamed the land and nature, he had to fall asleep sometime, and it was at night that all the creatures, both normal and paranormal, came out to play.

Anna took a deep breath of the chill air and smiled, looking out at the night-cloaked landscape she loved so much. It was easier to be overlooked in these hours between dusk and daybreak. Even if they used their magic to make themselves invisible, as they had, the cloak of darkness assured the creatures of the night an extra level of protection from the most dangerous animal on the face of the earth: man. Therefore, they felt happiest roaming about at night. The night was their time. The night was their friend. They all came out at night.

Anna, Lexei and Alix crept through every area of the park, and then walked out on the sidewalks for miles. They walked into the inner city, pausing there to hunt and feed on several homeless and broken individuals. They fed on the homeless because these were the people most forgotten by society, the ones who would not be missed. If half a dozen people turned up murdered by the same method in a single week, it would cause an uproar. But the homeless and forgotten were never missed. The People stashed their bodies out of sight, where they weren't discovered for a long, long time, if ever. The homeless were the invisible people, even in death, Anna thought.

It was a horror they brought to these people, whose last days were so fragmented, but the vampires had to feed. In some cases, they overwhelmed the minds of those they killed, bringing ecstatic visions and highs to their minds and bodies as they died, as the vampires fed, and those victims died happy. But only in some cases. If they attacked a person and that person looked into their eyes and there was a connection, perhaps such a mercy might occur, but more often than not, the victim struggled and kicked too much, or they hadn't delivered an incapacitating blow, so they hypnotized them to stop them struggling, to make drinking their blood easier.

A human who saw such a thing happening might recoil in horror and wonder at the cruelty of such creatures of the night, not realizing how much more humane a vampire is than the factory that processes meat for humans. Death at the hands of a vampire was far easier than it might be for an animal slain for human consumption: the cow or chicken or turkey hung upside down, panicking while its throat is slit, feeling everything without any hypnotic aid to ease its passing. There is an element of cruelty to every death a predator inflicts, all along the food chain. A moment of fear and terror, then the slumber of a welcomed death. The world was a terrible, wondrous place.

Anna sighed, content with her place in it. She kicked at a bush as they walked along, their bellies now full. Lexei straightened his tunic from where his victim had grabbed and tugged on it, before he could properly subdue him. That one had had a bit of a trip as they died, and Lexei voiced his worry that he was getting sloppy.

"Let's head along the waterfront," Alix said, turning down a side street to cut across to the bay. Seattle was a wonderful city for a vampire to hide in, full of all manner of alleys and nooks and underground shortcuts, some known to the humans, some hidden or merely forgotten. The three vampires headed down to the water and were soon flitting from rooftop to rooftop before landing on the wet sand.

Looking out at the light of the 2 a.m. city, they paused in their walk. It was a beautiful sight: the buildings, partially lit up, the streetlights, the few cars zipping along the roads. But they weren't finding what they needed.

Anna thought for a minute. "Let's go back toward the museum. They came out at that spot a week ago."

Taking to the air, they winged their way back to that area, looking down as they flew, searching for anything out of the ordinary. Landing back at the edge of the park, a few blocks from the museum, they decided to rest on the benches there before heading to the museum. Lexei lay on his back on the grass next to some trees, his hands locked behind his head, staring up at the moon. Alix sat beside him, on the bench, lying back as well, feeling dreamy after her feed, looking up at the trees and the leaves softly rustling in the night breeze.

Something skittered across Anna's toes as she leaned against a tree, and she looked down to see a dark cat looking back up at her. No, it wasn't a cat after all. It was a marten, its dark brown body almost rippling as it moved. It had paused in its sinewy path and stopped to look up at Anna, sniffing. It apparently liked what it smelled because it came closer and put one paw on Anna's leg. She studied it, bemused. *Such a creature*, she thought, *not afraid of one of the greatest predators on earth.* She leaned down and scratched its neck, and the marten purred in pleasure. It leaned against Anna, trying to reach higher up. Anna responded by rubbing under its neck and behind its ears.

"You've made a friend," Alix smiled, kneeling and petting the dark, beautiful creature.

"If I don't watch myself, it'll want to come home with me," Anna chuckled. The marten was rubbing its head and neck against her boot, scenting her, licking her booted toe before moving along on its nightly errands.

"You're his now," Lexei laughed. Anna smiled down at her brother. So distracted, they did not notice the shetani until the last second. It burst out of the trees and slammed into Anna, knocking her off her feet. It was the size of a small bear, and was of a species of shetani particularly adept at the silent hunt. It had Anna on her back before she knew what had happened, but just as fast, like a startled cat, Anna scrambled and shoved and was soon on top of the creature, which found itself pinned beneath her. The thing screamed and spat in her face, and she felt the spray of its mouth just as Lexei leapt and landed on its head. Alix was behind Anna and held its leg and tail. They had it immobilized within seconds.

"What do we do with it?" Lexei asked, as the shetani struggled under his weight. They hadn't thought of what to do next, really; they'd just wanted to see if they could catch one.

"I don't know, but we need to do something," Alix murmured, holding its bottom end. Her claws dug deep into the thing's flesh, making it scream in rage.

Anna looked down into its face, if it could be called a face. Three eyes and a mouth so full of teeth it couldn't close, and questionable intelligence. "Can you understand me, shetani?" She said in the old tongue.

It looked back at her, and raged and spat some more, struggling for its life. The three vampires held it down for several minutes, and it settled down a bit when it realized it couldn't escape. Anna continued looking into its face.

"I don't think it can speak, but it looks somewhat intelligent," Anna said.

"Well, overwhelm it with fear then. Flood it until it leaves us alone, for good," Alix said.

"Together then," Lexei said.

They all closed their eyes and concentrated. Fear, as real and palpable as a heavy fog, rolled out from all three vampires. Thick as a drenching rain, terror struck every living thing nearby, and they heard creatures running, racing, scuttling away, as fast as they could, away from the deadly vampires. The vampires' eyes glowed red with the ferocity of their auras. The marten screamed and raced away. Anna sensed three other shetani fleeing the area. She looked down at the one they held. It was looking into her eyes, unable to flee, unable to even lose consciousness in its fright.

Anna concentrated on instilling fear that would last a very long time; fear that would endure a lifetime. The fear she put into it and every other creature nearby was an instinct to flee from every vampire they would ever encounter, from that moment on. She hoped it would be communicated to every other shetani in the city. After some minutes, she sensed the thing's mind was close to breaking, so she let it up. They all retreated some steps from the shetani, and for a minute it lay still. After a while, it rose slowly onto its four feet. Unsteady, it slowly trotted off, weaving like a drunken bear. It allowed itself one more look behind it at the vampires and seemed to shudder, then disappeared into the forested area of the park, thoroughly traumatized.

"Well, I hope that does something," Anna brushed the dust off her legs and wiped her face on her wing. "Yuck. It was spitting."

Lexei laughed then, lighthearted and merry. Alix and Anna soon joined in. It was an odd feeling for them, to gang up on another creature like they were common hoodlums. They needed to feel happy again after the strong-arm tactics they'd just performed.

"Let's fly," Lexei suggested, still chuckling. They leapt into the air right where they were, bursting through the canopy of a giant liquid gold tree, and scattered leaves up and out in an impressive spray as they flew up into the night to play among the stars.

———————⋙⋘———————

Later that night, back home and relaxing, Anna made a decision.

"I am going to tell Eric my true nature. This week. I will choose a good time to sit him down and talk with him, and I will just hope for the best." Anna looked at her brother and mother. "I dearly hope he is not scared off." She looked at the ground, worried.

Lexei hugged her. "That is good. I hope everything turns out how we hope. Because I have a date with Julia next weekend."

The creature had landed in a redwood tree, where it roosted for the rest of the night. The tree was a hundred and fifty feet high, and stood in a small, forested, remote corner of a city park next to Lake Washington. As the sun came up, a dark cloud of fog remained in that part of the forest, effectively bringing a twilight darkness to the area that remained for the rest of the day. Birds and wildlife fled the dank darkness as the creature slumbered in an uneasy sleep shrouded by a night of its own making.

INTERRUPTED

Gretchen sighed as she bent her head to the task Mr. Ramsey had set for her that morning. Typing up the document's fifth incarnation, she hoped it would satisfy her demanding boss so that she could go home.

She reached for the steaming mug of tea by her side, and stretched her sore neck, stiff from a long day that had stretched far into overtime.

The office was quiet; everyone else had gone home hours ago. In the private Ramsey offices, the thick, plush carpet silenced any sound that dared carry to Ramsey's ears. Midnight hung in the air, thick and silent as a graveyard.

───────➤≈≈≈≈≈◄───────

In his inner office, Ramsey sat at his desk, lost in thought.

He'd finished his work ten minutes earlier, and had shut off all but the small, glowing lamp. The illumination was so slight it did not obscure the view from the huge window he faced over his desk. The lights of Seattle, bright even at midnight, sparkled in the night. Traffic flowed on arteries, winding its way around office buildings. The Space Needle could be seen off to the side, lit up against the inky blackness of the night.

Ramsey felt most at home in this nocturnal solitude. His supersonic hearing detected no sound from the quiet building other than Rachel's typing in the other room, and felt relaxed enough in the darkened, empty office to let down his shields. As he sat there, lost in thought, his face inscrutable, his mind drifted back. Back in time, back through a hundred scenes, back to the beginning.

As he remembered, he let himself recall the first time he had met her. She'd been a young thing then, barely 12. The promise of great beauty had been there, even then. Sparkling eyes, lush, wavy hair, and a laugh that had seemed to drip stars, enchanting him and seizing his heart in a grip like no other. With her creamy skin with flushed cheeks, and dark pouty lips, she was the picture of the young beauty.

Of course, she'd been protected, and when he tried getting closer, her father had warned him off. In his mid-forties at the time, Rasputin had been powerful, but he'd lacked the necessary status to court the pre-teen daughter of the tsar of Imperial Russia. So, he had worked to become close to the entire family, just so he could be closer to her. Ramsey sighed again, looking out onto the city, lost in thought.

He remembered the curve of her face, the way she had the habit of curling her fingers around her hair, and hooking it back behind one ear. Her ears, so delicate, had entranced him. Her softly blooming body, so new and fresh, had him staring at her almost constantly. He'd begun to fantasize about her. He'd taken to hiding himself in corners, watching her through the heavy drapes and tapestries. He couldn't help himself, he thought. She was enchanting, utterly irresistible.

Her sisters had taken to accompanying her everywhere when it was clear Rasputin had taken more than a passing interest in her. His frustration had grown when he couldn't see her privately.

When Rasputin had left the castle for some months, on a secretive trip to Paris, he guessed the family had breathed a sigh of relief, but then he had returned, visiting them at night, and he'd was different. Darker.

Rasputin scowled almost all the time after that, and he'd cozied up to her mother, who seemed to fall under his spell. But his unholy his desire for the young princess had never waned; she was always on his mind.

She was on his mind even now, after a hundred years of chasing them. Of chasing her.

He'd almost lost hope. But the heart's desire is a strong

thing, and the mind will go nearly insane to keep hope alive. Still, Ramsey felt overwhelmed with hopelessness now, and alone in his Seattle offices, he allowed himself a rare moment of raw emotion.

***

Out in the vestibule, Gretchen had just returned from refreshing her tea, one last cupful before she finally left for the night. She approached her desk, and was preparing to gather her purse and coat, when she paused. Listening for a second, she thought she heard the faint sound of a sob.

She turned to the heavy door that guarded the inner office where Mr. Ramsey still worked, late into the night. If Gretchen ever thought she worked long hours, she always reminded herself her boss worked even longer, seeming to toil far into the night. He rarely left before 2 a.m.

There. There it was again. It sounded like quiet weeping, barely there, coming from just beyond the door. Gretchen put her coat down, hitched her purse back onto her shoulder, and quietly crept up to the closed door.

***

Inside his office, Ramsey had laid his head down on his arms, resting on the desk, and, feeling overwhelmed with longing for her, had begun weeping into the arm of his jacket. Muffled against the material, he kept his voice quiet. His shoulders soon shook with his sobs.

Gretchen had her ear to the door, a concerned look on her face as she realized her boss was crying. Almost instinctively, she brought her hand up to the door and her knuckles rapped softly on the heavy wood. "Mr. Ramsey? Are you all right?"

Ramsey's emotions were a loud roar in his ears, and he did not hear Gretchen knock, nor did he hear the doorknob turn.

Gretchen's heart constricted in sympathy, she couldn't bear to see anything in pain. Her hand turned the knob, and she opened the door a few inches, poking her forehead through in concern. "Mr. Ramsey? Are you okay? Sir?"

The sight that first greeted her eyes was of the darkened office, the large window dotted with raindrops, and the city lights gleaming in the rain; then, the slight movement of Ramsey's shoulders shaking with sobs. He sat in darkness at his desk, seemingly lost in misery.

Gretchen breathed faster at the sight of the new senator engulfed in private grief. A powerhouse of a businessman, Mr. Ramsey had always appeared incredibly confident and authoritative to her, and this sight of him so compromised and vulnerable tugged heavily at her heart.

She crossed the thick carpeting and laid her hand on Mr. Ramsey's shoulders in a gesture of comfort and concern.

Ramsey, lost in his primal grief, weeping, ears filled with the sound of his own heartbeat and heavy breathing through tears, felt Gretchen's hand on him, and his sorrow fled, replaced by rage. How dare she intrude on him like this, when he was at his most vulnerable?

Ramsey's vampire aura surged outward.

Without thinking, he sprang from his chair with a roar, whirling around and lashing out with his arm in a flash. His deadly sharp inch-long claws hit Gretchen on the side of her jaw.

Gretchen never knew what hit her. Ramsey's superhuman strength rushed through him in a red-hot haze of anger, and he swiped at Gretchen with the power and strength of an enraged bear. The savage blow ripped into Gretchen, and her head went flying.

Hearing it land with a *thunk* on the other side of the room, followed by the heavier sound of Gretchen's body falling, brought Ramsey out of his berserk rage and back into the present moment. Looking around at the sight of his dead secretary, blood splattered across the finely furnished office, his eyes rested at last on her open purse, which had fallen off her shoulder and to the floor. A roll of mints had escaped and rolled off to the side a few inches; her keys had fallen as well, making the last sound he had heard before his eyes settled on the grisly sight before him.

"Damn," was all he said.

High up in the tree it crouched, waiting and slumbering. Biding its time was something it was used to doing, and it could rest and hide for weeks at a time, motionless, invisible, and lurking. If it didn't want to be noticed, it wouldn't be. Its belly growled ferociously. It waited patiently. Soon, a bobcat padded underneath the tree, and without warning, the creature dropped down onto it. Still clumsy with grogginess, the grotesque thing missed snapping the animal's neck and lost the chance to immobilize it. The bobcat whipped around and scratched it, slicing deep into the creature's front left limb. Filled with rage at the animal, it held it without killing it, and slowly ate it from the inside out. The bobcat only passed out and died at the last, as the creature bit into its heart.

REVELATIONS

"Eric?"

They'd been meeting before class for a week now, and this Monday, Anna fidgeted nervously, rehearsing what she planned to say to him. Eric was smiling broadly when he walked up to her and took her in his arms.

"Babe." He kissed her. "Saturday night was incredible, I've never felt so ..." he smiled, unable to articulate his feelings. He buried his face in her neck, her hair curling around him softly.

Anna hugged him warmly, feeling so close to him, yet at the same time worried he would freak out and break up with her over what she was about to tell him.

They walked into class together. "Eric," Anna whispered. "After class, I need to talk to you."

He looked at her with concern. "Is everything all right?"

"Yes, everything is fine. Don't worry." The look on her face was pensive though, and so all throughout class Eric worried, just a little. Class was fabulous, as always. He loved art, and with Anna there, the class was especially enjoyable. Relaxing.

After class, they wandered over to Lestat's and sat down in the secluded corner booth they'd taken to thinking of as "their spot." After chatting about class for a short while, Anna fell silent, a thoughtful look on her face. Eric watched her, a soft smile on his face.

After a few minutes, Anna spoke. "Eric, do you remember that evening in the museum?"

Eric did. "Yes, I remember. It was spooky in that exhibit."

Anna sighed. This had happened before. Humans who had never been exposed to the supernatural, often rationalized their first sight of it as something familiar, something their brains could understand. "Eric, it was more than spooky."

"That diorama. ... Everything seemed so real, because of the lighting. The fake vampires, the fake monster creatures, the forest moving in that fake wind. Very weird."

Anna tried another tack. "Eric, remember when we were in the forest after we left the gallery?"

"Yes, I remember." He looked over at his lady love and

smiled. "I'm not sure what happened Saturday evening."

"Do you remember anything at all?"

Eric looked slightly troubled. "What I remember is fuzzy, and I think it's wrong ... it has to be." He looked up at her.

Anna took a deep breath and dove right in. "Eric, I'm not like everyone else."

"Yes, I can see that." Eric smiled, his eyes crinkling with affection. "That's why I love you."

"No, what I mean is, well..." Anna stopped for a moment and thought about what Eric had just said. He was right. That *was* why he loved her. But the reason she was like this had a lot to do with her being one of the People. That was part of her personality, part of her very identity. Just as a dog is friendly and happy-go-lucky because that is part of the essence of being a dog, she was this way because that was how vampires were. Her own personality was a big part of her too, true, but she was who she was mainly because she was a vampire. She looked over at Eric and smiled.

Anna remembered how she had been before she'd been turned by her brother Lexei. She'd been a petulant, arrogant, selfish child who'd been spoiled beyond belief. As the daughter of Nikolai Romanov, the reigning tsar of Imperial Russia, she'd lived in a palace and had everything she'd ever wanted at her fingertips. She'd been a royal princess in an age where royalty was everything. That era had ended abruptly, along with any remnants of her childhood, but until then she had enjoyed a life of high privilege, surrounded by luxury and excess. And she'd been an incredibly self-centered spoiled brat.

Shortly after she'd been turned, everything had fallen apart. The tsar had been overthrown, and the royal family forced into hiding. The next few decades had been very different from her childhood, and had been instrumental in forming the woman Anna was today. She'd lived a lifetime since then, literally, and she looked back on her former lavish childhood and self-centeredness the way a hundred-year-old sea turtle might look back on the weeks after it had been hatched and was making its way to its new life in the ocean.

Yes, she knew that nearly everything she was now was because she was one of the People. She looked at Eric. "I love you, Eric. I want you to know that."

"I love you too, Anna," Eric lifted her hand to his lips and kissed her fingertips softly.

"Eric, there's no soft way to tell you this. The things you saw in the museum? In the park? The wings you said you thought you saw on me? Well..."

Eric leaned forward.

"Eric, I am one of the People. I have been changed from what I once was."

"The People? I don't understand. What you once were?"

"Yes. I was once like you, Eric." Anna took a deep breath and just said it. "I once was like you. Human. I am no longer." She looked at him.

182

Eric looked back, not sure what she was trying to tell him.

Anna looked around again to make sure they were alone. "Eric," she whispered, "I'm a vampire."

Eric blinked. He looked at the person across from him: Gorgeous, incredible. He'd loved her from the beginning; from the first time he'd talked to her on that foggy night so many weeks ago. His parents liked her, his sister liked her, he liked her mother and brother; they were all wonderful, just like her. He looked down at her feet; today she wore purple boots and a black gypsy skirt, with multiple dangly bracelets that tinkled when she moved. He looked up into her face, she had on little makeup, letting her natural beauty shine through. Her cheeks were still rosy from the cold outside. She was smiling. Eric smiled back.

"You're a vampire." He said it as a statement.

"Yes."

Eric thought a moment. "And all the odd things that have been happening, they aren't my imagination?"

Anna shook her head. "And the things that attacked us? In the museum diorama and in the park? Those are called shetani. In present day, they are known as African spirits or demons, because the last place they existed, before they became extinct, was in Africa. I believe they disappeared a few thousand years before the mammoths," Anna explained.

"Mammoths."

"Yes. But the shetani aren't really spirits, they are

animals. One of the last animals to have magic."

"Magic?"

"Some animals evolved with magic as a defense mechanism, mostly. Magic is one of the brain's powers." She looked at him. "Kind of like your sixth sense?"

Eric just looked at her. Anna tried again.

"Have you ever felt someone's eyes on you, before you knew they were there? Kind of a spooky feeling, when the hairs on the back of your neck spring up and your senses prickle?"

"Oh. Yes, I've experienced that." Eric was happy to have a point of reference in the conversation.

"Well, your sixth sense is one of your brain's powers. Probably one of the last magical ones modern humans have."

"I guess after civilization started, we didn't need some of our other ... senses? Brain powers? Not sure what to call them," Eric trailed off.

"Exactly. Humans were no longer alone in the forest, needing these skills and powers to survive. Civilization caused these traits to disappear. They were no longer needed." Anna sat back.

"I feel dumb," Eric grimaced.

"Oh, no no!" Anna laughed. "Civilization enabled humans to grow in intelligence. You may no longer have much magic, but you can reach the moon, build supercomputers, and operate on a baby inside the womb. These are things humans could never have achieved in their more primal state."

"I guess nature really does know what it's doing then. Huh. Evolution." He looked at her. "So, they were animals that attacked us? They didn't look like any animal I've ever seen."

"They wouldn't. They haven't been seen on this planet in an extremely long time. Over 750,000 years. In fact, vampires are distantly related to shetani.

Eric leaned closer, studying her. "Vampires are ... but ... you sure don't look anything like them."

Anna laughed. "Nor do you look anything like a dolphin or a tiger. And that's about how close we are to the shetani. But we exist, in present day. Not a lot of us, but more than you would think."

"And you really do have ... wings?"

"Sometimes. When I need to." Anna smiled gently at him.

Eric looked thoughtful. "Do I have anything to be afraid of?" he asked.

"No, not at all."

Eric remembered the incredible Saturday night they'd shared in his apartment. "Saturday night? That was incredible," he smiled at her and squeezed her hand gently. "That was ..."

"Part of what we felt was because of what I am, yes, but most of everything was just us, loving each other; and I hope to have many more nights like that with you." Anna leaned forward, took Eric's face in her soft hands, and kissed him, thoroughly.

Afterward, she laid her cheek against his and whispered in his ear, "I know this is an incredible thing to take in, Eric, but I want you to know that I love you, I don't want to lose you, ever." She brought her face back up to look into his eyes. "I love you."

Eric smiled back at her, looking relieved.

She moved to sit next to him on the loveseat, and they sat there together, embracing, and whispering to each other.

After a while Eric sat up again, "Anna, tell me more."

She smiled. "Well, we ..."

"You mean vampires?" Eric interrupted.

"Yes. We have this thing, a kind of power emanating from our minds, it's called an aura, and we can make it stronger or quieter; it kind of protects us, in a way. But part of it, because you and I share a love that runs deep, well ... What happened Saturday night back at your apartment was part of that."

"You mean, ...the way I could," Eric blushed, "feel what you were feeling?"

"Yes. And I could feel what you were feeling too, Eric," Anna blushed as well.

"Well, I loved that. It was incredible," Eric kissed her and held her closer.

They kissed again, long and deep. Eric shifted in his seat. "Anna, I want to see everything about you, everything you described. Wings, anything else, all the vampire part of you:

I want to see it all," his eyes danced with curiosity.

Anna laughed. "Eric, it's a very primal thing. The way making love with me was, well, everything about me is: very primal." Anna looked into his eyes.

"I've noticed a very primal aspect of your art in class."

"Oh, wait until you see my brother's paintings. That's one reason we were so intrigued by Julia's art; her paintings have a very primal, beautiful quality about them as well."

Anna paused a moment. "Eric, as a vampire, you realize that, well, I do have to feed. I mean, eat." She looked down at her cup. Today it contained hot chamomile tea with lemon. She brought the cup to her lips and wetted them, inhaling the scent of the tea, but not drinking any. She looked back up at Eric. Realization dawned on his face.

"You don't drink the tea. Or the coffee or hot chocolate, or any of them." He sat back, taking it all in. "I wondered ..." He looked intrigued. "Tell me more."

"Well, are you a vegetarian?"

"No. I like a good steak," Eric smiled.

"I do too, I just prefer mine raw."

The smile on Eric's face fell off. Anna sat back and laughed.

"Do you mean ...?" Eric seemed to searched for words, looking around to be sure, once again, that they weren't being overheard. "Anna," he said in a low voice, "do you drink blood to eat?"

"Yes." She kept her eyes on his.

Eric looked thoughtful. Silence ruled over their tiny corner of the café. Looking up suddenly, his eyes brightened. "Do you mean like in the movies, where there're people who willingly volunteer to be drained every now and then? And they partner with ... you, ..." His voice trailed off. Anna was shaking her head.

"No, Eric. That would not be smart. We hide, no one knows about us. If we had a network like that, dozens of humans who knew our secret, it wouldn't be a secret for long." She sat back.

Eric fell silent again. He looked at her. She was smiling across from him.

Anna watched the play of emotions on Eric's face. She could see him battling with the two conflicting emotions: love and horror, and watched as love won out. Her heart skipped a beat, and she closed her eyes in relief, thanking whatever deity there was that Eric was overcoming his revulsion at the undeniable horror of what a vampire must do to stay alive. Anna had been appalled herself at first, but when hunger set in so strong you nearly died from starvation, you got over it pretty quickly. She hoped he could, at least.

Eric put his arms around her and hugged her tightly. Then pulled back. "I'm sorry, I put my neck right in front of your mouth, I didn't mean to tempt you or anything."

Anna laughed then, she laughed so much she fell back in her seat and held her belly, her eyes closed in merriment.

"Oh, Eric ... No ..." She gave up trying to talk and just laughed, for a long time. After a while, Eric just sat there watching her and grinning. When her laughter finally started to subside, she put her hand on his leg, chuckling.

"Eric ... Eric, do you feel an incontrollable urge to grab a cow you see and chomp down on it?"

"No, but that's not the same ..."

"Okay, fair enough. Well, if you were really hungry and you saw someone on campus munching on a bag of chips or a hamburger, do you have the uncontrollable urge to grab their food from them?"

"No," Eric chuckled, "that'd be ridiculous. So," he looked at her, "do you mean that you don't look at every human and think, 'Ooh! Food!' "

Anna started laughing again.

"Okay, well..." Eric grinned. He stood. "I guess not, huh?" Anna had fallen back into the loveseat, laughing so much she couldn't speak. Weak-kneed, she wordlessly reached her arms out for him to help her. Eric grabbed them and lifted her to her feet. Laughing together, they both buttoned their jackets and left the coffee shop, arm in arm.

<hr />

They walked for a while in the cool evening breeze, hand in hand, not speaking, just communing with the night and deepening their bond. Stopping against a lamppost, Anna leaned back against the ornate surface and lifted her lips to Eric's as he stepped up against her. They kissed there for a long time, and Anna saw that creatures of the night, in the nearby bushes and trees, were watching them, smelling their love. The scent of it rolled out all around them, the heady essence of love and passion, thick in the air.

As the two lovers kissed and communed, one of the many animals watching them was so overcome with enthusiasm it screamed out to the night, startling Anna and Eric. They parted, smiling, then continued walking along the sidewalk.

Eric and Anna wandered along, hand in hand, until they came to the park. They kept walking, slowly, very close, whispering together every now and then.

"Anna," Eric looked at her. "Show me your wings. Please. I want to see all of you, every bit."

Anna hesitated. "Eric, I cannot bring out my wings without bringing out everything. Every part."

"What do you mean?"

"I have claws, I have fangs, I actually grow taller when everything comes out."

"You're kidding. Really?" Eric was grinning broadly.

Anna laughed. "You know, I think you're more excited than I've ever seen you. You can't wait to see everything, can you?" She smiled.

"I want to see it all."

"Are you sure? All of it?"

"Yes. Oh, yes, Anna. Please."

"Okay, but let's get deeper into the park."

Something screamed far off, making Eric jump in his excitement. "What was that?"

Anna rolled her eyes, "A peacock."

Eric laughed. They continued walking farther down the walkway as night owls flew across their path, silent as the wind. Eric was delighted. "They're so beautiful."

Anna made kissing sounds to the air, beckoning, and lifted her arm out. Within seconds, an owl flew out to them and landed on her arm. It was huge and brown and gorgeous.

"Oh my god," Eric whispered. "Can I touch it?"

"I'm sure she will let you. Just be gentle and respectful." Anna smiled.

Eric reached out and touched the great owl, first dipping his fingers lightly into its feathers, then, after a minute, running his hand down the magnificent creature's back, marveling at being so close to it. He turned his head slightly to address Anna. "How did you get her to come to your arm?"

"I'm acquainted with all the animals around here. Plus, we're both creatures of the night."

At this Eric looked deeply into Anna's face, his face alight with curiosity and wonder. The moonlight came through the trees and cast a mottled light on her face. Her eyes looked so alive they were almost glowing, and a rapturous smiled played across her lips. She laughed in delight, turning to face the owl, and the bird leaned over and playfully nibbled at Anna's pursed lips as Eric looked on in astonishment. Smiling, Anna lifted her arm high, and the owl jumped back into the air and was gone. They walked on for a while along the path, then she entered the woods and led Eric off into the wild, untrampled park.

They soon came to a secluded clearing at the back of the woods, far from any other people who might be on a walk that night. Anna stopped in the middle of the grass, where the moonlight came through the strongest, so Eric could see her clearly. She looked at him, and he looked back, smiling.

"Come sit with me." Anna sat on the thick grass and patted the spot next to her. Eric joined her, tilting his head back, and soon they were lying next to each other, stargazing. The forest air smelled clean and fresh and full of magic, and Anna felt wonderfully alive.

"I've wanted to have love in my life for a very long time," Anna said after a minute. "I've tried, but it just never worked out."

Eric shifted next to her, "Why not?"

"I'm not sure. I think I scared them off or something."

"It's weird, I guess, but I'm not afraid at all. I find all this so exhilarating! Exciting, wonderful, amazing, and utterly fantastic," Eric let out a WOOT! to the stars and laughed.

Anna laughed next to him. "Eric, you're wonderful. I love you." She took his hand and squeezed it lightly.

He turned to her again, "So the other guys got scared off?"

"All the guys and the girl I tried to date, too."

At this Eric's eyes widened. "Girl?"

Anna chuckled. "Yes, one girl. Her name was Evain and she was beautiful, inside and out. Gorgeous long, flowing red hair; a laugh like a faerie, and absolutely beautiful breasts." At this Eric laughed out loud. "We fell in love, in the only way you could in the 1930s. Secret rendezvous, stolen kisses, clandestine meetings, it was all very romantic and very forbidden. It lasted a fortnight. Then she was gone. The day after I told her, she was gone. I never saw her again. I went to her house, but she refused to even see me. Her family was very hostile. They even called a priest to answer the door. At that point, I stopped trying."

"Did you show her everything?"

"I never got the chance," Anna sighed.

"Man ..."

"It just got ridiculous, really. I mean, can you imagine me knocking on her door, and a priest answering and going straight into some kind of exorcist's chant?" Anna rolled her eyes. "What do I look like? A poltergeist?" She chuckled. "Anyway, after that, I just thought, 'Sweetie, you're not worth this much.' I mean, I felt bullied, for goodness sake." Anna gave a huff.

"Sounds pretty lame. I guess the '30s were really different than present day, huh?"

"Well, yes and no. Society was far more uptight, but people still did the things they wanted, they just went underground. She was just disingenuous. Something I hate."

"Anna, you've been through a lot."

"Well, nothing all that different than anybody else, I guess. Just maybe more of it."

Eric turned onto his side to look at her, and she turned to look at him. "Anna, I will not ever say anything to you that I don't mean. I promise you, when I say, 'I love you,' I mean it. And I do love you, I think it deepens every day I spend with you." He leaned over and kissed her.

Anna's hand came up, and she ran her fingers through his hair, kissing him back with feeling. Breaking apart, they looked into each other's eyes, love shining out.

"I think it's time I showed you everything," she said.

"Everything," he smiled, getting to his feet.

Anna stood, brushing the brambles from her outfit, and took off her jacket.

"Okay. Don't be afraid of what you see. No matter what happens, I'm still me, okay?" Anna cautioned.

"Okay," Eric took a step back to see better, and waited.

Anna knew she had to do this slowly, if she concentrated and popped everything out at once Eric would probably run for the hills. Slowly. Yes, she could do it slowly.

Closing her eyes, Anna concentrated as Eric watched her, waiting. The midnight breeze played with her hair, lifting it and ruffling her skirt as he watched.

The first thing that happened was that the breeze became supernatural. The wind blew in a circle, like a whirling dervish, and then changed its direction to blow upward, then outward. It seemed almost magical, and speckles of electricity popped at the edge of the clearing.

Vampiric power surged through Anna, and she began to glow softly. Her skirt drifted up slightly, as did her hair. She spread her arms, and her fingers, palms down, parted. As Eric watched, Anna glowed and *grew*, shimmering in the moonlight. She took a deep breath and *pushed*, and fangs began to grow out of her mouth: long canine teeth, right in front of her normal teeth. Her fingertips shimmered as her claws grew out of each fingertip, lengthening until each curved, razor-sharp talon reached out at least an inch.

As Eric watched, the air behind her shimmered in an ethereal light; and wings, huge and black, grew out of her back. They were shaped like a bat's wings, but they were covered with silky black feathers, iridescent with peacock highlights, and they were huge, dragging the ground behind her, even as she grew taller.

Anna's hair billowed out as she grew by six inches, and Eric found himself looking up into her face. Her mouth opened as the fangs grew, and she lifted her chin to the sky, emitting a quiet huff of power as she finally opened her eyes.

Anna hissed at the night in relish as she let everything out; she inhaled deeply, thrusting her chest out in happiness.

Anna could hear Eric's heart raced in excitement as he beheld her true form. Beads of sweat formed on his forehead, and his face flushed pink in the moonlight. He kept his eyes on her, unblinking and staring, amazed; and she reveled in the fact that at last he understood everything she had told him, everything she had explained. The Anna he had known up until now was just what she had allowed him to see. She was so much more.

Anna looked at Eric and smiled in glee, flexing her wings in delight. Eric stepped closer to her, his lips parting open.

Eric's hands reached for her as she watched him with glowing eyes. Her mouth was half open, so he could see her razor-sharp fangs, and her tongue dipping out to lick her lips. Swallowing hard, Eric began breathing faster; and she was breathing hard, too, and the rhythm of their breathing synchronized and became equal in intensity.

His eyes took her in, all of her. Reaching down, he ran his fingers along her muscled arm down to her elegant hands tipped in long, curving claws. She flexed and brought up her hand as he lifted his, and they locked fingers. Eric stepped as close as he could to her, and his mouth opened, his lips lightly brushing her cheek and moving to her lips, where they began a soft, intense dance.

Eric's other hand came around to Anna's back, the touch of his fingers raising goose bumps across her shoulders. Her feathers billowed as she arched her wings, and she tilted her head to kiss him more deeply as her tongue darted out to flick against the inside of his mouth. Eric pushed against Anna, and she thrilled in what she felt in him.

Anna responded by reaching her own arm around to Eric's back and pulling him hard against her. She arched her back, pressing against him until he groaned. With her other arm, she reached and began undoing his shirt. That was all the prompting Eric needed, and they were soon free of their clothing, a hindrance discarded on the grass next to them, forgotten.

Eric's kisses began trailing down from Anna's mouth and across to her neck and collarbone. She gasped and flung her head up in pleasure as Eric's mouth worked its magic. She grabbed his shoulders and began kissing his neck, hanging on for dear life. Anna's vampire soul, fully glowing in power, flowed freely, and her mind reached out to Eric's in ecstasy. Shuddering, he began kissing her intensely, holding her with both arms, imparting all the feeling he had for her in his kisses.

Eric reached and picked Anna up, and she brought her legs up and around his waist, drawing in the prize she craved. She wrapped her arms around his shoulders, and he carried her as they became one. Her delight was complete as they joined in their primal dance, a dance as old as time.

Eric gasped in pleasure and buried his face in her neck. Her soft hair tickled him as it fell onto his shoulders. Groaning in ecstasy, Anna looked down at Eric, her mouth open, her tongue out, her fangs gleaming in the starlight; and she flung her head back again as the sensations rolled over her. She could not contain her feelings. She didn't want to. She knew her passion flooded Eric's mind, combining with the sensations she felt from him, until they were both lost in pleasure.

Eric's arms held Anna around her waist and hips, and he arched his back in pleasure. Anna's vampiric aura surged, and she floated into the air a few inches, her long legs still wrapped around Eric's hips as he held her.

Her wings flexed back and forth as they both rose in the air, and the breeze began to turn them slowly as they made love. His lips stayed on her, loving her in the sensuous dance, and Anna lost her head in ecstasy as her body rode wave after wave of pleasure, reaching multiple heights in the cool evening breeze. Her mind was an electric wave of fantastic sensations as she felt Eric reach deeper and deeper, becoming so excited that when his body finally peaked, the release almost hurt.

"AHHHHH," He groaned loudly, his lips finally parting from her chest. The ripples of pleasure lasted a long time, and he buried his face in her ample form as he convulsed, his arms holding her around her waist, under her softly feathered wings, his groans dying in her heartbeat. She dropped her face onto the top of his head and exhaled in happy pleasure.

Some minutes later, she sighed softly as she loosened her legs and slid down to the ground. He reluctantly released her, burying his face in her neck, opening his mouth to taste her skin again. His arms stayed around her, and he held her close to him, and they communed this way for several minutes.

After some time, Eric brought his face back to look into her eyes, which still glowed with an unearthly magical light. Her smiling lips showed the tips of her fangs, and Eric brought his tongue out and tasted the long teeth. Anna opened her mouth further to allow his complete inspection, and Eric ran his tongue over the fangs, noting their sharpness and strength as well as their length and width. They were formidable weapons. Backing up a bit, Eric peered into her mouth and inspected everything with his eyes; she allowed this as well, wanting so much for him to accept everything about her vampire body.

Eric stood there naked in the midnight moonlight, taking her all in. He moved around to the back, inspecting her magnificent wings and how they met her shoulders. The black iridescent feathers grew smaller as they approached the base of her wings, and they were baby fine where they met her back and grew a few inches onto it.

The muscles and bones of her wings reached out from dual shoulder blades. It was as if she had turned into a creature with six limbs, except the top two pairs grew from the same area. At the base, her arms seemed nearly the same limb as her wings, but grew apart almost instantly, in a duality that worked as well as if nature and evolution had made them that way, and he told her as much.

"But that is how it did happen. Evolution. Vampires are from the same evolutionary branch as the shetani are, remember?" Anna explained.

"The shetani?" He asked from behind her.

"Yes."

"But those all look different from each other, I thought."

"Yes, but they are all interrelated. Just as dogs and cats and monkeys and humans all sprouted from the same primordial family branch of the evolutionary tree, vampires, shetani, even dragons, all grew from the same branch together."

"Dragons???" Eric sounded astonished and stopped his examination of her wings to come around to the front of her. Unfortunately for the conversation, his eyes fell on her chest, and Eric's train of thought was gone.

"Ohhhhh," he moaned, and dipped his head to feather kisses over her. Passions surged, and she felt the incredible sensation of Eric's mouth on her body once more. Her head went to the side, her eyes closed, and she was once again lost in the excitement he was producing in her. Eric almost instantly grew hot again, and his hands came around her to hold her again.

Anna felt weak in the knees, and they bent, lowering her to the ground. Eric's muscled arms flexed as he climbed over her, making love to her a second time. He reached down to kiss her again, his lips moving, his tongue entering her mouth, his throat unable to hold back the groans. His body moved faster and faster as he lost control, and her legs came up to wrap around his back as his body curled into hers, and they were lost in ecstasy once more.

After some minutes, Eric groaned and nearly lost consciousness as pleasure overwhelmed him. Anna kissed him, beginning on his mouth and face, and trailing down lower, dribbling light, tickling touches down his body, and began to lick and circle and nibble until Eric was shivering. He lay back, lost in sensation.

His eyes rolled up into his head, his hands reaching down and his fingers entwining in her hair as she moved, her mouth and tongue performing magic. His groans became gasps as she loved him, and he could not hold himself back any longer. With a gasp, she felt his mind fill with overwhelming pleasure, and she was lost in the sensations he was feeling, soon joining him in that ecstasy.

Anna fell back, her hair spread on the grass, her natural beauty irresistible. Eric bent over her again and kissed her, touching and caressing her everywhere. She gasped, opening her eyes and her mouth, and hissed in pleasure as his hands wandered over her. His eyes opened to watch her face; seeing what his ministrations were doing to her, he smiled in satisfaction. His kisses wandered everywhere, and Anna gasped and shuddered in happiness.

Anna lost herself in the sensations he was producing, and her whole body shivered where it lay on the grass. Her wings trembled as Eric kissed and caressed her, and soon her whole body was convulsing in sensations that made her heart race with pleasure.

Eric gently climbed atop her, and she reached up to him

with a smile. He leaned down and kissed her deeply and joined with her again, his movements making him groan in pleasure. Her heart swelled and she shivered in the dark forest glade, kissing him all the while, and her feelings for him cementing themselves in permanence. She felt they were bonded for life.

Lying side by side on the grass, the moon and stars as witnesses, Anna and Eric dozed off for a few hours. She smiled as she slipped into slumber, sensing the animals watching them from their hiding places in the tall grasses close to them. The last thing she heard was an owl gently hooting in the trees. The last things she saw as her eyes slid shut were the stars and moon as they kept watch on the young lovers.

───────※◆◆◆◆◆※───────

It was about an hour before dawn when Eric was roused by the sound of a wild rabbit sniffing out tender shoots in the grass a few feet from them. Opening one eye, he peered out, and his gaze settled on the furry creature. He could only see the top of its back and its long ears. Chuckling, half asleep, his subconscious nudged at him insistently with a detail he had heard earlier. Suddenly his eyes opened wide.

"Anna, did you say 'dragons'?" Eric stared wide-eyed into the starry night sky, wide awake now. He heard the rabbit run off into the forest, and turned on his side to face her.

"Babe, did you say you were related to dragons??"

"Mmmmph. Bbbbblrbbbggd."

Smiling, Eric pulled his pants on, stopping to breathe in the crisp night air. It had been warm lying against his ladylove, but now he was beginning to feel a bit cold. He turned to look at her, still lying in the grass, asleep and beautiful. Buttoning his shirt, he studied her. She lay on her soft feathery wings, which had been very warm and nice to lie against. Anna's eyes came open just then and she blinked, still sleepy. Eric reached down and kissed her, and she smiled.

"You're still here. You haven't left." Her statement was obvious, yet happy. He chuckled.

"I'd have to be insane to leave you, Love."

She smiled wider, and was suddenly fully awake. In a quick movement, she leapt into the air, wings spread wide, held aloft by mostly magic, wings beating back and forth slowly, making the air whistle gently through the trees. She smiled down at him from several feet above, looking into the trees all around them before lowering herself back to the ground and reaching for her clothes. She gave a slight shiver, and Eric saw her wings, fangs and talons slide seamlessly back in to her body, leaving no trace they were ever there. Eric blinked in amazement and smiled.

As Anna busied herself dressing, Eric spoke.

"So, dragons?" He said.

Nodding as she balanced on one foot, she deftly put the

other straight into her boot and stomped it into place on the ground. "Yes," she looked at him. "Dragons."

"Maybe I should be satisfied by everything you've told me, but I'm more curious now than ever. I especially want to hear everything about your family tree. All I can boast about are cousins who are apes." He laughed.

"I am a font of information, and I am at your disposal." Anna bowed deeply. Rising, she smiled. "Let us explore all the information I have gathered in the last hundred years."

"What? A hundred years? You've been alive for a hundred years?"

"Yes." She put her arm around his shoulders. "Oh, Eric. I have so much to tell you. So much. For instance, you remember my mother and brother?"

"Yes, I really liked them. Oh! Are they like you? Vampires?"

"Oh, yes. Yes indeed." Anna smiled.

Eric stopped. "This is so extraordinary." He stood there thinking for a minute, a hundred questions floating in his brain. "Oh, I meant to ask: can I see Lexei's paintings?"

"Oh, I'm sure he will love showing them to you. After all, Mother and I are the only ones who ever really get to see them. It's hard when you produce art and no one sees your work. Creativity is fed by others' appreciation of the artist's creation."

"I certainly understand that, especially being Julia's brother," Eric said. "When she started showing in galleries and people began really appreciating her paintings, and buying them, she just blossomed. Her art blossomed, too. She began painting some really amazing scenes, really taking some chances on her instinct. The results were incredible. Well, you saw."

Anna nodded. "I can take you to see Lexei later; he'll like that." She looked up at the sky. "Right now, though, I must go home. Dawn is coming soon." She looked at him, waiting for his reaction.

The night wasn't so pitch black anymore. The sky would be grey in a few minutes, and the pink of dawn would be there in a half hour. "Are you in danger?"

"No, but I must go, now. Right now." She took his face in both her hands and kissed him deeply before laying her cheek against his. "We will talk more soon, don't worry." She smiled. Taking a step back from him, she shivered, and her wings popped out behind her. Blowing him a kiss, she jumped into the sky.

Eric watched her leap into the morning air, her huge wings flexing in the predawn sky. She flew up out of the trees, then she turned and was gone like a shot, flying very fast, homeward. He sighed, smiling, and walked home alone, very happy.

Seven miles away, a dark cloud finally left the park, surprising a family of ravens, which chittered and scolded as it crawled past them. Falling out of the tree was bad enough, but falling and hooking the large wings you'd forgotten to retract onto the crook of a large tree branch, and getting stuck like that for an hour, was the worst. Frustration had transformed the creature into red ball of rage, and, as it finally gathered its senses and morphed into dark smoke to escape, fury had shaped its path for the next several minutes. It glided along the forest floor, hovering five feet off the ground. An early-morning jogger, earbuds and Bluetooth plugged in and wired to the hilt, had made the mistake of inattention, and had run on a paved park path and right into the dark mist that was the creature. There was a loud snap and buzz and a scream, and the jogger fell to the ground, headless. The creature morphed back into its corporeal form, and crouched, nervously lapping up the runner's blood as it flowed out of the severed neck onto the asphalt. It looked up frequently as it fed, bent over the body, exposed on the jogging path; before finally transforming into smoke again and leaving the park, the sound of scolding ravens behind it.

VISITOR

Alix sat on the tall stool in her kitchen, Lexei beside her, both staring down at the stone disc on the counter. When the dragon had given it to Alix it had been glowing softly, but then it had been nighttime; here in the bright kitchen of their home on Mercer Island, it looked far plainer.

Darkened, weathered stone with runes carved into both sides, it was about the size of a compact disc, and about an inch and a quarter thick. The runes carved into each side were dug about an eighth of an inch in, and the grooves held s kind of hardened black substance, possibly creosote. The whole thing was covered in some manner of muck they couldn't identify.

Lexei picked it up and brought it to his nose, sniffing. "I think this thing has spent some time in a grave." He wrinkled his nose and set the runestone carefully down again. "It stinks of the ancient dead."

Alix stuck her tongue out and made a face. "It was in my leather satchel, which I will now have to fumigate."

"Gross," Lexei said. He looked at the clock on the nearby wall. "Anna better get back soon, it's nearly dawn."

"I think I hear her at the door right now." Alix walked over to the hallway, where Anna was just opening the door. "Anya, did you have a nice time tonight?"

Anna was smiling broadly. "The best I've had in a very long time, Mama." She gave Alix a long hug. "Eric is wonderful." Anna twirled around in the small living room, her arms out like a ballet dancer.

"Oh. Did you tell him?"

"Yes," Anna sat down and started pulling her boots off. Her sock had gotten a bit damp from the forest grasses and the boot stuck.

"Here, let me help," Lexei grabbed her boot and began tugging as Anna sat back.

"He seemed very fine with the news. I think he is mostly fascinated and curious."

Alix looked at her daughter. "And he is not afraid? Not at all?"

"No, he didn't seem to be." Anna snapped back in her chair as the boot came off. Lexei grabbed hold of the second boot and began pulling. "I think it really helped that we got to know each other before he found out." The second boot came off and sent Lexei tumbling backward.

"Well, good. Maybe this one will stick around to discover how wonderful you are, my daughter." Alix leaned forward and kissed the top of her daughter's head, then stood back and looked into Anna's eyes earnestly. "Now. I think we are going to have to put the runestone back where it came from; it's still pulsing, and it could get to the point where it opens another doorway wherever it may happen to be at the time."

Anna thought for a moment. "That's not good."

"Tell me about it," Lexei said. "It could open a tesseract at any moment. It could open one right here, in our living room." He grinned.

Laughing, Anna pushed her brother gently, "You would enjoy that, wouldn't you?"

"Well, it was exciting, not the same dull old nights. And I loved the dragon. I wish he'd told us his name."

"I think that is a secret he keeps very closely guarded, my son." Alix pointed at the runestone, "Look." She shut off the lights. The runestone was definitely glowing; it was very slight, but as Anna's eyes adjusted to the darkness, she could definitely see a faint illumination.

That evening, an hour after sunset, Anna, Alix and Lexei found themselves flying high above the city, trying to find the grave the runestone had been taken from. They'd already tried three different cemeteries in the area, but had had no luck. Alix held the stone in a small pouch at her waist, and she could feel the heat coming from it, warming her belly.

Anna gestured to the others and pointed down at the next graveyard they planned to check. It was surrounded by a large wetland area and was, in fact, part of a nature preserve. The graveyard hadn't been in active use as a burial ground for decades, but the area's beauty and history drew joggers and nature lovers for a hundred miles around.

Alix flew toward the oldest section of the cemetery, situated at the top of a hill, and the others followed. Flying low, the three of them glided over the graveyard and Alix, feeling at the pouch holding the stone, felt it grow warmer. She nodded to the others and gestured, and they landed among the overgrown weeds and began walking among the tombstones.

Alix held the old artifact in her hands and studied it like a compass as they walked. An owl screeched and flew overhead, sounding a greeting. The fog curled around their legs as they walked and carried with it the smell of old, rotted corpses and decomposing vegetation.

The city council had allowed the nature preserve to grow wild as a way of protecting indigenous species, and although the nature paths that wound through it were kept clear and in repair, the cemetery itself had become overgrown. Caretaking had fallen off further as winter approached. Lexei kicked at a dead bush as they walked, and Anna wrinkled her nose at the smells greeting her nostrils. The stone Alix held suddenly brightened as she turned to the left around a tombstone, and she stopped.

"This way, I think." She turned back to the right and took a few steps, and saw the glow fade ever so slightly with each stride. "Yes, definitely this way." She turned back to the left and began walking in that direction, Lexei and Anna following closely. After maybe 30 or 40 feet, they came close to the edge of the cemetery and stopped, looking around the area. Overgrown bushes pushed against the wrought iron fencing, which leaned to the side precariously.

"There?" Lexei pointed to a low, dank, partially collapsed crypt next to a dead tree. The door was wedged closed against the stone walls, which had begun to topple over. The rear of the old crypt had fallen over sideways to such an extent that it was almost to the ground. Weeds crowded the front entrance and the old crumbling wooden door, obscuring the lower half of the small building. It was built into the hillside about five feet, the entire thing roughly a dozen feet long, and half again as wide. They approached the front entrance, and Lexei tried prying open the wooden door, but it wouldn't budge.

"It's an illusion," Alix said, studying the runestone in her hands. It had begun to shine even brighter at the proximity to its old resting place. "This door was recently opened. It had to be, to get the thing out of there. Pull it hard."

Lexei shrugged and yanked hard on the rotted wooden door; it finally flew open, sending weeds, bushes, dirt and rocks flying. "Oops. Sorry," he said, brushing the debris out of his hair. He reached out and pushed the door back, then kicked rubble out of his way. Stepping into the crypt, he concentrated and sent his aura surging out. He began to glow, filling the small mausoleum with light. Alix stepped in after him, eyes still on the runestone, and made her way to the back of the tiny chamber. Anna followed them both, her eyes looking everywhere. She reached up and pulled away a few cobwebs and turned to the side coffin, leaning over to study the inscription carved into the top.

"This is fascinating." Anna moved to the coffin on the other side, brushing off the dust accumulated over a century to read the words carved on this coffin as well.

Lexei moved to read over Anna's shoulder. After a minute he whispered, "My god."

"Mama, these two here," Anna gestured indicating the two coffins on either side of the door. "These were knights from the Middle Ages." Alix looked up at her from where she stood farther in.

"The inscription reads, 'Here lies Sir Henry, protector of our Lord David Robert, youngest son of Prince Edward, the Black Prince of Wales, late charged of protecting the witch's runestone and bearing it to heaven, praythee...' The other one identifies it as the coffin of Sir William." Anna looked up at her mother.

"These are knights' tombs, moved from medieval France over a hundred years ago." She gestured at the plaque on the inside wall of the crypt, directly inside the rotted wooden door. "Look, it explains when and why they were moved on that plaque." Lexei brushed the dust and dirt from the plaque and saw a faint coat of arms engraved on it. As he rubbed, shiny gold began to appear from under decades of grime.

He looked at the ceiling and walls of the tiny crypt. He brushed his hand across the wall, and a dusty film clung to his fingers. He examined it for a moment before rubbing his fingers together, then brushing them against his pants.

"It's incredible," Anna murmured, looking at the coffins again. "People must have just stopped coming. They were eventually forgotten." She moved to look at the plaque on the inside front wall again.

"It says the old crypt was originally in France, and was vandalized starting in the mid-19th century, during the Victorian Era. Something about hysteria and witch hunts. The descendants of the knights decided to move the whole crypt here in the early 20th century to protect what was left of it." She looked over at the last coffin. "Lord David Robert," she whispered. "Son of Edward, the Black Prince of Wales."

"I didn't know there was a second son of Edward, other than Richard II," Lexei said.

"There were several instances of noble children born from wartime dalliance," Alix peered down at the last coffin. "This lord was probably the son of Edward the Black Prince during his time in France when he fought there with his father, Edward III. Illegitimate children would often enter military service to prove their honor."

She stood there, reading the carved inscription on Lord David Robert's coffin. "I daresay his father and grandfather raised him, from the looks of it. He was probably knighted by his father, the Black Prince, and charged with carrying the runestone to heaven after he fell in battle." She looked up at them. "They would have thought it would be safe there. Safe from misuse anyway."

Lexei moved forward then. "I think it's time to replace it back in Lord David's hands, so he can bear it to heaven." He began to carefully lift the coffin lid. "Yup, it's recently been opened, look: The coffin nails have been removed." He pushed the coffin lid aside completely, and they all looked inside.

"Oh, dear," said Anna.

Inside the knight's coffin, the body had fallen in on itself, and much of it had turned to dust. Alix looked at the disc, which still glowed strongly. "Well, maybe it'll still be okay." She placed the runestone carefully where she imagined the hands of the knight had crossed over his chest, which was now mostly collapsed. The ancient stone rested on what remained of the decayed corpse's chest, teetered there a moment, and then fell through in a small puff of dust. The light appeared to go out completely.

"Oh, gross," Lexei said, holding his nose.

Anna leaned over, peering into the cavity where the

runestone had fallen in. "It's only down a few inches. She wrinkled her nose. "The body is completely decayed, though."

"I wonder if it's safe," Alix mused. "The vampire who took it could just come back again and take it a second time." She looked behind them and shivered.

"Really, Mama. I think we are a match for whatever idiot came and got it in the first place. After all, we are three, and all over a hundred years turned." Anna looked at her mother.

"Hey, this is weird," Lexei bent his head over the knight's decayed corpse. "I think the body is decaying further."

"Well, of course it is," Anna looked over his shoulder. "Wait..."

"Hmmm."

"Turn off your glow for a minute."

Lexei pulled his aura back in, and they were plunged into pitch darkness.

"Oh ..."

"Wait, what is that?"

"Um, Anna?" Lexei was again bent over the corpse, his nose inches away from the dust and bones of the chest cavity. "Wait ... oh no ..." Lexei's body jerked. "Oh ... Ah, ah, AH ... !!! CHOO!!" Lexei let out a massive sneeze right into the middle of the decayed corpse.

Crumbled bone dust from the decayed eight-hundred-year-old corpse flew up in a small cloud faster than the three vampires could react, and each of their faces was instantly covered in the muck. Alix was farther back and reacted first, bringing her hands up to wipe her face.

Anna shook her head, trying to dislodge the specks that had invaded her eyes, nose and mouth, "Oh, god ..." she sputtered, wiping herself.

Lexei, who'd had the worst of it, fell backward and scraped at his eyes first, then moved to clear his mouth. "Ewww." He finally got most of it out.

"Ugh..." Each of them spent a few minutes clearing their faces. Anna, finally fed up with the whole thing, concentrated and transformed herself into smoke, drifting up to the ceiling of the small crypt for a minute, then settled back down and rematerialized, clean again.

"Oh," Alix repeated her daughter's actions, cleaning herself by dematerializing. "Good idea, my daughter."

Anna rolled her eyes as her brother morphed into smoke, drifting about for a few minutes before settling up near the ceiling.

Lexei rematerialized finally. Clearing his throat, he apologized. "Er, sorry about that." He leaned over the corpse again.

"Hey."

"Wait."

"No, I'll be careful, I swear," Lexei protested as their hands grabbed his shoulders, trying to avoid a repeat of the sneeze fiasco.

"We don't want the knight's essence all over Seattle."

"I know, but look, I saw something." He looked closer, holding his breath this time. "There's something there."

Alix and Anna both held their breath and leaned over, cheek to cheek with Lexei.

"Hmmm," Alix squinted as she dipped her hand into the knight's chest cavity, where the accelerated decaying process was still occurring. She had to dig for a few seconds; the more she tried to grasp the runestone, the farther it slipped down. Finally, she had it, and drew her hand out of the corpse, standing up again. They each looked at the stone she held. They thought the light had completely gone out when it had been placed back into the knight's hands, but it was still giving off the faintest glow.

Lexei blew on it, then brushed off the muck of decaying matter it had picked up inside the rotting corpse. "Hmmm," He looked at it.

"Wait, what's that?" Anna approached the runestone in her mother's hand and leaned over it. The faint glowing was uneven, and an almost invisible stream of magic flowed out from the side; it looked like miniature purple sparks, dribbling out from a tiny crevice in the artifact, then drifting down like dust motes. "May I?" Anna took the artifact from her mother's hand and lifted it up to see better.

"Hmmm." Alix and Lexei stared as well, and the three vampires made a small circle around the runestone, and looked up at it, studying it closely in the pitch darkness.

A soft light emanated from the entire runestone. But on

the side, through the tiny crevice Anna had seen, small glittery particles were flowing, almost too small for even their keen eyes to follow. Anna lowered the artifact to their eye level, and they could see into the tiny breach and a faint light.

"Well, it's definitely magic. I can feel it." Lexei rubbed his nose again.

"Me, too. It's like someone left a heat lamp on inside there." Alix confirmed.

"Do you see that?" Anna brought the stone circle up close to one eye and peered in intently, squinting to get better focus. "Oh, my god," she mumbled. "Oh, this is not good, not good at all." She handed it to her mother, who lifted it to her own eye to look.

"Oh, no," Alix sighed.

"What is it?" Lexei asked. His mother passed the artifact to him and he squinted into the crevice to look.

Eyebrows raised in surprise, Lexei smiled. "Well, hello there."

Eric was jogging, trying to clear his thoughts. Ever since Anna had told him she was a vampire, he'd been filled with energy and excitement. The knowledge that his girlfriend was a supernatural creature made Eric feel so exhilarated he couldn't contain his energy. Unable to sleep, he tried spending time reading with Jinx by his side, but even then he was restless.

Finally, he knew he had to run it off, this extra energy. He couldn't sit still, let alone sleep. Strapping on his running gear, he headed out of the city, to the nature preserve where he loved to run. The birds and wildlife that lived in the protected wetlands made him feel at peace and close to nature. The fact that it was the middle of the night did not deter Eric. In fact, the quiet peace of the dark night drew him onward, like a magnet.

If anyone had happened to be jogging and had come upon the fallen runner, head missing from its torso, they would have seen a figure in rags, skin mottled white and grey, looking like something out of a nightmare, crouched over the corpse, and licking the blood still dribbling out of the severed neck. And it would have been the last thing they ever saw.

ATTACK

"Well, well, well, what do we have here, Claude?" Anna, Alix and Lexei froze. A soft light entered the old crypt and shone on the vampires.

"Looks like a couple of grave robbers, Triss," drawled Claude. "What do you think, Emil?"

"I think dinner has been served." Emil smiled.

Anna gave her mother a look, then winked at Lexei, who slowly crouched behind the old knight's tomb. Alix nonchalantly dropped her hand holding the artifact down and handed it off to Lexei as he disappeared behind the coffin.

Anna and Alix turned to face the three vampire thugs.

"Fellas, I'd hate to battle in such a confined area; these old coffins would be destroyed if we did, so can we step outside?" Alix said in an unconcerned voice.

"Battle?" Emil began to giggle. "You want to battle us?" Tristan began to laugh.

"You two ladies are about to die a painful death," Claude looked Anna up and down as Tristan played the weak flashlight beam on her and her mother. "But first, maybe we'll have a little fun."

"Like hell you are, you loser!" Eric's voice came from behind the three vampire thugs, out of sight. Shoved hard from behind, Emil came tumbling into the small area inside the crypt. Anna, Lexei, and Alix made the most of the distraction, turning into smoke, and rapidly drifting out the front, over everyone's heads.

Tristan began giving hurried commands. "Dammit, they're getting away! Claude, grab that guy! Emil, get the hell up!"

"You're gonna die, asshole," Claude turned and grabbed at Eric, but he was too fast, jumping backward and racing away. Claude was after him in a moment, through the foggy night.

Eric ran through the dark cemetery. The graveyard was thick with weeds and half-fallen tombstones, and wet from a recent rain, making the ground slick and muddy in places.

He scrambled several times, tripping once on an exposed root and going down on one knee in the mud before he recovering his footing. Finally, he reached the top of the hill, and whirled around to face the vampire thug chasing him. Pulling a hunting knife out of his belt, Eric brandished it at the hooligan, waving it in Claude's face, making him jump back, startled.

"Okay, everyone; calm down," Tristan's voice came out of the fog as he walked up to the pair. His wings, fangs and claws were out, and his eyes glowed red in the darkness. Emil emerged from the mist beside him and one step back, and the two vampires walking toward Eric were a formidable sight. He swung his knife in an arc in front of him, and wished he had something more deadly to use, outnumbered as he was.

"What do we have here?" Tristan said quietly, walking up to Eric until the point of Eric's knife was pushing into the vampire's jacket. Looking down, he smirked. "Wow. If I'm not careful, you might hurt me with that." Looking back up into Eric's face, he surged and his eyes glowed even brighter. Eric backed up a step. Moving forward to match him, Tristan yelled, "BOO!"

The three vampire thugs were focused on Eric, laughing and taunting him.

Anna was high in the air, huge wings out, and angry as hell. From the looks of the three vampires below her, she could tell they'd been just recently turned. These new changelings were no match for Anna and her family, whose wings stretched out twice as far as Tristan and his cohorts. Power emanated from within Anna, Alix and Lexei, and strong magic pulsated out from them.

The three vampires began their dive from a hundred feet

up, and by the time they leveled out, they were going faster than a jet engine. At this speed, they were nearly invisible. And angrier than they'd been in a long, long time. Flying level to the ground now, Anna tucked her wings close to her body, and reached out, hands curled into fists as she slammed into the three vampire thugs, who were by this time, standing so close together that she hit them as if they were bowling pins.

Anna, Alix and Lexei slammed into the three thugs with the force of a freight train. Bones were crushed. Spines snapped. Skulls caved in. Blood splashed out from the impact.

The three pulled up sharply; they didn't want to keep flying so low at that speed. Flipping back into the sky, they twirled to slow themselves down and then gradually returned to earth, wings beating to ease the drop.

Anna landed next to Eric. She immediately put her arms around his neck and kissed him hard. "You acted to protect me."

He smiled at her, his hands resting lightly on her hips. "Yes."

Alix and Lexei landed next to them. "Eric, my man!" Lexei high-fived with Eric, and they both laughed. Alix just shook her head, smiling.

"How did you happen to be here tonight?" Lexei asked the question they were all wondering.

Eric shrugged. "Just good luck, I think. I've been jogging

for the last hour through the preserve, mostly down below. I just decided to run up here and saw those goons bothering you." He looked at Anna and kissed her soundly. "I've had a hard time sleeping since your news, Babe. I was restless." He smiled.

Anna turned to look at the bodies of the three vampire thugs. Her mind, without being prompted, began playing, 'Let the Bodies Hit the Floor' in her head, and she grinned to herself.

Tristan, Emil, and Claude lay on the ground, bloody and twisted, their bodies broken in too many places to count. Tristan's legs curled back in a way that legs should not bend, and the side of his face was caved in. Blood dripped out of his eye socket, and through his hair they could see what looked like a portion of his brain peeking out. His arms were splayed out sideways, and appeared to have sprouted multiple elbows, bending, like his legs, in a manner that arms did not normally bend. Incredibly, his head moved slightly, and he groaned.

"He's still alive?" Eric was incredulous. He looked over at the other two bodies, similarly broken, and saw they were stirring slightly as well. Looking at Anna, he was speechless.

"It takes quite a lot to kill a vampire, Eric. Even newly turned vampires like these who make incredibly stupid, brash mistakes." She kicked at Tristan, and the thug's whole body shook in pain. "They will heal, eventually. But it will take a very long time. And it will be excruciating." Leaning over his face, which by this time had the one good eye opened and looking up at her, she put her hands on her hips.

"You're going to hurt for a very long time, pup." Anna, grinned, walking around to Tristan's other side while she talked. His good eye followed her progress. "If you ever heal, come see me when you're worthy." She kicked his head. "But don't ever taunt one of the People's companions. Next time I won't be so merciful." She hauled back and kicked his shoulder so hard he flipped over, groaning. Glancing at Claude and Emil next to Tristan, she spat and walked away.

Alix and Lexei had pulled back, away from the fallen thugs, and had gathered near the old knight's crypt with Anna and Eric. Alix went in and shut the coffin lid. When she re-emerged, she shoved the crypt's door hard into the stone, wedging it so tight it would be hard for any mortal to open. They did not want it disturbed again, not for a long time.

Lexei stood talking to Eric, holding the runestone up for him to see. "It's got something, or rather, someone, in a small crevice in its side."

"What?" Eric studied the artifact in Lexei's hand. "How...?

Anna explained. "Eric, this runestone is what opened the doorway at the top floor of the museum." At this Eric looked at her sharply. "Yes, it really was there." He nodded. Anna continued. "Look at us," she gestured at her mother and brother. "You are seeing things you've never seen before."

Eric looked at Lexei and Alix and smiled. "You guys look so badass." Lexei threw his head back and laughed. Alix just smiled and looked at the tips of her boots.

"Anyway," Anna continued, taking the stone from Lexei's hand. "This thing, it was through the doorway and buried near the opening at the other end. It was retrieved to close the doorway. The tesseract."

"Tesseract?"

"Yes, a tesseract is a portal through time. Literally, the fourth dimension, to get scientific."

"In the museum?" Eric asked.

"Yes, and it should hopefully be back to normal. But some shetani came through before we closed it. They're what attacked us." Anna turned the artifact over in her hands. "We were trying to return it to the grave it came from, seal it back up, when we noticed the light coming out of the side." She held it up for him to look.

"I don't see anything."

"It's very faint. You have to look really closely in the pitch darkness for it to even show up." Lexei said.

"What if there hadn't been any light coming from it?"

"Then we would have returned it to the tomb it was taken from, that of an ancient knight charged with bearing it to heaven, and we'd have sealed it so it was once again invisible to the human eye." Anna explained.

"Wait, 'heaven'?" Eric seemed incredulous.

"Well, heaven as 14th century monks would have

described it."

Eric swung his head toward the old crypt. "There are 14th century monks buried in there?"

"No," answered Anna. "There are 14th century knights buried in there. They were moved from France here to Seattle more than a hundred years ago, probably by the Catholic Church, to protect the coffins from further vandalism. The church was much more powerful back then."

Eric was speechless. He looked down at the runestone. "This thing was in the grave of a 14th century knight?"

"Yes."

Eric looked at the old crypt. "It looks so plain and nondescript."

"They would have wanted it that way. To hide it in plain sight."

"Eric," Alix said, "the runestone is a Thing of Magic, and even medieval humans could tell it had power. They would have interpreted its power as something evil, and they apparently wanted to protect themselves and history from its effects."

"It probably caused all kinds of trouble for them back then," Lexei looked at the stone thoughtfully.

"If it did anything like what it did here, opening a tesseract to another time, with those people's superstitions? They probably went nuts," Anna said. "They would have thought the shetani coming out of the past were demons."

"They do kind of look like something out of a nightmare," Eric said.

"Even though they are just animals, nothing from hell or heaven," Anna shrugged. "Like vampires are just animals, albeit, both are infused with magic."

Lexei turned to Eric. "Magic infused animals are still a natural product of evolution, Eric. Yes, we were hunted to near extinction back thousands of years ago, because of people's superstitions, but still..."

"This is incredible," Eric said. He squinted at the runestone. "I wish I could see the light you described." He looked up at the partial moon and shook his head slightly.

"Well, here, let's go into the tomb again; you can see it really good in there." Alix opened the door and led the way to the knight's crypt, and they were all soon crowded inside.

"I probably should be worried, being trapped in a tiny tomb with three old coffins and three deadly vampires, huh?" Eric laughed. Anna turned and kissed him. Lexei rolled his eyes and smiled.

"Okay, everyone, go dark," Alix said as she turned and shut the old door behind them. They all made their way to the back, where the knight's coffin that had held the runestone sat. The three vampires bent down and stared at the runestone. Everything was still and quiet, and Eric stared steadily at the artifact and waited for his eyes to adjust to the total darkness.

"See?" Lexei whispered.

"Oh, my god," Eric said softly, staring intently at the runestone. He fished in his pockets and came out with a pair of eyeglasses. "Magnifiers," he mumbled. Slipping them on, he leaned in close and peered at the side of the small stone circle. "Ah..."

"Do you see it?" Anna whispered.

"Yes. At least I think so." Eric glanced at Anna. "Is it ...?" He looked back into the tiny crevice. "Is that? Is that a dragon?"

Purple sparkles, slightly heavier than the air, so they slowly drifted down after emerging from the runestone, flowed out from the crevice. As they looked inside, squinting, staring until they could properly focus on something smaller than a ladybug egg, they all saw the same thing: what appeared to be a baby dragon.

As four sets of eyes crowded together for a glimpse of it, the tiny creature became aware it was being watched, and it slowly lifted its head, yawning as it turned to look. To the tiny creature, it looked like a several giant moons were looking through the entrance to the small cave it had taken refuge in during a rainstorm. Being sleepy, it stood, arching its back like a stretching cat, turned around in a circle, and lay back down again, closing its eyes and promptly falling back to sleep.

They each let out a sigh of delight and contentment, as if they were observing a very small, very cute, fluffy kitten. Small curls of smoke drifted up from the baby's nostrils as it slept. Anna sighed and smiled. It was adorable.

They investigated the rest of the inside of the crypt, Eric used his cell phone as a light source, taking in the three coffins and their inscriptions, and reading the plaque on the inside wall of the tomb. He agreed that the Catholic Church had likely moved the coffins and built the crypt to keep the three knights' bodies safe.

As they left the stone building, carrying the runestone and sealing the door behind them once again, they discussed it.

"More than a hundred years ago, they may have thought this cemetery was safe enough, compared to anything in Old World Europe." Eric looked around, and spied an old abandoned abbey far down at the bottom of the hill. It was tiny and forgotten, and half collapsed. He pointed. "There. There's your proof. Old Catholic abbey, long abandoned, decrepit, falling down." One stone wall had fallen in.

They climbed down and entered the little sanctuary; it was so tiny there was only room for a few windows and an altar, and three tiny rows of pews. Old ivy and vines climbed its walls, entering the building where the windows were broken. Old leaves and brambles layered the floor, and it had a forgotten feel about it. The air smelled stale and damp.

"I wondered..."

"Long since abandoned. Probably forgotten." Anna kicked at a stone wall.

"Not completely abandoned." Alix crouched and pulled

some vines and leaves away from a corner. A mouse squealed and scurried away quickly. She chuckled and pulled the leaves back over the spot, then stood up, brushing the dust from her hands.

"Well, the mystery of the knights' crypt is solved. We just have to figure out what to do with the runestone, and the hitchhiker riding inside it." Anna said. They all walked back up the hill to the cemetery. Anna and Eric held hands and snuggled together as they walked.

"Anna, I am so glad you and your family are okay. Those thugs…" Eric whispered to her as he walked alongside her.

"Oh, Eric," Anna hugged his arm as she walked. "That's one thing you needn't ever worry about. As vampires, we are very strong. And because we've been turned for over a hundred years, we're stronger than most other vampires. It would be very rare to meet another vampire as old and powerful as we are. And to meet one who wants to battle, well, that would be extraordinarily unlikely. Vampires usually aren't that stupid."

She looked over at her mother and brother as they walked. "We're an uncommon breed. There are hardly any of us left in the world, we old ones. That may be why some of us are creating this new breed." She kicked at the ground. "But really, to turn human thugs into vampires, that was very stupid of whoever did it. Incredibly stupid."

"Why would they do it?" Eric asked beside her.

"Well, I really am not sure. Unless…" Anna lifted her head.

"Mama?" Alix looked over. "Do you think those thugs…?"

"Let's go ask them," Alix smiled, showing her long fangs in a deadly grin. Eric made a mental note of thanks that he was on the good side of these deadly vampires.

As they topped the hill, they walked over to where the thugs' bodies still lay, broken, sprawled on the bloody ground. Alix flapped her wings a bit, rising seven feet or so and landed on the neck of the nearest one. A loud crack resounded as the vampire's neck broke. He screamed weakly.

"Who sent you here? WHO?" Alix rested all her weight on his neck and chest, and crouched there like some giant bird of prey, rocking up and down on her heels, making him gasp with pain repeatedly. "Who, vampire?" She spat to the side. "Who sent you here to this place of death?"

"Don't tell them, Claude," Emil gasped at his side. Lexei hopped up and slammed his feet down on Emil's chest, silencing him. Lexei spread his large black wings to steady himself as he rested on Emil's chest, heels digging in, looking like a giant vulture hooding its kill.

"If you don't tell me, I will remove your head from your body," Alix whispered to Claude like a lover, smiling and caressing his bloody face as she spoke. "And I will do it slowly, so slowly. …" She winked at him. Claude's eyes closed in pain and fear.

"It was … Mr. …" Claude gasped.

"Claude! No!" Emil gasped. Lexei sat on his face.

Alix gently took hold of Claude's lower face, hooking her thumbs on either side of his jaw, and applied pressure. He screamed and urinated in fear. Alix wrinkled her nose at the pungent smell and removed her hands from his mouth so he could speak.

"It was Ramsey! Mr. Ramsey! He works out of the black mirrored high-rise in downtown Seattle! Ahhhhh!!! Let go, please!" He begged.

Anna, Alix and Lexei all looked at one another. Anna turned her back and started swearing as she walked away to the edge of the clearing, kicking at the brush as she went. Eric walked over and put his arm around her shoulders.

Alix looked down at Claude again and spat to the side. "I should have known." She looked into Claude's eyes, now flooded with blood inside, the whites no longer showing. "And did this 'Ramsey' come take the runestone in the first place?" Her hands gripped Claude's head tighter and began to apply pressure again.

Claude felt his bowels voiding in fear and tried to nod. The way Alix held his jaw, he couldn't get his mouth open to speak. She relented so he could: "Y-y-yes! He took the stone, and we placed it in the museum! He said an incantation and a passage opened. We even went through it into the jungle and met the big dragon!"

"You met the Dragon Lord?"

"Yes! He almost ate Emil! Then he released us and ... and ... took the stone from us and forced... forced... us to leave thr-

thr-through the passage!" Claude gasped and swallowed, in incredible pain. "Mr. Ramsey will pr-pr-probably kill me for telling you," he whispered.

"Well, I could kill you now, if you like." Alix looked down on him. "As a favor." She studied his face. "But I think I will not. You attacked one of our companions, and for that you will always be marked by our clan. I suggest you leave Washington. Go south, when and if you can. Stay far away from us. Spend the rest of your days gaining wisdom, and stop taking orders from corrupt, insane vampire lords." She got up and stepped off of Claude's body, a look of disgust on her face, turning her back on him without another glance.

"Come, my children, let us leave these fools to their pain." Alix leapt into the sky, her huge wings expanding and filling with air as she beat them to gain height.

Lexei leapt directly off of Emil's body, making him groan in pain, and rose into the sky after his mother. Anna turned and, embracing Eric, wrapping her arms around him firmly. She spread her huge wings and jumped up after her mother and brother, lifting Eric with her as easily as one would lift a baby; and they were aloft, all of them, and in flight across the hills and back into the city, back to their Mercer Island home.

The creature had crawled back into the trees after drinking its fill of the runner's corpse, and had fallen asleep under some bushes. After a few hours, it rose and stretched, and took to the sky again, flying silently through the thick fog. Back on the forest ground, the leaves and grasses where it had lain looked withered and black, and nothing would ever grow there again.

EXPLANATIONS

The three vampires landed on the roof of their house on the secluded Mercer Island cul-de-sac, entering the home through a small upstairs window. They did not speak, by mutual agreement. Eric stayed silent as well, sensing that there was something important to discuss, and that they would not speak of it until they were back in their lair, safe from intruders.

Since they flew with him, and took him to their home, he also understood that the vampire family was accepting him into their inner circle, something that, he would learn later, hadn't happened in nearly a hundred years. He sensed this, and smiled, and his heart warmed with love for Anna. She must have told them about us, he mused as they flew.

During the short flight across the countryside, he could see across to the far end of Seattle, to the Space Needle. It was exhilarating and incredible, and Eric's eyes teared up with the wind as he watched everything. Anna's arms held him tightly, and he never felt any fear at all. She kissed him on his neck and hair as she flew, snuggling him to her.

They all gathered in the cozy living room on the first floor, the vampires morphing into their mundane forms and taking a few minutes to relax on the sofas there. Lexei lit a small fire in the fireplace, and it crackled merrily as they sat and relaxed. Eric sat on the sofa, on the end next to the fire, Anna next to him, still holding his hand. Lexei sat facing Eric on the second sofa and stared moodily into the flames. Alix paced and finally sat next to Lexei, and gazed off into space, deep in thought.

Anna was silent, her head leaning against Eric's shoulder. After a few minutes, a tear silently rolled down her cheek, slowly making its way down her jaw to drip from her chin onto the dark leather of her jacket. Alix's stare slowly focused on her daughter, and she gave a low groan and rose from where she sat. She settled herself next to her daughter on the couch, gathering her up in an embrace.

Anna put her arms around her mother and rested her face on her shoulder; Eric could hear quiet sobs coming from Anna. He was not sure what had happened to create this dark, somber mood and make Anna cry, but he reached out and put his hand on her back, slowly making swirls as he rubbed it, trying to bring her comfort. Lexei saw his sister crying, and his brooding gaze darkened, and he glowered in his seat for a while, his eyes growing redder with each passing minute.

Eric sat in silence as Anna wept softly into her mother's shoulder. The sleek black form of Anna's cat Gypsy padded into the room and leapt onto the sofa, settling herself on Anna's lap. As the cat's purrs filled the room, Anna put her hand on the soft feline, her fingers disappearing into the shiny black fur. Gypsy's purrs deepened and she rested her chin on her mistress, closing her eyes in contentment.

The whole house was still save for the crackle of the fireplace and the purring of the cat. Eric studied the room. Two comfortable sofas upholstered in a dark, ruby red fabric that was almost a burgundy sat on a thick, rich, creamy white carpet.

Several paintings hung on the wall, exquisite landscapes depicting a forested land and countryside with castles. It dawned on Eric that they were probably Lexei's work. Rubbing Anna's back one final time, he rose and soundlessly made his way closer to the paintings to study them in more detail. Most were landscapes, but he spied one in the corner, almost to the kitchen, that was a portrait.

As he approached the painting, he saw it was exquisite, in the style of the old masters. Against the dark background, the subject's face and chest looked as though they were illuminated by a soft light. Eric studied the face in the painting. The merry eyes were dark, piercing, and seemed to look straight into his soul. A strong nose, and a laughing mouth, corners turned up in merriment: This person had been a jovial man, a man who loved life. The figure was dressed in royal clothing of a bygone era: rich blues and golds, with reds and ermine trim. He looked like royalty.

"My father," Lexei said quietly beside him.

"You painted this?"

"Yes, about ten years ago," Lexei studied his own work. "I couldn't get him to stop laughing, so I made it part of the painting." He chuckled and looked at Eric. "He was always laughing."

"What happened to him?" Eric asked.

"He was murdered. By the vampire that turned those thugs," Lexei studied Eric's shocked face."

"By the...?" Eric looked back at Anna and her mother, both now sitting up and wiping their eyes.

They rose and came to join Eric and Lexei by the painting of Nikolai Romanov. Anna put her arm around Eric's waist as he studied the painting; his own arm reached around her waist in turn.

"He looks ... he looks so happy, so regal," Eric said softly. "He looks like a king." He turned to look at Lexei.

"He was," Lexei said simply.

"Eric, perhaps you'd better sit down." Anna looked at her mother, who nodded. "We will tell you everything," she said, pulling him by the hand back to the sofas beside the warming fire.

They all sat down again. Lexei had pulled the painting

from the wall and set it down beside him on the floor. He sat there studying his father's visage, an inscrutable expression on his own face.

Anna began talking. "So. You know we are vampiri." She looked at Eric, and he nodded. "We," she indicated herself, Alix and Lexei, "were turned over a hundred years ago." Eric took this in.

"So, you are all over a hundred years old."

"Yes."

Anna continued. "For the first half of the 20th century, we stayed in our homeland, hidden away in a castle of one of the People. But the reason we hid wasn't only that we were vampiri, it was that there was a revolution in our country we were fleeing, a deadly revolution." Anna stopped here, uncertain how to continue.

Alix inhaled and let out a sigh, then seemed to draw herself up, looking regal. "Eric." He looked over at her. "Eric, we are the Romanovs." Eric's eyes widened.

"What???"

Lexei turned to Eric and slowly thrust his hand out to his sister's mate. "Hello Eric, my name is Alexei Romanov. Please to meet you." He smiled grimly. Eric slowly shook his hand.

"Wait, you are all the... the..." Eric tried to wrap his mind around the concept.

Anna laid her hand on his arm. "Eric." He looked into the face of his lady, the woman he loved, his mate. "Eric, my name is Anastasia Romanov and I have been alive for over a hundred and fifteen years." She smiled gently at him. "We were turned in the year 1916, in the late spring, I believe," she looked to her mother for confirmation. "The year before the Bolshevik Revolution began in earnest."

Eric looked astounded. Anna leaned forward and kissed him softly, and he relaxed a bit. Looking into Anna's beautiful eyes, he whispered, "I love you, Anna." Then he thought for a moment.

Turning to his lady's mother, Alix, Eric said, "Ma'am?" She smiled. Eric had always thought there was something different in this family, in Alix, and now he realized. She looked gently regal.

She held out her hand to Eric, "Hello Eric, my name is Alexandra Romanov, and I am very pleased to meet you." She chuckled as he took her hand and placed a gentle kiss on the top of her knuckles, a bemused expression on his face.

"So, that means ..." he looked down at the painting against Lexei's leg.

Anna gestured at the portrait. "Our father was Nikolai Romanov, tsar of Imperial Russia."

Eric studied the painting, speechless.

Anna smiled, tears in her eyes. "And we loved him very, very much." Her voice caught in her throat, and fresh tears ran down her face as she smiled.

"Were you all ... was he also a ... a vampire?" Eric asked softly.

"Yes. The monster who killed him was responsible for our turning," Alix said.

"What?" Eric turned to her.

"Have you ever heard of Grigori Rasputin?" Anna said.

"Yes." Eric looked down, thinking, then looked up again, and began counting off fingers. "He was a madman, I've read. Took a lot to kill him? 'Seduced the Romanov family and was partially responsible for them being overthrown and murdered?' " Eric remembered.

"Most of that is true." Alix said quietly. "He is a vampire as well. They did not kill him; that was a cousin who resembled him a little too much for the poor man's own good. I think he was a blacksmith before the mob took him."

"Rasputin befriended our family. He misrepresented himself. He was, and is, a master of deception. A sociopath. And quite insane."

"Rasputin first turned poor Lexei," Anna hugged her brother tightly, kissing the top of his head. "Then, in the first insanity of becoming vampiri, Lexei bit each of us."

Eric looked at Lexei, who hung his head.

"No, it is not his fault. The first days after turning are painful, and the bloodthirst is a kind of insanity. He is not to blame." Alix hugged her son until he smiled.

"The point is," Anna said, "Rasputin is going by the name Greg Ramsey in present day."

At this, Eric spoke up. "I've heard of him."

Anna nodded and continued. "He's a very powerful man,

and he is hunting us. I fought him in Manhattan this summer. He lured me, telling me he'd captured Lexei, and I fell for it. I fought him and a dozen of his vampire cronies. He'd trapped me, using me as bait in order to kill my father. He hates all of us; he blames us for his downfall."

"Wait, but you said he turned your family, not the other way around," Eric said.

"Like I said, he is quite insane, and has been since we met him."

"If anything, he's gotten worse."

"Much of what happened in the Revolution can be attributed to him or his followers. His maniacal quest for power nearly destroyed our country. It destroyed our family. He has caused our us untold distress and harm; he's incredibly dangerous. At this point, all we want is for him to leave us alone. But he is obsessed."

"He trapped me," Anna continued. "And lured my father there, and they fought. I escaped while they were fighting, but Father didn't survive..." Tears rushed into Anna's eyes again. Alix hugged her, and Lexei joined them, sitting on the arm of the sofa and leaning in. The couch became very crowded.

"It was strange," Anna said, muffled by tears. She blew her nose onto a tissue Alix handed her.

"Why was it strange?"

She looked up at him. "Because my father was very powerful, their strength was pretty much equal. Rasputin should not have been able to kill Father without help, at the most it should have ended in a stalemate, with both retreating wounded." A tear ran down Anna's cheek. "I think he was distracted, it was my fault ... he died. ..." She buried her face in her hands.

"Anna, my daughter, you must not blame yourself. Your father would not have wanted that. He went there to help you, to save you. He would want you to go on with your life and thrive." Alix put both arms around Anna and held her tight, trying to hug the pain out of her daughter.

"I will be okay. It's just, this mess has brought back memories." Anna sat back, sniffing and clearing her throat. She glanced at Eric and smiled through watery eyes. "I do not want you to think me weak, Eric."

"Babe, I would never think that. Not after what I've seen you do." He glanced around at all of them. "What I've seen all of you do, it's ... it's really incredible." He smiled, then chuckled, his arm around Anna. "You're an extraordinary family. I'm very glad to be friends with you all." He glanced down at Anna and kissed her. "In some cases, more than friends." He kissed her again.

Lexei rose from his seat with his painting, lost in thought, and went to hang it in its place on the wall. Walking back to the living room, he seemed distracted. As he sat down, he pulled something from his pocket and gently set it down on the coffee table in between the two sofas: the runestone. Then he shut off all the lights. The curtains were thick and drawn, and there was not a hint of light in the room, except for what came from the stone. It shone faintly from the small crevice in the side as they watched.

Lexei sat back down and began to speak. "This disturbance, this time period, is killing this small creature. The light is growing weaker. It's very subtle, you can hardly tell, but I see it, just from earlier tonight. Whatever the reason, maybe it's the radiation in the present world, the lack of certain isotopes in the air. ... Who knows? But if we don't do something right away, she is going to die."

"I sensed it was female as well. Double the reason for helping her," Alix said. "We must return her to her own time. We must reopen the doorway and bring her through again."

Eric turned to Anna and whispered, "What does she mean, 'double the reason?'"

Anna explained, "In the distant past, life was not civilized. Creatures died, and were born, at a more accelerated rate. As a female, this small creature would have, will be able to, create many more of her kind. Without her to do this in her own time, without all those future generations, great and terrible changes may ripple forward to her future, to our present."

Eric sat back, nodding, deep in thought.

"I propose we go back to the old cemetery, perhaps even inside the old knight's crypt." Lexei said. "It will be better hidden there."

"Agreed. Who knows why Rasputin used the runestone in the museum? Opening a tesseract right in the middle of a public place was exceedingly irrational," Alix mused.

"He *is* irrational," Lexei looked disgusted.

"Or perhaps he is crazy like a fox." They all looked at Anna as she explained. "He opened the doorway in the middle of the city. I think he wanted shetani to flood present time."

"But why?"

"To create chaos?"

"To find us," Anna sat back suddenly, understanding dawning on her face.

"What?"

"Listen," Anna explained. "He is already here, so he must have known we'd fled to Seattle, he just didn't know exactly where. The shetani coming through the doorway would have been strongly attracted to us."

Anna turned to look at Eric as she continued. "We are distant genetic relatives, and there are no others here in present day." Turning back to address them all, she continued: "And look how some of the creatures were attracted to Eric and me at the park, in the middle of the city, near the museum. Rasputin was trying to locate us by drawing other paranormal creatures into the present time. He knew they would eventually draw close to us." She sat back.

"He is hunting us, still."

"Again."

"You are surprised?"

"Not really. But I don't think I'll ever get used to it."

"I know."

Alix rose and began to pace. "Okay, then it's settled. We use the runestone one last time. We return to the cemetery, to the knights' crypt, and we open a tesseract. We return the dragon." She drew aside the heavy curtain and peeked outside, frowning.

"It will be dawn in an hour." Lexei yawned. "We must rest soon."

Eric turned to Anna. "I should return home. I will meet you back here at nightfall."

Anna hugged Eric. "Babe, are you sure? If you'd like you can sleep here," she indicated the overstuffed couch.

Eric glanced down. "Well, maybe. I did leave enough food and water down for Jinx ..."

"Oh, yes: I love your Kindred. He came to sleep alongside me when I slept over, he is really special," Anna kissed him. "So, you should stay."

Lexei poked his head into their tête-à-tête, "Did someone mention one of the Kindred?" He smiled.

"Eric has the most fabulous cat," Anna grinned. "Wait till you meet him."

Alix came just then, her arms laden with several thick quilts and a pillow. "Eric, sweetheart, you must sleep here tonight. It is not safe for you out there." She began tucking a sheet around the cushions of the ample couch.

"Not safe? Oh, I'm sure it's fine ...," Eric began.

Alix straightened and surveyed her work, then leaned over to straighten one corner.

"Eric, Rasputin is a very dangerous vampire, and he will know of your connection to us soon, if he doesn't already. Those vampire thugs we left injured at the graveyard will get back to him and fill him in." Anna paced.

"Already?" Eric was astonished.

"Oh, yes. They will have psychically called their master to them after such an attack," Anna looked grim.

"Ass-whoopin' is more like it," Lexei balled his fist at the memory. "And I'll do it again if need be."

"So," Anna turned back to Eric, "Rasputin will likely add you to his list of targets, I'm sorry to say." She kissed him. "Since we are together, you and I, he will consider you part of our clan."

Eric grabbed Anna and kissed her back, holding her close. His mouth nibbled on her neck as he held her, making her shriek with laughter.

Alix smiled broadly at them. "So, Eric." She finished spreading the blanket on their couch. "You will sleep over, it will be very good. And we can get an early start right at sunset." She smiled at the young man, her hands on her hips.

Eric looked at Anna helplessly and shrugged. Anna laughed. Lexei suddenly opened the door and left, closing it firmly behind him.

"Eric, tell me about how you came to be owned by one of the Kindred." Alix sat down on the opposite couch and settled down for a good long story.

"Mama, not now. He must bathe first," Anna said.

"Oh, no, Anna, I'm sure that ..." Eric protested.

"Eric, look at yourself." Anna gestured at his pants. Eric looked down and saw they were covered in mud where he'd almost fallen, having gone down on one knee as he fled the vampire thugs. His hands had dried mud on the edges.

"Hmmm. All right, I guess I'd better shower," Eric said, feeling embarrassed.

Anna led him to a luxurious bathroom and handed him a thick towel, winking at him as he shut the door. Eric was smiling as he showered under the steamy spray, soaping himself thoroughly. Five minutes later, he was toweling his hair dry. Stepping back into the living room wrapped in a soft oversized thick bathrobe, he was greeted by Lexei coming through the door with a bag.

"Thought you might be hungry, my man," he said, handing Eric the bag. Looking inside, Eric spied a thick burger with onion rings.

"Oh, my goodness," Eric's stomach rumbled loudly. Looking up as Lexei handed him a fountain drink, he was speechless.

"Best all-night burger joint in the city. You're going to need your strength," Lexei said, smiling. "Eat up, big guy."

As Eric wolfed down his food, sitting at the dining room

table, Anna chuckled.

"Guess I didn't realize how hungry I'd be," Eric grinned sheepishly. "Thanks, Lexei."

"My pleasure, Eric."

Alix walked up then. "Okay, Eric? We are going to retire now, and we will see you again at dusk." She indicated the front and back doors. "They are alarmed, so please do not open them; they will rouse us from our sleep. This should only be done under an emergency, because it could be dangerous for us. It will definitely be dangerous for any intruder." She smiled.

"Gotcha. Keep the doors shut."

Alix kissed him on the top of his head where he sat. "I like this boy, Anna." She winked at her daughter as she retreated. Anna laughed.

Eric finished his meal, and cleaned his place at the table, before turning to Anna. "Babe," he kissed her. "Mmmm."

"Good night, Eric." Anna smiled and retreated.

Lexei finished sealing the doors and setting the alarm. "Okay, everything's set." He patted Eric's arm. "Goodnight."

"Goodnight Lexei."

It had lost the scent, and it circled, high in the sky, trying in vain to sense where the magic had settled. Diving down into the countryside again, it growled in frustration, white teeth gleaming in the moonlight as it glided above the cloud cover. In an ancient time, some might have mistaken it for a small white dragon, but it was not. It was nothing so regal. It had survived for many millions of years, slumbering in caves and remote mountains, biding its time. Waiting.

NEW DOORWAY

Dusk found them again gathered in the living room, well rested and ready for anything. Eric was dressed in his newly laundered clothes and was finishing up another meal of fast food that Lexei had brought him.

"It's almost like you're feeding a pet, dude." Eric laughed and burped softly.

"Not my pet, my sister's pet," Lexei rolled his eyes. Eric's smile dropped off his face, and his eyes narrowed.

"Eric, he's teasing you," Anna stage whispered beside him.

"Oh, right." Eric yawned.

Lexei laughed and patted Eric's back. "Naw, man: you'd do the same for me, wouldn't you?"

"If you, a vampire, were a guest in my home?" Eric put his hand on his chest. "You'd better believe it," he said laughing.

"Okay, everyone ready?" Alix walked up, pulling on her coat.

"Ready."

"Yes."

"Ready, Mama. Let's do this."

Climbing the two flights of stairs, they exited through the tall window in the attic bedroom, sealing it behind them and lining up on the roof. The vampires, all dressed head-to-toe in black, were invisible to all humans but Eric. They stood flexing large, black feathery wings in the cool evening breeze, their eyes closed, their faces turned up toward the night sky. Eric could see waves of heat rising from their flexing wings as they stepped around the roof, stretching and bending their legs. He made a mental note to ask about that later.

"Eric?" Anna called to him softly. He went to her, and she stepped behind him, hugging him tightly and kissing his back. "Ready?" He nodded, and she launched herself into the air. The others followed quickly, jumping into the air with glee, pumping hard with their wings to gain altitude. Eric saw Lexei tuck his wings in and twirl several times, laughing in exuberance, and he smiled as he flew with Anna.

After leveling out high in the air, just under some clouds, the vampires began winging their way toward the cemetery.

Glancing up at the white clouds just above their heads, Eric turned his head and asked Anna, "Why don't we fly through the clouds? It's not raining."

Glancing down at him, she smiled. She turned over as she flew, flying belly up, and Eric found himself right-side up. He laughed in delight and raised his head, closing his eyes and enjoying the night air. Anna rose a dozen feet, barely touching the first fluffy, opaque edge of the bottom of the cloud, and Eric found himself with a wet face, hair dripping with moisture.

Laughing, Anna dropped again so he was out of the cloud, and continued flying on.

"Okay, I admit, that was a stupid question," Eric laughed, wiping his face. "I remember now: Clouds are water vapor."

"Now, now. There are no stupid questions," Anna chuckled.

As they approached the old cemetery, the vampires flew overhead, circling the hillside and the lowlands surrounding it. It was dead quiet, and the moon was a faint glow in the sky, barely visible through the cloud cover that was settling over the area. Anna loved the marine layer that hovered almost perpetually over the Seattle area, and this hillside was no exception. The moon hardly ever made an appearance, though not for lack of trying, and Anna reveled in the darkness that was so convenient – it hid them well, saving them the trouble of going invisible.

She glanced around. The countryside was dark in shadows, and the nocturnal animals were in high spirits. Great horned owls flew silently over the meadow next to the old graveyard, the wind ruffling their wingfeathers as they coasted on the night air. Coyotes ran in a small pack after prey, yipping in unison as they caught it and ate an evening snack. Skunks, raccoons and opossums skittered and waddled in the trees on the side of the hill as the vampires flew low overhead.

They landed halfway down the hill and found themselves alone; they saw no sign of the vampire thugs, not even a mark to show they'd been there.

The graveyard was inky dark.

Alix glanced at Anna and nodded, then closed her eyes and amplified her vampire aura to clear the area, and a palpable sense of fear blasted out in a half-mile radius from where she stood.

"Oh, god. Man, even I felt that," Eric dropped to one knee, trying not to vomit. Anna came up to him and rubbed his back, easing his distress.

"She is very powerful," Anna smiled at him. Eric nodded wordlessly and stood up. After collecting his wits, he turned to Anna.

"Anna," Eric spoke quietly to her. "How is it that your mother is more powerful that you and Lexei are?"

"Oh, I did not mean to suggest that she is. All three of us are extremely powerful." Anna looked straight at Eric. "And that," she gestured to indicate what Alix had just done, "wasn't even as forceful as she might have been. All three of us can project an aura of fear so intense that it would make you lose consciousness. Kill you even, if we really tried." Eric gulped, and Anna just smiled. "But the point was to clear the area, not make the animals pass out." She kissed him and patted his cheek. "Don't worry, Eric. You are very safe with us."

Lexei strode over to the site of the previous night's battle.

Kicking at the spot where he remembered they had fallen, Lexei mused, "Well, looks like the trainer came to pick up his dogs." He spat on the ground.

"Come," Alix said, and they made their way to the knights' small crypt. The door was still sealed, just as they'd left it.

"Looks like he didn't disturb the old tomb, I'll give him that much."

"He probably didn't want to have them after him."

"I know, right?"

Eric turned to ask, "What? 'Didn't want to have them after him'? Who?"

"The corpses."

"What???"

Anna giggled. "Don't worry, you're in no danger." She turned to him with a finger against her lips. "But don't disturb the knights' corpses."

"WHAT?"

Anna dissolved into laughter. "Sorry, sorry, I couldn't help it." She bent double, holding her middle and giggling in mirth.

Grinning, Lexei patted Eric's back. "Don't worry, you'll be fine."

"You two stop this silliness; you're scaring the poor boy," Alix pulled open the door to make room for them, and ducked her head inside, sniffing. "Seems okay. Come on."

Still laughing, Anna stood up again, pulling her coat straight. "Coming, Mama."

Lexei walked in last, behind Eric, closing and sealing the door behind him; he waved one clawed hand over the entrance and muttered some unintelligible words under his breath.

They all gathered at the far end, behind the knight's coffin. There was a small alcove, and after a slight drop of a step, it opened into a small, closet-sized room where several of the knight's possessions had probably been stored. They were long gone now; the tomb was somewhat safe from vandalism by religious zealots, Anna thought, but old crypts such as these were tempting targets for grave robbers, who cared little for what coffins themselves contained, preferring to steal nearby valuables stored alongside them. The alcove was bare, but the perfect place to open the tesseract.

Lexei removed the runestone from his bag and handed it over to his mother, who held it aloft. She glanced at them all in turn. "Now, it will happen suddenly: be prepared."

They all nodded. In unison, the three vampires extinguished their natural luminescence, and the small room was plunged into total darkness.

Holding the stone artifact aloft, the faint light shining through the crevice, they could all see it was far dimmer than it had been the night before. The dragonling was dying. They could wait no longer.

"Anya, protect your man. The blast will be hot." Alix placed the runestone on the lowest shelf, about three feet off the ground, up against the back wall, and then stood up. She closed her eyes and placed her hands in front of her, the fingertips of her left hand touching the fingertips of her right. She was silent for a minute, then began whispering ancient words as she slowly raised her head. Eric heard the words and tried to remember them, but they slipped from his mind as soon as he heard them. Try as he might, he could not recall even a syllable of what Alix was quietly chanting. Her voice rose little by little as she raised her head, until she was looking straight ahead at the runestone, commanding it in a strong voice that filled the tiny chamber. The runestone began to glow, slowly at first, but as the command from Alix became insistent and forceful, it could no longer resist. It became so bright Eric had to look away. Anna touched his shoulder and nodded toward the runestone.

"Watch the changing. Do not look away."

It became brighter and brighter until the light flooded the chamber. Alix's voice rose to a crescendo, commanding the tesseract to open. Her voice held such strength, such authority, that Eric felt relieved that the magic she commanded was not directed at him. His eyes squinted at the brightness, but he kept them on the runestone. Alix's arms were raised above her head as she commanded the artifact, and then she cried out a final command and threw her arms out, her hands pointing all ten fingers at the runestone. And the stone responded.

There was a bright flash of light and heat, and flames curled out suddenly, licking at their faces. Anna held Eric protectively behind her, her body shielding his, as he watched over her shoulder. The flames were swallowed back inside the new tesseract, the edges of which sparkled faintly, and the center of which was the blackest space Eric had ever seen. That darkness seemed to swallow every speck of light in the room, and hunger for more.

An imprint of the bright flash remained in his eyes for a moment, pulsating, but the newly formed doorway had swallowed up the flames. The near-blinding light had faded slowly, receding into the back wall until all was darkness. The shelves along the wall still appeared to be in place, creating a natural camouflage for the doorway, which, though invisible, was now fixed just beyond the darkness.

Lexei reached forward to touch the shelves, and his fingers disappeared into the breach. Looking back at them with an infectious grin, he stepped forward and vanished. Anna still braced an arm against Eric, holding him back, waiting. They all were breathing hard, most of all Alix; the creation of the doorway had taken its toll on them.

After a minute, Lexei stepped back through, still grinning, the runestone in his hand. Nodding, he gestured to them. "It's okay. Come on." And they all stepped through into the past.

They emerged on the other side near the lake where they had first encountered the Dragon Lord. Looking up, they could see his cavern on the far side. It was early evening, and the sun was descending in the western sky. It would be sunset soon.

"The sun returned; this is good." Alix looked toward the cavern. "We should make this fast. I expect he will not be pleased at the return of the artifact that wreaked such havoc on his land before."

Anna turned to Eric. "I will extend my aura into your mind enough so that you may understand the ancient language we will be using."

Understanding and trusting her, Eric nodded.

"Let's fly then," Lexei jumped into the air, flapping his wings to gain height before heading toward the cave entrance. The others followed, Anna carrying Eric with her. Eric was silent, his eyes taking in everything in the primal earth before him.

Anna pointed things out as they flew. "That way is where the museum doorway was opened. We were actually in this world together, during the eternal night that fell because of the runestone's presence." She pointed. "And over here is where we found the dragon roosting high in the cave."

"Is it dangerous?" Eric asked.

"Not to us."

"Why? Because you're vampires?"

"No, because we're respectful."

They all flew to the cave and entered near the top, gliding to the Dragon Lord's ledge, where they could see him resting. He saw them approach and raised his head in greeting. As they landed, one by one on the edge of the nest, smaller shetani scattered and fled to the rear of the dragon's bed.

Alix approached the Dragon Lord and bowed deeply, greeting the massive creature. "My Lord."

The dragon bowed his head in return, "Madam Vampire. What brings you back to my realm again?"

Lexei walked up, holding the runestone out, and Alix took it from him.

"My lord, we discovered an unintended hitchhiker within the runestone's cracks. We brought it back home." She held out the artifact to the Dragon Lord.

He extended his massive clawed paw and delicately took it from her. Alix glanced back to the others, and they all extinguished their auric brightness, and the cave ledge was plunged in further darkness. Seeing this, the dragon closed his eyes and dulled his own magic light until it vanished completely.

There was no light on the ledge. The cavern entrance was so far away, and the sun had descended even further so that the faint orange sunset glow that touched the cave's entrance failed to reach them where the Dragon Lord had made his nest. The dragon turned around, the vampires moving with him, placing the bulk of his body between the runestone and what little light remained.

They all waited a few minutes as their eyes adjusted to the dark and they could see the glow from the artifact's crevice. Far fainter than it had been before, the purple light shone out of the small breach, so faint they all leaned in to see it better.

There was a deep huff as the Dragon Lord inhaled a surprised breath. "You were correct in returning her, Madam Vampire. She barely clings to life."

He cupped the runestone in his massive paws, curling his talons around it, and exhaled onto the artifact. At first, the Dragon Lord's breath was a warm air, but it grew hotter until it ignited in flame. As the vampires watched, dragon fire enveloped the runestone until it grew hot and glowed from the heat. Then the Dragon Lord stopped, and they all waited.

After a few minutes, the purple glow from the artifact's crevice began to brighten. Sparkling glitter sprayed out from it in tiny geysers that grew gradually larger, until finally, the Dragon Lord spoke to it.

"It's all right. Come on out, you are home. Come out, little one," the dragon said in the gentlest voice.

As they watched, a tiny, tiny being looked out from the breach, then stepped out, hopping onto the Dragon Lord's paw. Climbing to the top, she sat there, stretching and yawning. The Dragon Lord smiled. He handed back the now dark runestone to Alix. "Here, it is empty now. Please take it from this land; it does not belong here."

"With haste, my lord," Alix bowed.

They all watched the tiny creature for some minutes. She was adorable, mainly because of her small size. She had grown since emerging from the runestone's crevice, and measured about three millimeters in length now, her skin mostly green with blue patches.

Lexei finally spoke up. "What is she?" he asked.

"She is a cousin to the dragons." The Dragon Lord smiled, his eyes crinkling. "This," he indicated the tiny creature, "is one of the smaller fae."

"She looks like a baby dragon," Lexei leaned forward to see the small faerie better.

"She is from a nearby branch of the same family tree, much as you are, littling. This wee faerie is similar to myself in the same way a monkey is similar to a human." The Dragon Lord chuckled.

The small creature suddenly stood up, stretching as tall as she could, and squeaked at the Dragon Lord. Then she raised her back, arching it and producing four small purple iridescent wings that began vibrating faster than the eye could see.

"She reminds me of a miniature hummingbird," said Lexei.

The faerie rose an inch, hovered there, then settled back down on the Dragon Lord's paw.

"Very well, I will take you back home," the dragon said quietly. Looking at the vampires, he asked, "Can I escort you all back to your tesseract? The little one here is still weak, and asks to be carried home."

"Yes, thank you."

"I see you brought a human with you this time," the Dragon Lord looked curiously at Eric, who raised his head and looked directly into the dragon's eyes, each of which was bigger than Eric himself.

"Yes," Anna said. "He and I are mated, my lord."

The dragon looked impressed. "A fine catch, sir. My congratulations." He said, addressing Eric.

Eric smiled and dipped his face momentarily.

"Tell me," the dragon continued. "What are you all called?"

Alix looked up sharply.

"Do not fear, Madam Vampire, I will not misuse the naming magic. I will respect and honor you if you divulge your names." The Dragon Lord bowed.

Still Alix hesitated.

The dragon then sighed, "I understand. As a show of good faith, I will tell you that my own name, the name given to me by my own mother, is Zrandengthalull." He bowed again. As the word left the Dragon Lord's mouth, the air itself tingled, and a spray of gold sparkles shot out from his tongue. The dragon batted at these as they floated out over his head. "Silly. Ridiculous." He muttered.

Alix tried to hide her smile as she looked back at Lexei, Anna and Eric. They exchanged glances and all nodded. The show of trust the dragon had offered was indisputable. In the wrong hands, and with the right magic, the name of the Dragon Lord could spell deep trouble for him. Of course, it could also spell life-saving magic, but this was very rare.

Turning back to Zrandengthalull, Alix bowed deeply before rising again and speaking. "You honour us, my lord. My own name is Alexandra Fyodorovna Romanov." She curtsied deeply before reaching her hand out to the Dragon Lord's massive claw. He took her hand in his, very delicately, and brought his massive snout down to it. As they watched, the dragon's enormous mouth pursed and he gently kissed the hand of the Empress.

Eric let out the breath he hadn't realized he was holding and gave Anna a look of relief, which quickly changed to mild alarm as she stepped forward next.

"Greetings and felicitations, my lord," Anna bowed deeply, then rose and stated, "My name is Anastasia Nikolaevna Romanov. I am very pleased to make your acquaintance," Anna said, smiling broadly as the Dragon Lord took her hand and delicately kissed it as he had kissed her mother's.

Lexei came forward then, thrusting out his hand in friendship. "And I am Alexei Nikolaevich Romanov. I am also very pleased to make your acquaintance, even though last time I was here you cradled me inside your mouth," Lexei finished, giggling. Smirking, the dragon extended one great claw, which Lexei curled his hand around before shaking it. The Dragon Lord then threw back his head and laughed in delight. Lexei laughed with him, holding his middle.

Eric stood back from all of this and shook his head, smiling.

"And who is this last new friend I am to make name-acquaintance of this fine day?" The Dragon Lord said as he settled his eyes on Eric.

Gulping, Eric decided to make the most out of the situation. *I mean,* thought Eric, *how often do you meet a real-life, honest-to-gosh Dragon Lord?*

"*Probably not that often at all,*" said a laughing voice inside his head.

Eric looked up at the dragon, and the dragon winked back.

"I'm Eric James Wallace. Pleased to meet you." Eric bowed deeply, one hand in front of his waist, the other behind his back. Rising again, he saw the Dragon Lord bow his head in return. Extending his hand in friendship toward the great dragon, Eric felt a shiver travel up his spine. The hair on the backs of his arms and neck stood up, as if electrified, as he shook the Dragon Lord's great claw. A shudder traveled through him from head to toe.

"That is the naming magic," Lexei said beside him. "We are all now connected."

Eric smiled.

"Now, let us fly." The Dragon Lord crept to the edge of his ledge and tipped forward, launching himself off and spreading his wings as he fell, catching the air and gliding toward the large cavern opening next to the lake. The vampires followed him, riding on thermals that rose up from the cave floor hot springs. As they glided out and over the lake, the dragon ahead of them, Eric in Anna's grasp, the sun dipped below the horizon, below purple and orange-red clouds.

Zrandengthalull banked to the left and glided over hundred-foot-tall treetops, startling a flock of large silver reptilian looking birds as he flew. After a minute, he dropped out of the sky and landed in a clearing, and the vampires were soon on the ground beside him.

"It's just ahead," the Dragon Lord said. "Come, you will enjoy the sight." Despite his massive size, Zrandengthalull deftly squeezed around dozens of tall trees without bending a single one. They arrived at a particularly old, particularly tall tree that looked like an ancestor of the Sequoias. A large amount of brush surrounded it, fallen branches and forest growth, as well as several large boulders. The dragon reached over all these and stretched himself nearly 75 feet up the tree. He looked very much like a cat stretching against a scratching post.

Looking down, he said, "Come see this."

With leaps and flutters of their wings, the vampires, with Eric, flew up and landed on Zrandengthalull's shoulder and saw what the dragon wanted to show them.

It was a tiny city, in the small, hollowed-out middle of the tree. Faeries, hundreds of them, were flying all around the edge of the city like bees buzzing around a hive. The city, built of what looked like twigs and grasses, reached down inside the tree for several yards.

Tiny castle keeps sprang up from below, and reached eight to twelve inches up, with smaller towers built alongside them. Smaller buildings surrounded the taller ones, and many of the fae traveled busily along the many pathways in between.

Small branches, thick with leaves, had been trained to grow out over the small city, shielding it from the elements. This deep in the forest the light was nearly gone and they could see the fae in the city as tiny spots of light. Some were purple, some blue, some red, some green, some yellow. Anna, Eric and the others marveled at the sight of the tiny creatures flying together, in a buzz all around the city.

Zrandengthalull leaned out and gently placed the little faerie onto the outer wall of the city. She stretched, and her wings vibrated as she flew down to her home. The dragon chuckled and watched for a minute longer.

"That city is exquisite," Alix murmured.

"Isn't it? I could watch it all day," Zrandengthalull chuckled again.

"Are there more of them around?" Lexei looked around. "Or are they rare?"

"This is the only collection of these tiny fae in this part of the world. They are rare this far north; they are more readily found in warmer climes," the dragon answered.

"They're precious," Anna said.

"Actually, they are extremely fierce," the Dragon Lord said as he made his way back through the trees, "if you get them riled. I wouldn't want to battle them. That city goes all the way down into the tree; there are hundreds of thousands of them in there. They attack together, armed with barbed spears dipped in a sap that neutralizes the nerves."

Eric shook his head, looking over his shoulder. "I had no idea."

"I wouldn't worry now, little one; we brought her back, she is very happy. I imagine that she is, at this very moment, regaling her fellow fae with her tales of adventure in the land through the tesseract. I think soon we will have the friendship of the entire city."

"That's a lot of friends," Lexei chuckled.

It raised its head, closing its eyes and sensing, sniffing the air. The magic was active again. It opened its eyes, and a smile formed on its face that was more grimace than grin. Gathering itself, it began making its way toward the source it had been waiting several million years to find.

DRAGON FIRE

Zrandengthalull flew with them to the doorway and they landed as the last bit of sunlight left the land. The night sky faded from indigo to velvet black and was soon sparkling with a million stars.

The tesseract glimmered faintly in the darkness, if they looked at it out of the corner of their eye. Straight on it was invisible, with only the suggestion of a shimmer around it, like hot air above a desert highway.

"Madam Alexandra," Zrandengthalull bowed his head as he spoke. "Once again, I am in your debt for bringing the wee faerie back home before she died. I will not soon forget this kindness. Such creatures are very important to the balance of life in my land, and their tribe would have suffered greatly had she been lost."

"It was our pleasure, sir." Alix bowed deeply, her nose

touching her outstretched leg.

"I would like to give you a token for your kindness, but nothing I can think of can come close to repaying you for saving the life of a faerie." The dragon thought for a moment. "We are already friends, and we reside in times much separated. The mountains around my realm will be much changed in your time, and many of the creatures who live alongside me will be extinct, or gone to better worlds, by the time yours comes along."

He seemed to think for a moment longer, idly scratching at his side as he pondered. There was a pattering below him, and he glanced down, brushing the scales that had fallen aside. The large rainbow-hued, crescent shaped scales were about the size of a bat'leth. Lexei picked one up and examined it. Smiling at him, Zrandengthalull said, "My apologies. I'm molting."

"You mean, you're going to grow larger?" Lexei said.

"Oh yes, little one," the dragon chuckled.

"May I have one of these?" Lexei examined the changing shades of color on the dragon scale.

"Yes, of course. Take as many as you like." The dragon thought for another moment, then addressed Alix. "Madam Alexandra, I am in your debt, and it can never be repaid to my satisfaction. Know here and now that I will always be your friend," he moved his great head to indicate all of them. "And I will always come to your aid."

Alix bowed deeply again. "You honour us,

Zrandengthalull." She then leaned forward and her hand brushed the side of the huge dragon head.

The dragon dipped his head in happiness, and they saw the scales on his face darken to a rosy purple as he blushed.

Anna reached up and gave Zrandengthalull a kiss on his great cheek, and the sides of the dragon's mouth curled into a smile at the corners.

"Farewell, Zrandengthalull."

They turned to enter the doorway. Taking a deep breath of the cool, crisp primeval evening air, Eric looked around. "I'm going to miss this land." He smiled at Anna, putting his hand around her waist.

Anna turned to enter the tesseract with him.

Before they could do so, something came bursting through the tesseract, catching Anna around the throat in an iron grip.

Rasputin leaped out of the time portal. Grabbing Anna, he hooked an arm around her neck and screamed a challenge. Eric was tossed aside as Anna and Rasputin tumbled to the ground amid the ferns. Rasputin jumped to his feet, releasing Anna, and sprang at Alix.

Rasputin screamed, spittle flying from his mouth as he turned and reached with a clawed hand to grab Alix. Latching his arms around her neck, he locked them together at the wrist.

"No!" Lexei reached to pull his mother from the madman's grip.

Two-inch-long fangs, deadly and dripping with saliva, reached for Alix's face. Rasputin's mouth was opened so wide it seemed grotesque, making him look like something out of a nightmare. He reached down and bit, hard, locking his jaws on the side of Alix's face. His fangs were buried in her flesh down to the bone, and blood ran down her neck as she screamed in surprise and pain.

"MAMA!" Anna sprang up from the ground and grabbed Rasputin's face, trying to pry his jaws from her mother.

Lexei jumped onto Rasputin's back and grabbed the maniac's neck and shoulders.

Alix screamed again, pain and fury mixing in her voice.

Anna felt a surge of panic as her mother screamed again, and shifted her grip on the vampire's face. His teeth were all razor sharp; if she reached into his mouth for the correct leverage, her fingers would be severed before she'd be able to apply any kind of pressure. She heard Zrandengthalull and Eric scrambling behind her, but kept her full concentration on her mother's face, now covered in blood.

Alix's eyes shone from the depths of massive amounts of blood, and for the first time in her life, Anna saw fear on her mother's face. Anna dug her fingers into Rasputin's eye sockets and pulled on his chin, applying massive amounts of pressure, trying to open his jaws, but they held fast.

Rasputin growled angrily in his throat, and lashed out with hands ending in claws, tearing at Alix's vulnerable middle, ripping into her flesh, making her scream in agony.

Lexei's hands squeezed Rasputin's throat, trying to strangle the monster into unconsciousness, but it was taking too long. Somewhere in the distant background, he heard the dragon and Eric talking in hurried words, but his full concentration was on choking the madman who was killing his mother.

Rasputin had his hands on Alix's shoulders now and was applying pressure, trying to pull her head from her body. A loud crack sounded in the clearing as her neck broke, the backbone separating from the skull. Alix's screams trailed off as she lost consciousness. Lexei reached down and grabbed his arms, pulling them back at the elbows and anchoring his grip on Rasputin's neck in a full nelson.

Lexei strained, pulling as hard as he could at Rasputin's arms and shoulders, using leverage to stop the mad vampire. A second later, the first arm broke at the shoulder with a resounding crack. Then, moments later, the second. Both hung uselessly at Rasputin's side, but his teeth, buried almost an inch into Alix's skull, still had a death grip on her face.

Anna and Lexei gripped tighter, trying to force Rasputin to release his mouth from Alix's face, when Eric burst the fray. Wielding one of the dragon's scales in his hands, and he wiggled the sharp tip into Rasputin's mouth, and pried, using it as a lever. Rasputin resisted as his teeth met the dragon scale, but its hard surface would not yield to him, and his mouth slowly began to open. He screamed again in fury. Lexei heard the dragon behind him.

"Here, let me try," said the Dragon Lord.

Taking the scale in his own great hand, the dragon thrust upward it with such force that Rasputin's jaw was flexed back to his neck. Now it was the madman's turn to scream in pain. Lexei pulled Rasputin's head up while Anna and Eric extracted Alix's head from Rasputin's teeth. Their assailant fell back, jaw dangling uselessly, and Alix collapsed, Eric cradling her and falling beneath her.

"Step back," Zrandengthalull's voice was quiet and grim in the evening darkness.

As Rasputin struggled on the ground, Lexei and Anna withdrew to where Eric lay with their mother. Zrandengthalull pushed his head forward and, taking a deep breath, exhaled a tremendous blast of blue-white dragon fire that completely enveloped Rasputin.

So vast were the dragon's lungs and so great his fury that the assault lasted several minutes, and blew the crazed maniac back several hundred yards, leaving a long line of charred trees in its wake. Startled forest denizens squawked and flew up into the air or ran off in surprise as the huge flame tore through the undergrowth, pushing the writhing figure ahead of it. The body finally hit a small granite hill and stopped cold. The dragon fire kept coming, and it didn't stop until all that was left was a heap of molten rock that all but encased an unmoving ball of charred flesh that had once resembled something alive.

As he finished, the Dragon Lord turned to look at Alix, then cast his gaze on her companions in concern. "Is she ... is she dead?" he whispered.

"No," Lexei said through a tear-streaked face. He sat down next to his mother.

Anna cradled Alix in her arms and sobbed. Eric sat, stone-faced, his lap supporting Alix's head and shoulders. Tears ran silently down his cheeks as he stared off into space, unable to look at the mangled former empress.

"Mama," Lexei sobbed softly, trying to wipe clear the blood from his mother's face.

"Here," the dragon handed Lexei a large bucket-shaped flower, half-filled with water. Lexei splashed a bit on Alix's face.

She was very pale. "She's lost a lot of blood, and her neck ..." Eric swallowed. "I think I heard it break."

"She's breathing," Anna said haltingly. "But she is in immense pain. Heart-stopping pain."

Lexei sobbed again, heartbroken. He patted Alix's hand.

"Here, take these." Zrandengthalull handed Eric five small pods, each about the size of a large peanut, hanging from the stem of a branch he'd broken off. "Steeped, they will provide a healing sleep from which even a shetani cannot wake. It will give her body time."

Eric took the branch. "Thank you," he choked out.

A high buzzing filled the glade where they had gathered, and they saw what looked like a cloud of miniature fireflies approaching. The faeries. Zrandengthalull turned and began communing with them, and then turned to the vampires.

"They want to help," he said, turning back to the swarm of lights and talking with them further. The vampires waited expectantly. Nodding finally, the dragon turned to them once more. "Will you let them approach her?

"Yes."

The swarm of lights, bright in the night air, flew up to Alix and settled on her, their wings vibrating, their lights winking on and off in the night air. As they all watched, the faeries' wings moved faster and faster, producing a hum that rose to such a high pitch it was soon inaudible to Eric. But not to the vampires.

The lines of worry on Anna and Lexei's face soon vanished, and their eyes closed, their features relaxing, until they looked as if they were dreaming. Eric looked down and saw Alix's damaged face reflect the same calmness, pain draining from it like water from a sieve. After a few minutes, the faeries rose from her, and, in a tight swarm, flew from the clearing and disappeared into the night.

Anna and Lexei opened their eyes, still looking serene and peaceful, yet amazed. They looked down at their mother and saw her face was no longer contorted in semiconscious agony. She was tranquil and she looked at peace.

"The fae use supersonic sound to soothe discomfort and relieve stress," Zrandengthalull murmured.

"Please thank them for us, when you can, Sir Dragon,"

Lexei said.

"I will."

"We have to leave; we have to take her home," Anna said.

"I understand, littling," the dragon said quietly.

Nodding, they gathered Alix up and departed through the tesseract. On the other side, Lexei held his mother close, and they left the knight's crypt, sealing the doorway behind them, leaving a solid wall no longer touched by magic. They sealed the tomb's wooden door as well; Anna waved her hand across the entrance, whispering the words as purple magic flowed from her palm. "Now no one can open this again, ever."

Lexei held his mother close, like a small child, and launched himself into the night air. His huge wings seemed to blanket the sky as he beat them to gain height.

Anna looked around once more at the old cemetery with a tired sigh. Then she turned quietly, took Eric up in her arms, and launched herself into the air after her brother, her wings blacker than the surrounding night, her heart heavy with sorrow. They both flew hard and fast, traveling quickly. Eric turned his face into Anna's shoulder to shield his eyes from the buffeting winds, his tears mingling with hers as they flew.

They made their way across the sleeping city, through

the misty clouds and winking starlight, back to their Mercer Island home. Anna and Lexei settled Alix on her bed, cleaning her up and changing her into a snowy white nightgown.

Gypsy padded into the room and immediately curled up next to Alix, snuggling against the injured vampiress's side and purring loudly. Alix's long hair lay spread out on the pillow surrounding her ravaged face. Eric busied himself brewing the tea from one of the pods the dragon had given them; trying and failing to restrain tears that fell into the cup. Anna came and poured some blood into the tea, mixing it with a spoon as she stared into space, lost in thought.

Carrying the mug to Alix's bedside, Eric looked down at her ravaged face as he handed the steaming mug to Lexei.

"How is she?"

"The fangs dug deep into her face, cracking it in one place, and her neck is broken." Anna arranged Alix's hair around her face.

Taking the mug, Lexei gently opened his semi-conscious mother's mouth and dipped spoonfuls in. She swallowed automatically, groaning. "This will help you with your pain, Mama."

Eric sighed, his heart constricting. Fresh tears ran down his face as he watched son feeding mother. After a few minutes, Alix seemed to relax into the pillow, her head lolling to the side. Anna held her mother's hands and bent down to kiss them. Rising, she pulled the blankets up to

Alix's shoulders, and patted them down near her feet. She took her mother's hand and laid it on Gypsy's back, pushing Alix's fingers deep into the soft fur. The cat's purr deepened.

"Help her heal, Gypsy Girl," Anna murmured softly.

"What do we do now?" Eric asked quietly.

"She needs time, a lot of time," Anna wiped a tear from her cheek. "We wait."

Lexei leaned down and kissed his mother's cheek, and they all left the room.

Back near the cemetery, down the hill and next to the road that bordered it, the creature came. Crawling, hopping, leaping, it made its way up the side of the hill, through the dead leaves and fallen branches and under the barbed-wire fence that bordered the cemetery on the north side. It crawled up to the top and sniffed around, then settled on top of a huge, partially fallen over statue of an angel. Claws clung to old lichen-mottled stone as it rested there, waiting.

ENCOUNTERS

Anna sat in art class next to Eric, staring off into space, silent and unmoving, lost in thought. The white canvas before her was blank, waiting for color. Mr. Newcomb watched the two from the other side of the room, a worried look on his face. Mr. Wallace had explained that there had been an assault on Miss Roman's mother, and that they were all very stressed out, and asked for patience from the old professor. Mr. Newcomb was in his sixties and understood; he told them to take time, and suggested they use art as a balm for their souls.

Eric's brush played across his own canvas, dabbing purple across a landscape of trees as he tried to capture the details of the Dragon Lord's primeval forest from memory. Anna's brush, dipped in black, hovered over her canvas as she stared off into space, lost in thought. Eric sighed beside her, and her eyes slowly came into focus, bringing her into the here and now, and settled on the blank white expanse in front of her.

Anna had told Eric she disliked the whiteness of a blank canvass; she said the stark void made a statement in and of itself, of emptiness, and she had the urge to fill it with color. She slowly brought her brush up and began to move the tip on the canvas. An intricate diamond shape slowly took form, an exquisite, three-dimensional filigree design. Anna's brush dipped to her paint board to pick up deep ruby red, and she used this to paint the shape of a gem in the middle of the filigree.

When the design was complete, she began to paint a delicate neck above it, and a soft, comforting torso below it. But the focus of the painting stayed on the shape she had first put on the canvas, which Eric soon recognized as the brooch her mother sometimes wore. It was a portrait of Alix, with the ruby brooch as its centerpiece. Anna painted in a shadowy form in last, on the lower left side, and up-close Eric was not sure what he was seeing. He was about to ask her, but when he turned to her to ask, he saw she was painting with unshed tears in her eyes.

"That's beautiful, Miss Roman," a quiet voice said from behind them. Eric turned and saw Mr. Newcomb standing five feet back, studying Anna's painting over her shoulder.

Anna mumbled a thank you, wiping tears from her eyes, and turned to clean her brushes. Eric took the opportunity to walk to where their teacher silently stood. From there, Eric could see Anna had painted a picture of her mother's torso, the brooch shining bright, a deep red ruby surrounded by filigree artwork. The shadowy form of a small child lay against the Alix's lap, her arm reaching across her mother's waist, and mother's arm held the child close.

As Anna put her brushes away, she sighed, a heavy feeling in her chest.

***

Anna and Eric walked in silence from the campus in the crisp night air. Crickets sounded in the bushes, still wet from an earlier shower. The air smelled fresh and clean, and the night sky had cleared momentarily, the clouds parting to reveal a deep black velvet fabric with jewels of light embedded in it.

"I've always thought our night sky was beautiful, the stars winking in a sea of inky blackness, but now I think I will always remember the sky from the past. I think of it as Zrandengthalull's land, primitive and unpolluted by man." Eric's arm half encircled her waist as they slowly walked along, and Anna's head lay on his shoulder, her arm entwined in his. She remained silent, not looking up, lost in thought again. Eric held her close as they made their way to his apartment across campus.

As they ducked in to his front door, it began to rain again.

Eric made Anna comfortable, settling her in a loveseat, a soft wrap tucked around her legs. Jinx came to investigate almost immediately, sniffing the smell of the evening air that had settled on their clothes and hair, eventually curling up in Anna's lap and purring. Her hand absentmindedly came up and slowly stroked the cat's fur, her fingers dipping into the soft strands, and Jinx's purrs deepened and became louder.

Eric fixed two cups of cocoa and came to sit next to them, sipping his warm drink, not speaking, just allowing Anna to heal. The cat's purrs seemed to help, and her fingers slowly moved through his fur, Jinx dipping his head sideways to bring them to his ears, and rubbing back and forth as she held her fingers steady. Eric smiled, thinking of what Anna had said about his cat last week.

"Oh, Jinx is special," she'd said, running her fingers down his head and back. "Aren't you Jinxy?" She kissed the top of the cat's head as he purred. Jinx had reached up and began licking the side of Anna's chin, purring madly. She'd grinned at Eric over the top of the cat, chuckling when he reached his paw up to touch her head.

"He loves you," Eric had told her. "He really has taken to you. Normally he's suspicious of strangers."

Anna had smiled a knowing smile. "Kindred can sense one of the People; they love us. I think we must have a connection, some kind of psychic bond."

She'd picked up the cat, and lain down with him on her

chest. Petting him, she smiled again. "Cats are similar to vampires. We both hunt for prey, and we are both most alive at night; we both find happiness in the gothic nature of the creatures of the night. We have a definite connection." Eric had chuckled at this, leaning forward to kiss her.

As Eric watched Anna now, silent, brooding, troubled, cat purring on her lap as she absently stroked it, he wondered at the connection. After a minute, she shifted and lay down on the couch, her face and torso stretched alongside the huge, black cat. Jinx purred loudly as she snuggled against him, her eyes closed; the movement of her fingers as they idly twirled the cat's fur was the only sign she was awake.

An hour passed as Anna rested. Eric finished his cocoa and sat there staring out into space, lost in thought as rain began to pound against the window in earnest. The cat ceased his purring as he fell deeply asleep.

After a while, Anna sat up. "I am finished moping," she said, turning to Eric.

He smiled. "Just like that?"

"Just like that," Anna said firmly. "Mama is strong, and she's already showing signs of healing. I need to heal, too." She stood up with Jinx in her arms, kissed him, and set him down gently on the sofa. Grabbing her jacket, she stretched. "I need to walk. I need to find nature."

Eric jumped up after her, grabbing his own coat against the chilly winter temperatures. "Where are we going?"

"Don't know, Wallace, but we're going there fast."

"Cool," Eric grinned, excitement surging through him like electricity.

They ran out into the night, into the rain, into the wind, exhilarated by the storm. Raindrops stung their faces, and they laughed as they ran. Anna made a beeline to the city park, running all the way, Eric behind her. They stuck their tongues out as they ran, and rainwater soaked their hair and dribbled down their backs.

As they made their way up the pathway into the trees, their cheeks were flushed a vibrant red. Anna wore a grin that threatened to split her face in two. Eric felt so happy he laughed out loud. They jogged a hundred yards in before they stopped, and as they ran into their clearing, the rain stopped. Anna laid her jacket on the grass and sat down, and Eric did the same beside her. Eric's heart was beating so fast his brain buzzed.

"Eric, I am worried a bit."

"About what?"

"You." She looked at him sideways.

"Me? Why?"

"The world is dangerous, especially around vampires," Anna's brow was furrowed.

"Well, yes, but we left Rasputin a million years in the past."

"More than a million years, actually." Anna smiled.

"So ... we should be out of danger, at least mostly,

shouldn't we?"

"Well, yes and no." Anna thought for a moment. "You should know there are other vampires around. Not a lot, but it's not unheard of."

Eric looked alarmed. "I've ... I've never seen any, at least I don't think I have."

"You saw me before you knew my true nature."

"That's true enough." Eric paused, deep in thought.

"Paranormal creatures are very, very adept at hiding," Anna said. "You will not see them if they don't want you to. Even if you do see them, you will not know their true nature unless they reveal it."

"Okay. But they are rare, right? Very rare?"

"Not as rare as you think."

"What do you mean?"

Anna wrapped her arms around her knees and laid her head on his shoulder. She was quiet for a moment. Then, "You know Jordan? In art class?"

"The quiet girl? She always wears a braid?"

"Yes, that's her."

"What about her?"

"Well, don't let on that I told you, but..." Anna paused, then continued. "She's one of the People."

"You're kidding."

"Not at all," Anna said, laughing at his tone.

"That girl is a vampire? I saw her waitressing at a downtown restaurant." Eric looked shocked.

"Well, yes. I think she does waitress downtown. But she is also a vampire."

"She looks so ... benign," Eric seemed at a loss for words.

"We don't all have the same personality. Some of us are extremely shy. Quite a lot of us, actually. Jordan, from what I can smell, has been turned for a decade. I believe she lives alone, which is quite understandable."

Eric remained silent, lost in thought.

Anna shifted. "Eric, I want to tell you how to defend yourself. I don't mean to scare you, just equip you with the resources to protect yourself."

"Okay. Are you going anywhere soon?" Eric laughed.

"No, silly," Anna pushed his shoulder lightly, laughing. Sobering up, she continued. "But what if what happened to Mama, happened to me? I'd be laid up in bed, recovering, for a week or more. You'd be out there, defenseless ..."

"I'm not completely defenseless. I've picked up some skills, ya know."

Anna smiled. "Well, if you meet another vampire, and *if* they aren't thugs, like those patooties back at the cemetery, identify yourself as a mate of one of the People, and they should leave you alone. In fact..." Anna rose on one elbow and look at Eric, thinking. "I can put a mark on you that will be a sign to other vampires, and most other paranormal sentient beings, that you are of our clan, under our protection. Claimed. But it is only done rarely. It's almost kind of like ... a commitment, sort of. Very serious. There's a long process involved."

"Okay, well that actually sounds like something we are already moving toward," Eric said. "But Anna, if you get injured and are laid up, I will be by your side. I will never leave you. I love you. I'm not going anywhere."

Anna seemed relieved. "I love you, too, Eric." She kissed him. "That's why I want you to learn, well, not only how to defend yourself, but how to see, really see. If you use respect, you will stay free from harm, at least most of the time."

"How do you mean?"

"Well, have you ever been camping?"

"Yes," Eric smiled. "Years ago, with my parents."

"So, you know, for instance, to watch out for things that may normally be nearly invisible. Like a wasp's nest, for instance."

"Oh, I see what you mean. Like, 'respect the wasp's nest' and 'stay away from bears,' that sort of thing."

"Exactly. I want to help you so you will be aware, so you won't get hurt. You need to learn to see the other paranormals around you; it will be eye-opening," Anna said. "For instance, here, now, do you see anything around you?"

Eric looked around at the damp clearing around them. It was dark and quiet, and the cloud cover blocked most of the light. But his eyes had adjusted to the blackness present at the middle of the night, and he could make out the trees and undergrowth around them. He could hear several creatures far off, and crickets chirping nearby. He turned to Anna, and waited.

She smiled. "Close your eyes," she said, taking his hand in hers.

Eric closed his eyes.

"Now, listen. Really listen." She paused a minute. "Can you hear your heartbeat?"

"Yes," Eric said, feeling very relaxed. His heart was loud in his ears, thumping strongly in his chest. He quieted his mind further, and his breathing slowed. Eric imagined reaching out with all his senses into the forest around them. He remained like this for many minutes. Then ...

"Did you hear that?" Anna whispered.

It was a scuttling sound, and a tiny thrumming. Eric opened his eyes. Because they'd been closed, and resting, when he opened his eyes they took in more than he imagined.

Anna moved forward and gently parted the nearby bushes. Whatever had been there zipped away in surprise, and then came back to investigate them.

The creature looked like a cross between a centipede and a dragonfly, with wings folded tightly against its back. A trail of tiny lights flickered all along its spine, running from its head, which had double antennae, down between two sets of wings, to its tail. It was several inches long, and its body was a brilliant silvery-blue.

Anna reached her finger out to it, and the tiny thing hopped up and ran along her hand and halfway up her arm, where it stopped and reared up half its height, chirping at her. She let out an answering trill, and the little thing jumped into the air, its wings coming out to vibrate like a hummingbird's. It dashed around them in delight, dancing through the air several times on purple wings before flying straight up and into the high tree branches, where it perched, looking down at them.

Eric smiled in delight. "What was that?"

"That's a tzippa, one of the magical creatures humans don't focus on. It's a kind of sprite, sort of a cross between bird and insect. Very playful. Now that you know what they look like, you will see them." Anna looked into Eric's eyes. "Always be respectful. They can sting and paralyze you for hours."

Eric's eyebrows rose in surprise. Looking up at their new friend, he said, "I certainly will."

"Another thing I want to show you," she said, looking around them. Spying something deep in the bushes, she began a low humming, more vibration than sound. Eric focused on the spot she was staring at, but Anna stopped humming and whispered abruptly, "Don't look straight at these. They can spit in your eyes from ten feet away. Wait until it comes to us; that means it's not scared." She began humming again. Eric waited.

Slowly, out of underneath the closest bush, what looked like a winged lizard came zipping out. It ran out about a foot, then back under the bush, then out again, a little farther, coming to rest by Eric's knee. It looked up at him, and paused there, as if to get a good look at the newcomer. This gave Eric a chance to look right back, and what he saw was amazing.

The creature's body was black and green, and covered from head to tail with tiny reflective scales. A small, fine ridge of sharp spines began at the halfway point on its head, which looked like a lizard's head, and ran all along its back and down to the tip of its tail.

From nose to tail, it was about six inches long, with wings sprouting from its shoulder blades. The wings were a lighter, emerald green, with black finger bones between each sail. Tiny black claws ended each finger bone, looking like shards of obsidian.

Eric glanced from the lizard thing to Anna, who was smiling. "What is it?" he whispered.

"She's called a winged makara, although a miniature variety that lives on land. She's of the lizard family, but she also has a little magic."

Anna held out her arm, and the makara hopped up onto it, aided by her wings. From there she ran up Anna's arm, across the back of her shoulders, and down the other arm. She paused there and looked up at Eric with intelligent eyes. Anna nodded to him, and he held out his arm.

The makara's wings hummed, and she hopped into the air and onto Eric's wrist. From there she ran up to his shoulders and stopped to examine Eric's face. She was extremely curious and placed her front legs on Eric's chin, leaning in to see better, her whiskers tickling Eric in the process. Eric's eyes crinkled in mirth as he tried in vain not to laugh. As he silently chuckled, middle heaving in spasms, the creature retreated and sat perched on Eric's knee, watching them both.

"Watch this." Anna began humming again, very low at the back of her throat. After a few seconds, the little creature answered, humming back at her, and began vibrating its wings. As Eric watched, the makara's wings began to glow.

"Oh!" Eric whispered. "Very cool," he said, smiling.

Anna continued to hum as she slowly got to her feet, and the makara rose in the air to follow her progress. Eric stood as well, and watched as the beautiful creature's glow illuminated the entire clearing. In the air she looked for all the world like a miniature dragon from mythology. As Anna stopped humming, the makara twittered over to her and settled on her head, making several circles before settling down to sit.

Eric smiled as he reached his finger to the little creature and touched her front paws, which were crossed in front of her like a cat's. She leaned forward and delicately licked Eric's fingertip with relish.

Anna stepped to the edge of the small clearing and leaned over to touch her head to a low tree branch, and the makara delicately stepped onto it. Smiling, Anna turned back to Eric. "Not only are we surrounded by these magical creatures, there is magic in the very air, in every place on earth. The creatures you saw just now? They have a natural camouflage, and that's the main reason most humans can't really see them. These magical creatures appear even more densely in a wild forest. Like in the nearby redwood forests: they are thick there."

"This explains so much. Like when I was a kid and walked my dog, she would sniff every few feet, especially walking through a park or forest."

"Most animals are extremely perceptive: They sense everything around them."

"And Jinx, he is always looking at different things out the window, things I don't see, but he seems frozen to the spot, watching them," Eric said.

"Jinx sees everything. Most cats do, and," Anna held her finger up, "not everything they see is small and cute and friendly. All magic is wild. Some of it is quite seriously dangerous."

She inhaled deeply, closing her eyes and smiling. "And they can see what's happened in a spot before."

"What do you mean?"

"Well, every place, every single place in the universe, holds every single moment that ever happened there; holds it in the place's embrace, and it is there, always." She wrapped her arms around her elbows and seemed to hug herself, smiling broadly. "There is no such thing as time, from a certain point of view."

"How do you mean? Do you mean time travel?

"No, I mean everything that happens in a place leaves an imprint, a kind of echo that can be seen again if one has eyes to see."

"Eyes to see?"

"Come here." She drew him to the edge of the glade, their backs to the trees, then turning him around to face the clearing. "Now, close your eyes and remember that night we made love in this very same spot."

"Mmmm," Eric closed his eyes and smiled, remembering.

"Now focus on one thing, from your memory, just one moment of that experience. Got it?"

"Mmmm, oh yes. I'm picturing you rising in the air, when you wrapped your legs around me."

Anna chuckled, "That's a good memory. I'm thinking of it, too." Anna took Eric's hand, and squeezed it. He felt a warmth growing in his chest, and felt tears come to his eyes.

"Eric, open your eyes," Anna whispered.

Eric slowly opened his eyes and looked into the clearing and gasped.

They were there, both of them. Ghostly images of the two of them making love shimmered in the night air in the clearing. Anna's huge, black wings flapped slowly as she rose a few inches and wrapped herself around Eric, cupping her body to his as they joined. The edges of the images sparkled, as if their substance was not truly there, and yet he saw them there as clearly as he saw his own body. Seeing himself making love to Anna, he blushed and felt a surge of love for her. He made a mental note to propose to this incredible woman at the earliest opportunity.

"Amazing, isn't it?" Anna said next to him. The couple appearing before them did not react to the sound of her voice, and Eric fully realized that what he was seeing was in the past.

"Yes," Eric said reverently. "It's incredible." He turned to Anna and gathered her into his arms and kissed her, long and slow, his eyes open and watching over her shoulder as the ghostly pair from the past continued their dance, a dance as old as time.

Back in the cemetery, the pale creature slumbered on the old boulder. Waves of repelling aura pulsing out from it as it slept, undisturbed. At the bottom of the hill below, a fat raccoon paused in its shuffling gait to sniff the air, then abruptly turned and ran back in the other direction, away from the ancient thing at the top of the hill.

EXPLORATION

Anna and Eric walked hand in hand down the path out of the park and toward the town center. As they strolled, arms entwined, Anna's head on Eric's shoulder, Lexei ran up to them from behind.

"Hey! What are you two up to?" He put his arms across their shoulders, poking his head between theirs. Laughing, Eric grabbed Lexei's head and rubbed his knuckles on the top.

"How's Mama, little brother?" Anna said, smiling.

"Oh, she's sleeping. I brought her noms, and she fell right to sleep."

" 'Noms?' " Eric asked.

"Blood," Lexei explained.

"Ah," Eric looked at the ground. He'd never inquired too closely about the vampires' feeding details; it was an uncomfortable subject. He caught Anna smiling at him.

"I was about to take Eric to the redwoods," Anna began strolling again, and the men followed.

"Ah, cool. Can I tag along?"

"Sure," she draped her arm around Lexei's neck.

"Anna, I have some questions about what we were talking about before," Eric said.

"Ask me anything." Anna smiled, then turned to her brother. "I was explaining the nature of magic and earth memories."

"Very interesting subject," Lexei stopped to pick a flower, stuck it in his mouth and continued to walk beside them.

"Well," Eric began. "You know how you said that every place holds the memories of what happened at that spot before?"

"Yes."

"Well..." Eric seemed at a loss for words. Anna squeezed his hand gently, encouraging him, and he continued. "All the war. All the death. All the sorrow. The earth must be weeping. Some battlefields ran red with all the blood spilt in wars." Eric shook his head. "Humans are idiots sometimes."

"No," Anna explained. "All the bad is minuscule compared to all the good, all the beauty, all the magic moments, that ever happen in each place. Modern humans have only been on the earth for a fraction of the time since it formed, billions of years ago. Yes, the horror is there, and let me tell you, horror does not only come from humans. But it is overwhelmed by all the good moments. There are some places, which, if you stand there and dwell on the battles, nightmares will appear before you, but you have to really work at it."

Anna continued walking a bit, thinking. Then: "Tell me: did you ever fight with your sister when you were kids? In the house you grew up in?"

"Well, yes, but very rarely." Eric blushed.

"But your memories of your childhood, especially the times growing up in your family home; aren't they mostly good?"

"Of course."

"You probably only remember the good parts with clarity, because there were so many of them, huh?"

"Pretty much, although there was this one time when she jumped on top of me while I was sleeping ..." Eric laughed. Anna joined in.

"Oh, you!" She chuckled.

"But I see what you mean," Eric said. "I never thought of it that way." He looked around them at the trees and clouds drifting across the dark sky. "This planet has been here for so long, gathering memories." He smiled.

"Hey guys," Lexei said, "It'll be dawn in a few hours. Eric, some incredible things are best seen at dawn. Tell him, Sis."

"Lexei is quite correct, Eric." She turned to look at him. "Would you like to see the dawn? It's been a while since I've gone to watch it. In a wild forest especially: it's magical." She smiled, remembering.

"Sure, it sounds great! But Anna: I thought vampires couldn't be out in the sunlight. Doesn't it burn you?" Eric asked.

Lexei began laughing, holding his belly.

Anna smiled. "No, Eric. That's just a myth."

"Really?" Eric's eyebrows rose, and he punched Lexei in mock anger. Lexei jumped on Eric, and the two rolled around on the grass for a few minutes. Lexei stuffed dandelions down Eric's shirt, and Eric rolled over Lexei, howling and laughing.

"Okay, cut it out, you two." Anna waited on the sidelines for them to finish, her arms crossed, right hip stuck out, a smile on her face.

"Do we have to?" Lexei asked, dirt and grass falling from where Eric had put it on his head.

Anna rolled her eyes and smiled, then turned and began walking away. The two jumped up and followed.

"Okay, seriously: Why does your family only go out after dark, then?" Eric asked.

"It's much easier to remain unseen when our wings are out, especially when we're flying," Anna explained. "The invisibility is more of a cloak, works much better at night; but aside from that, the fact remains that vampires are simply nocturnal."

"Nocturnal?"

"Yes. Ever go to a zoo and try in vain to find the tiger in the enclosure, only to be told they're nocturnal?"

Eric nodded.

"Well, if you wait until twilight, quite a lot of animals in a zoo will wake up and get very active. It's just how they are." Anna finished.

"So, sunlight?"

"Is not a radiation burn for us. Not any more than it is for you."

"Radiation burn?"

"Yes, radiation burn. Also known as a sunburn."

"You can get sunburn?"

"Well, of course." Anna smiled. "I remember one time, years ago, we were at a carnival that went on for three days. I got a bad sunburn on my shoulders. I had a sundress on, and for a while there I was so red I resembled a tomato. It was July in Cannes." She smiled, reminiscing.

"Vampires vacation in the south of France?"

"Of course. We vacation wherever we happen to be near, actually. That year, we were in Digne, and it was a warm summer. There are many secluded places in those mountains, much safer for us."

"Safe? Were you in danger?"

"Fifty years ago, yes. We moved a lot, then. We needed to stay hidden. People would attack us. We're talking pitchforks and torches." Anna grimaced.

Eric's eyebrows moved up. "Man ..."

"Hey," Lexei piped up. "Enough of this downer talk. Let's fly."

Anna chuckled. "Okay, little brother." She turned to Eric. "Come see the forest at dawn?"

"Sure."

They moved to a dark alley, transformed, and were soon in the air. Eric could see the edge of Seattle pass under him as Anna rose higher, wings barely straining. As they passed much of the city and flew out over water and toward the large redwood park, the air was sparkling and fresh. High above the earth, held safe within Anna's arms, Eric could see the faint beginnings of daybreak at the horizon, while below them, the trees were still shrouded in darkness.

Lexei gestured, and they began descending over the forest. Trees as tall as skyscrapers grew thick and deep in this nature preserve. Eric inhaled the sweet forest scent and smiled. The forest was utterly wild here, and civilization seemed a million miles away. They landed in a thicket surrounded by dozens of saplings and hundreds of trees, where the grass grew thick and wild, and sat down to wait.

It didn't take long: The sun soon changed the blackness of complete night into a dark grey shimmering air, with the magic of twilight at daybreak. They sat silently, Eric took his cues from the two vampires, who both held their wings tightly folded against their backs as they waited.

A purple-grey sparkling soon filled the forest air, and suddenly, a breeze began to blow through the trees. And creatures began to appear.

Eric watched in amazement as an assortment of paranormal life appeared before him, shimmering in the light. He saw makara, tzippa, and sprites, and many unfamiliar forms, skittering on the ground and flickering through the air. Some of the creatures floating on the air came down to twirl around the saplings, dancing with joy. He was speechless as he watched, and the vampires next to him watched in silence as well, just as mesmerized.

Eric noticed that the creatures were only truly visible in the half-light present just at this time. If he looked down at the darker ground, the creatures would change from visible to nearly invisible, distinguished by little more than the sparkles and shadows that followed in their wake. Up higher, in the brighter air, the crowds of flittering paranormals disappeared entirely. He could tell they were still there, but as one sprite he focused on rose in the air, it seemed to disappear as it passed into the brighter light. The sunshine was camouflaging them, Eric realized in amazement.

Anna stood and began walking into the clearing, arms at her side. Eric rose but remained where he was, as did Lexei. As Anna stepped among the magical creatures, she lifted her arms and began to sing, trilling a wordless tune that was both soft and beautiful. The creatures were drawn to her, and landed on her arms to listen.

She looked back at Eric and motioned with her eyes for him to come. Eric stepped slowly forward and stood next to Anna. Lexei joined them, and the two vampires stood there, arms raised, both now singing to the forest. As Eric watched, he could see streams of pale morning light filtering through the trees in stripes; and magic, electric and incredible, sparkling in the air, almost purple.

Eric focused on Anna's arms, which now carried dozens of small creatures, crowding in together and settling down, looking calmed, as if in a trance. Anna continued singing for some minutes, until the sun shone brighter, and the creatures were asleep. As the sunlight descended through the trees, Eric saw the little animals disappear, although he knew they were still sitting on her arms.

Anna herself looked odd in the sunlight. Her skin looked especially pale and translucent, almost ethereal. Her lips darkened, and her tongue appeared bright red as she sang. She finally quieted, her song drawing to a close, and as the last notes fell from her mouth, she walked back to the shadows beneath a thick copse of trees, where the sunlight had not yet reached.

As she crouched there, she was plunged in darkness again, and the creatures on her arms appeared once more. She bent and leaned against the thicket's side, and they reluctantly hopped down and ambled off into the woods, scattering in all directions.

One small creature, looking like a tiny squirrel with six legs and two tails, seemed reluctant. Its fur was a soft light brown, and its ears and eyes were huge. It avoided Anna's eyes and wandered up to her shoulder, where it sat under her ear, pulling the vampire's long hair over it like a blanket. It sat there, and watched them from under Anna's face, half hidden in her hair, and chittered at them.

"I am sorry, little one." Anna said. The creature chittered softly some more.

Eric dug in his pocket and brought out a half-eaten granola bar, holding it out to the little paranormal. The creature fixed its eyes on it, watching Eric. Anna reached up and pulled her hair to the side, exposing the little furling, and Eric moved closer with the treat.

Slowly, reluctantly, the magical creature came out from atop Anna's shoulder and walked down to the treat to smell it. Eyes went wide, little paws grasped the treat and, chittering at them, it scampered down her hand and off into the forest, tightly clutching the granola bar. Anna smiled and rose, and walked down to where Lexei waited with a smile.

"I wasn't sure if he was going to let you go." He chuckled.

"You might have had a new pet to take home," Eric smiled.

"He wouldn't be happy in the city," Anna said. "Not enough grubs in rotten logs for him to find."

"Anna, that was amazing," Eric said.

"The crowd you saw included makara and tzippa like the ones we saw in the city park, but also sabbiors, twelling and rabaniffe, as well as some new ones even I didn't recognize. They are all part of the natural life of the planet. Each has families, homes, and adventures of their own. To the mundane world, and most human eyes, they are invisible."

"I see that now. It was incredible how they were most visible in the half-light of twilight. Just incredible." Eric realized Anna had been right about the magic and the good outweighing the bad.

"All the wonders and beauty everywhere dwarf the bad. All life, all creation, all Wild Magic, overwhelms every place, takes it over, makes it its own." Anna smiled, hugging herself.

"It's so extreme and different from the world of human civilization," Eric said. "If they knew of this, they'd try to control it, cage it, and would eventually kill it, I think."

"Most people only see the moments that are so huge and overwhelming, that they catch their attention, and so most people miss the quiet moments of everyday magic that happen, that overwhelm the bad with good, with Wild Magic," Anna said.

Lexei spoke then. "I think most humans are angry about what they think is their mortality, and so they try to shape nature into their own thing." He looked down at the forest floor around them. "But nature laughs and goes back to its original plan, and mankind fails." Lexei looked up again at them. "But what man doesn't know, hell, isn't even aware of, is how all the beauty and magic of life, of everything, remains."

Anna nodded. "It stays in each place. Even the beauty that humans create and the good that humans do, it all stays. So, without realizing it, human beings are immortal, as is everything." She smiled at Eric. "Nothing is ever lost. And all the beauty and magic that's ever been can be found again, if you have eyes that see."

"And the magical creatures that we saw?" Eric asked. "They are part of that Wild Magic?"

Anna nodded, hugging Eric.

"And the cool thing is, they're all still here, all around us," Lexei looked pleased. They began walking down a slope, and Lexei slid a bit, tilting sideways and sliding down the forest undergrowth with the skill of a professional surfer. He used his wings to stabilize his decent, extending them here and there where he needed to.

At the bottom of the small hill they walked farther, enjoying the forest morning, talking and walking and bonding. Anna fell silent after a few minutes, looking around as they walked, smelling, listening.

"You okay, Babe?" Eric asked quietly, letting Lexei walk on ahead.

"Yes, I just..." Anna looked around again and tilted her head, sensing something. "Something seems off."

"Anna, Eric, look here," Lexei had stopped and was crouching down looking at something under a large manzanita bush.

Eric and Anna ran to him. "Don't touch it," Anna cautioned.

Under the large bush, the leaves and grasses looked withered and black. The area reeked of dead things and the decay of rancid graves.

"I've never seen anything like this," Anna said as she knelt by the area.

"It smells as if the land here has been dead for a long time," Lexei said.

"But that bush is growing nearby," Eric wondered. "What could do something like that?"

"Whatever happened here, I think it happened recently," Anna looked at the bush. "It's just now spreading to the bush. Look. It's killing it." Part of the trunk of the manzanita bush was red, but farther down it was turning dark, and near the ground, not a foot from the withered blackened area, the burnt swath reached up to the wood of the bush, like acid spreading after a spill.

"It's almost like something radioactive was lying here and brushed up against that bush," Eric said.

Anna rose to her feet. "This does not bode well." She looked around and brushed her hands off.

"I don't like this at all," Lexei murmured, still staring at the blackened forest floor.

After dropping Eric at his apartment, Anna and Lexei returned to the house on Mercer Island and found Alix still sleeping, dark circles under her eyes. Anna brewed more tea from the pods while Lexei sat with Alix, looking worried. As Anna returned with the healing fluid, Alix opened her eyes.

"Mama, how are you feeling?" Anna asked as she dipped tea into Alix's mouth. Groaning, Alix moved her lips, but her children could not make out what she was saying. Straining her neck, she gulped the tea and tried to communicate with them, but she was too weak and fell back onto her pillow, exhausted.

"Well, I think her bones have fused, that's good," Lexei said quietly.

"I am glad. It was so scary when that monster ..." it was too horrible for Anna to articulate what Rasputin had done to their mother. Anna finished spooning the liquid into Alix's mouth and propped her mother up on some pillows. Lexei grabbed Alix behind the arms, and they soon had their mother sitting up in bed.

"Mama, we saw the strangest sign in the far redwood forest this morning," Lexei began.

"There was a spot on the forest floor that was blackened and withered, like it had been burned with radiation," Anna chimed in.

Alix's eyes widened. Trying to speak, she finally gave up, and Lexei brought her a pad of paper and a pencil. She wrote: "Tell me more."

They both described what they'd seen, relating how the dead forest patch had crept up into part of the bush.

"We'd taken Eric out to see the dawn paranormals, and we were walking in the forest."

"It was just after the sun rose, but it was in a darker area where the sun had yet to hit."

"I don't think that part of the undergrowth would ever get much sunlight anyway."

"It smelled like a rancid tomb, Mama. It was a horrid smell."

"It smelled of rotted animal decay, or something."

Alix looked alarmed. She wrote: "Oh no! Your father and I saw something like this once, in the Black Forest. In a remote cave, we found an old animal den filled with rotted carcasses; it had been there for hundreds of years."

Back at the cemetery, the creature had tunneled under the large lichen-covered boulder it had napped on, and now nothing was visible but a large, partially caved-in den hole. The dugout looked like a badger den, with pulled-up weeds and undergrowth across the opening to camouflage the hiding place. The creature was more comfortable waiting in the dark. Because it shared the earth with an old cemetery, the soil was partially rancid, and the creature found itself sniffing and then tunneling down a few feet more, eventually breaking through the side of an old wooden coffin. As it settled to wait, it gnawed on a femur, chewing off the dried-out flesh and cloth that covered the bone.

NIGHTMARE

The clock moved silently toward 3 a.m. as Eric slept; Jinx lay at his side, washing himself. The moon shone into the room through a break in the clouds, playing across the bed in patches. Just then, a large shadow passed in front of the window, interrupting Jinx's relaxed and contented.

The cat gave a start, his paws spreading and gripping the bed as he swung his head toward the window. Curtains obscured his sight, but a shadow was falling where a minute ago the moonlight had been cascading in, bright and strong. Jinx stared, eyes wide and unblinking, irises wide so that his eyes looked nearly black, the hair on the back of his spine rising in alarm. A low growl came from the back of Jinx's throat, and he hissed, ears going back.

On the bed, Eric's eyebrows pursed in concern as he slept, and he moaned in his sleep. Tossing and turning to his side, he seemed to be in a nightmare. Jinx turned to stare at his human, then turned back to the window behind the curtain.

A scratch sounded, like a claw slowly dragged down a pane of glass. Jinx hissed again, back arched and ears flattening again. The scratching stopped, and Jinx waited.

Slowly the cat rose up and, fur standing on end, stepped toward the window. Eric mumbled something in his sleep and tossed again, and the sheet wrapped around his legs further.

Jinx slowly stepped across the bed to the window, his steps slow and measured. Ears back, his tail puffed up like a bottlebrush, the cat approached the window. He sensed incredible danger there, and fought the urge to run out of the room and behind the chair. But his human lay sleeping on the bed, and that was Jinx's pet. He would not abandon Eric without a fight.

As he reached the edge of the curtain, Jinx could see the shadow on the other side of the curtain shift again. Jinx hissed in warning, then growled again, ears flat against his head, hissing once more in warning to the nightmare that lay beyond. He did not part the curtain to see what it was, but stayed frozen on the bed, his arched back a shield between the curtain and Eric.

There was a loud thump against the window glass, and Jinx jumped straight up, landed and scrambled for footing, half off the side of the bed. Looking away, he saw Eric's eyes open wide as he suddenly awoke.

"AHH! ... Wha?" Eric rubbed his eyes, his heart beating rapidly in response to the nightmare from which he'd been startled awake. As he fumbled for the light, Jinx saw the shadow leave the window and moonlight flood the area again. Zipping his head between the curtains, Jinx could just see the black thing that had threatened the household flee around the corner and down the hill. Just then, Eric found the lamp switch and flipped on the light, flooding the room with illumination that turned the hillside dark for Jinx.

Anna walked into class and sat down next to Eric. A week had passed since they'd visited the forest, and as they worked on new sketches, they talked.

Eric glanced at her. "You okay? You look worried."

"I am worried," Anna said, biting her lip. She leaned over to whisper in his ear. "Mama's recovery is not progressing very well."

Eric's eyes grew wide as he looked at her. "What do you mean?"

"She should be mostly healed by now, but she's still so weak she walks with difficulty," Anna sketched in a dark moon on her canvas. Leaning over again, she murmured,

"We ran out of the tea yesterday, and today she looked worse."

Eric looked sharply at Anna. "The pods?"

"Yes."

"What are we going to do?"

"Lexei and I've been talking. We're going to go back. We're going to get more."

"You're kidding?" Eric looked astonished.

"No, I'm completely serious."

"But I thought you said you sealed that tomb so no one could ever get back in," Eric asked.

"I did," Anna sketched in some clouds, shading with white charcoal pencils. "But we still have the runestone."

"You do? I thought you got rid of it."

"Lexei and I decided we couldn't just throw it away. It is priceless, and very powerful."

"So, where's it been?" Eric began broad vertical strokes, filling in what looked like moonlight through a window.

"It's in our vault at Gringotts Bank, in Diagon Alley."

Eric looked sideways at Anna, who looked back innocently. After a minute, he said, "What?"

Anna laughed. "Just kidding. We have it stored in our basement. It's protected. But I can use it to open a new tesseract. We can go through, get some more pods, and be back in an hour. It can't be helped. Mama needs more medicine. She's not getting better. And she was, with those pods."

Eric nodded. "Can I see your mother tonight?" he whispered.

Anna bit her lip. "Yes."

Eric took her hand and squeezed it, then turned back to finish his sketch. Anna filled in more broad strokes on hers as well. After five minutes, Eric spoke again.

"You know, last night was freaky."

"Really?"

"Yes. I was asleep, and I swore something banged against my window. It woke me up, nearly scared me half to death."

"Was it Jinx?"

"No. Jinx was freaked out as well. He was on the bed with me, and nearly fell off, he was so scared," Eric filled in more on his sketch. "It didn't help that I was having a terrible nightmare at the time."

"A nightmare?"

"It was surreal. I was at the bottom of a huge empty room, a box really, and the only way out was a tiny door at the top, at least fifty feet up. No other windows or doors." Eric shifted on his stool. "The horror of it was, the longer I looked up at the door, the farther away it was. The feeling was of flooding, intense horror at the situation." Eric shuddered.

Anna leaned over and hugged him, rubbing his back, trying to soothe him.

"And then the big bang at my window. Plus the cat freaking out. I mean, Jinx did one of those startles where he flips backward and up. Totally unexpected."

"Man."

"Yeah, a real fun time last night. You totally missed it." Eric grinned at her sideways and reached for a grey charcoal stick.

————————————————>≈≉≋≈≋≉≈<————————————————

The creature slumbered, a nightmare in the hole, cradling the corpse's femur like a baby.

TESSERACT

Eric looked down at the former tsarina of Imperial Russia, noting the dark smudges under her eyes, and the weak smile she gave him. Her eyes were half closed in pain, and the skin of her face and neck was so pale it looked translucent. Gypsy lay by her side, purring deeply and kneading against her, while Alix's fingers caressed the cat absentmindedly.

"Eric, dear one," Alix whispered, barely audible, "how are you?"

Eric knelt beside the bed and took Alix's hand in both of his. "I'm just fine," he smiled at her. "Everyone's fine. We're just worried about you, that's all," he whispered.

Eric studied her injuries. Alix's ravaged face was pale, and the black and blue bruises had faded to green and yellow. The holes where Rasputin's fangs had pierced her to the bone had closed into dimpled, scarred skin. She smiled at him weakly.

"How are you feeling, Alix?" Eric asked, patting her blanket in place worriedly.

"I'm fine, really." Alix struggled to move her head, finally raising it off the pillow and lowering it again. It was obvious she was weak as a kitten. "Just need to sleep some more." She closed her eyes.

Eric rubbed her hand gently in his palms, thinking about what Anna had planned. He studied the Empress's face as her eyes slid shut. He watched her until her breathing slowed to an even, quiet rhythm and fell asleep. They all retreated to the outer room, Lexei closing the door carefully behind them.

Once in the living room, Eric turned to the vampires. "Maybe you're right. She looks bad."

"She is very weak; her body is still struggling to heal itself."

"We need to leave at once, and return quickly." Lexei looked ready to fly.

"Are we all going?" Eric asked. "Can she stay here alone?"

"We will seal her in. No one will be able to enter. We can seal the house so that no one will even know it's there," Anna paced. "The only danger will be if none of us returns. She would be sealed in forever."

"That's not going to happen; you know that Anna," Lexei said, determined. "Let's go and get this over with." He looked at his sister. "You have the stone?"

She indicated her leather pack. "Right here. And I know what to do. Mother showed me weeks ago, just in case."

"Then let's go."

———————◦◦◦◦◦———————

They landed at the far end of the cemetery and swiftly made their way to the side where the old crypt lay.

"This will have to be fast, in and out." Anna studied both men's faces. "You both understand?"

"Yes," Eric nodded.

"Yes, let's do this."

"Okay," Anna walked to the lee side of the crypt. "The inner entry is closed, but this hillside is the other side of where Mama opened the tesseract before. It is already charged with magic." She knelt and dug into the leaves and dirt, burrowing a few feet into the side of the hill before hitting the old concrete of the crypt's outer wall. She pulled the artifact from the leather pouch at her side, holding it with thumbtip and forefinger as if it were white hot, and carefully placed it in a flat depression she'd formed with her digging.

Anna stood back and began to inscribe an intricate glyph in the air before the wall. After a minute, the runestone began to glow. Anna continued wielding her magic, chanting in a low voice, words that Eric heard and immediately forgot. A purple glow sprang up from the old runestone and formed the doorway, before going blank again. A shimmering was visible on the outer edges of the tesseract if he looked at it out of the corners of his eyes; otherwise, the night was dark and the cemetery quiet.

An owl hooted down below them. Anna turned toward the sound, her eyebrows pursed in distracted worry.

"Come on," Lexei whispered.

Glancing at Eric and nodding, Anna stepped through into the past one more time. Eric followed her, and then Lexei went through last.

Down underground in the grave it had dug itself into, not fifty feet from the tesseract the vampires had opened in the side of the hill, the creature's eyes popped open. They glowed with an unearthly yellow-green light, still rimmed with blood-red. Its heart began to beat more rapidly than it had in centuries. Moving its limbs, stiff with cold from its underground slumber, it slowly began to crawl out of the hole in which it had taken shelter.

Anna landed in a wet spot, in the lowlands of the ancient past. Splashing up the embankment, she reached down and pulled the others up as they came through. They gathered to get their bearings and spotted a dark swath of charred vegetation running past them. "Look here," she indicated. They cut through the forest and walked up to the burned path that Zrandengthalull had burned to eradicate Rasputin. It looked fresh.

"I think we've landed in the right spot, and at the right time," Lexei said as he studied the charred earth.

"You mean we might not have?" Eric sounded worried.

"Well, it's not an exact science," Anna explained.

"I heard of a magician who went back through a tesseract, and then tried to return to that spot, but ended up on an entirely different continent," Lexei said grimly.

"A different continent?"

"Yes, well, it was the same spot, but at a different time, a completely different time," Lexei said. "The continents move, you know. If you wait long enough."

"Let's find the pods, guys." Anna began hunting through the underbrush, and the men joined her in the search.

The graveyard was black as night and quiet as only the dead can be. Clouds scuttled across the sky, dancing in front of the moon, creating shadowy splotches that raced across the graveyard. The huge lichen-covered boulder shone white and grey in the uneasy light. Down below it, out from an indentation where the dirt had fallen in, a dead white, clawed hand began to dig itself out. Soon, another hand joined it, and the creature dug and scrambled and finally stuck its nightmarish mottled white head out of the ground. It soon pulled its body out, extricating itself from the grave it had tunneled into, discarding the femur it had been gnawing on, and crouched there in the half light, shaking the dirt off its back like a mangy cur. Sniffing the air, it soon sensed the open tesseract, and began scuttling toward the opening the others had gone through not five minutes earlier. It began breathing in ragged excitement as it moved, the wait of millions of years now almost over.

Anna, Lexei and Eric had moved almost a hundred feet from the other end of the tesseract, searching in vain for the pods to make the medicine to save Alix. Lexei was growing more and more frustrated. This was supposed to have been a ten-minute trip through the doorway, and instead it was becoming long search. Where were the damn things?

"Why can't we find any?" Lexei straightened up and stretched his back. "Anna, do you remember where Zran pulled them from?"

"I wish I did, my brother."

"Hey, maybe it was farther up the trail, on higher ground," Eric said from under a bush where he was crouched, looking. He backed out of the bush, brushed off his knees, and stood up.

"Actually, they were down the other side of the hill," said Zrandengthalull from behind them.

"Zran!" Lexei ran to hug the dragon, managing to wrap his arms around one toe.

Chuckling, the Dragon Lord stuck the tip of his tongue out and ran it up Lexei's back, nearly knocking him over. "How are you, little one?"

Lexei straightened, grinning from ear to ear.

"Not so good, Lord Dragon," Anna said. "Mother is not doing well. We need more pods to make the medicine tea with."

"Oh. Well then, hold on here, littlelings, I will go get some."

Eric dug in his coat. "Here, you can fill this." He handed the dragon a net bag that expanded when filled.

"Good idea, Sir Wallace." The dragon flew off.

"Let's go back to the portal and wait there, so we can leave and return to Mother that much sooner." Anna said. They began to hike back the way they'd come. They chatted as they walked, for the first half, then: "Wait. Shhh." Anna held her arm out to stop Eric and Lexei from moving forward. She ducked behind a huge tree, motioning them to join her.

Through the trees they could see a horde of shetani gathered at the doorway, attracted by the magic. Most were of the smaller sort, about the size of a man or smaller, but there were three that looked larger than giraffes. They were all blacker than the blackest night; their razor-sharp teeth chittered as they moved, and claws as long as human fingers dug into the wet dirt.

Backing away, Anna, Lexei and Eric retreated a dozen yards to hide behind a large copse of trees to discuss strategy.

"I really don't feel like killing all of them."

"Why don't we just wait for Zran to return?"

"He'll definitely scatter them; then we can go through."

"Okay. We wait."

Their eyes wandered over everything around them as they sat waiting. Eric pulled a purple flower from its stalk and began examining it closely.

<hr />

The creature made its way to the edge of the top of the cemetery hill and began its descent down the side, sliding on the underbrush as it went. Scrambling over dead leaves, sensing the source of the magic's emanation, it finally reached the tesseract. Crouched before it, nearly delirious as it inhaled the magic streaming from the portal, the creature shuddered, raising itself up on two legs, its eyes half closed in ecstasy. A rivulet of dark urine ran down its leg as it stood there. Then, resolute, it crouched and sprang, launching itself through the doorway and into the past.

Exploding through the doorway into the ancient forest, it landed in the thick of the shetani horde. The nightmarish shetani fell back in surprise at the newcomer, then, sensing what it was that had arrived in their midst, most of them screamed and scattered, fleeing in terror.

The three left, the larger shetani, were farther back than the rest had been. Startled, feeling waves of fear at this monster that had popped through the tesseract, they paused. They were not used to fleeing from many things. This creature was definitely not a dragon. The closest shetani tentatively approached the pale creature, which was crouched three feet in front of the doorway, dazed and studying its surroundings. The shetani towered above the creature, and lowered its nightmarish mouth, muscles rippling as it moved, and sniffed the creature that had just come through the portal.

So quickly no eye could follow it, moving purely on instinct, without thinking, the creature swung its head toward the shetani and bit, then turned to face the other remaining shetani. Black blood sprayed across the area. The shetani's huge head and long neck lay where it had fallen, severed from its body, which lay twitching a half-dozen feet away. The head had a surprised look on its face. It had not seen its death coming, and was just becoming aware of it, as consciousness faded from its brain.

The other two large shetani turned and ran, fleeing without thinking.

"Did you hear that?" Lexei's head rose from where it had been down, studying a plant he'd been examining.

"Uh ..." Anna looked disconcerted.

"I'll check it out," Eric got to his feet.

The creature, still crouched from where it had killed the large shetani, jerked its head sideway, listening. Fear rippled down its back, fear it had not felt for a long, long time. Fear of ancient things best not disturbed.

Across the forest, Zrandengthalull flew overhead, approaching the area, clutching pods and tubers in his arms.

The pale creature sensed the massive dragon approaching, and its heartbeat raced so fast it threatened to burst out of its thin, white chest. A hormonal cascade flooded its sympathetic nervous system, and without the ability to even think about it, the creature let out a supersonic scream in fear and jumped back through the tesseract, fleeing into the night, down the cemetery hill and across the marsh toward the lights of Seattle.

———————◄━━━━►———————

"What the heck was that?" Lexei jumped at the thing's scream, then swung around as Zrandengthalull landed next to them, and dropped his armload on the ground.

"Okay, here is your bag of pods, Mistress," the Dragon Lord handed the net bag bulging with a dozen pods to Anna, who took it gratefully, cradling the precious medicine in her arms.

"And here," the dragon indicated the items on the ground. "These are the roots of the trees the pods come from. If you grind them into a paste, and cook them, they are a stronger concentration of medicine than even the pods. Be careful, though."

"Careful?" Anna asked. "You mean don't overdose on them?

"Well, being a natural substance, you can give her bowls full morning and night. But if she gets too much, she might get sick," the dragon said. "When I was a fledgling, my mother dosed me with it, and I ate too much and ended up befouling our nest through voiding. She had to clear everything out."

"Ah," Lexei smiled. "Gotcha. Too much can give you the runs."

"Explosively."

"Sir Dragon, we are once again in your debt," Anna bowed, clutching the bag of pods.

Eric helped Lexei gather up the tubers, and they said their goodbyes.

Zrandengthalull walked them to the doorway, sniffing at the dead shetani next to it. "Hmmm, looks like something happened here while I was gone."

"We heard several screams and animals scrambling around, but decided to stay back out of sight," Anna explained.

"Probably wise," the dragon said, sweeping away the bloody leaves and dirt to make a clean path for them. "It was good to see you again, my friends. I am glad to help. Tell Madam I wish her well."

"I will," beamed Lexei. "I will miss you, Zran."

"And I you, little one," the dragon said fondly. "Do not worry, these pods and tubers will be just the thing your mother needs. I know she will be feeling much better very soon."

Lexei smiled and stepped through the tesseract to his own time, Eric and Anna close behind.

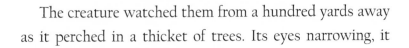

The creature watched them from a hundred yards away as it perched in a thicket of trees. Its eyes narrowing, it studied Lexei and Anna with Eric as they launched themselves into the sky on huge black wings, flying south. After a minute, the creature jumped into the sky itself, pale white wings looking spotted with disease and age, and followed them.

———————————⟩⟨———————————

The wind whipped and buffeted Eric's face so hard he had to close his eyes, as the vampire siblings flew faster than they ever had before to their home on Mercer Island. Spurred on by the desire to see Alix well again, they arrived in a matter of minutes.

Eric and Lexei immediately set to work in the kitchen, cleaning and grinding the tubers into a mash. They added blood, then decided to fry the fragrant substance into delectable brown, crispy tidbits; hoping to entice Alix to eat as much as possible. Eric brewed the dragon's medicinal tea as Lexei cooked the tuber mash mixture while Anna kept Alix company with Gypsy. The house was soon filled with a delicious smell, and treats lay piling up on a plate next to a mug of steaming hot tea, which Anna carried to the bedroom and began spooning into Alix's mouth. The medicine worked quickly, and Alix's eyes were open and alert by the time Lexei and Eric brought in the food. They all sat around her as she ate.

"These are delicious," Alix murmured between bites.

"Hopefully they will heal you without upsetting your vampire digestion too much," Lexei said. "I added plenty of blood to them before frying."

Alix reached for another and began chewing. "Mmmm."

Alix stayed in bed for another nine days, drinking the tea infused with blood, and eating the tuber mash mixed with blood, prepared in a dozen different ways. Anna and Lexei stayed with her, only leaving in shifts to feed. Gypsy spent most of the time sleeping against her recovering mistress, purring madly, and Alix had one hand on the cat most of the time. The cat's presence was helping the healing process.

Eric was there more than he wasn't, keeping watch and helping prepare the medicines so that Alix had round-the-clock care and infusions of the Dragon Lord's tinctures. At the end of the nine days she was strong and nearly back to normal, and Anna decided she would go on a walk with Eric.

In a tall tree about fifty feet from the Romanov house, the creature held on to the topmost branches; perched there, swaying and watching the house with intelligent eyes. After waiting nine days a hundred feet up the large tree, feeding off of stray birds and squirrels, it was ready to move. As Eric and Anna left and began walking toward town, the creature's eyes followed them with interest and intent. It began scrambling clumsily down the tree, stiff from not moving for so long, falling more than climbing down, tumbling over each branch, making so much noise the animals around it scattered and fled.

SAVAGE

Eric and Anna walked slowly hand in hand, talking and laughing for several miles, savoring the time alone together. They stopped under a streetlamp near the park and stood there, kissing softly. It began to drizzle, but they didn't notice at all, and a fine mistiness settled on their hair as they kissed. A car drove past them and slowed, the passengers leaning out and hooting something at the couple, and still they continued kissing. After some long minutes, when the rain threatened to deepen into a downpour, they parted lips and turned to run, laughing as they went.

Pushing open the door of Lestat's, they stopped to brush off the rain and laughed and kissed as they made their way to the same corner table they always sat at.

"Eric! Anna! What'll it be?"

"The same, Bob," Eric called.

Anna laughed as she took her coat off, draping it across the back of her chair. "I am in such a good mood, Eric." She smiled.

"Me too. I just know Alix will be okay now."

Outside, crouched atop a nearby building, the creature watched the coffee shop door and waited. Rain dripped down its back, but it didn't notice. Its eyes were on Eric and Anna through the glass. Unblinking and unwavering, it stared. After a minute, its mouth opened slightly and it began to pant.

Alix drank two more mugs of brewed tea and ate five more of the fried tuber paste, as she sat in bed talking with Lexei as Gypsy purred by her side.

"Tell me again about the attack," she said, sipping more tea and petting the soft purring kitty absentmindedly.

"Well, it was Rasputin, as I said, and he was crazy, as usual. He jumped on you and bit your face and tried to rip your head off," Lexei explained.

Alix reached up to touch the puckered and scarred skin on the edge of her face. "Oh," tears appeared in her eyes. Gypsy's purrs deepened.

"Mama, you're alive. That's all that matters."

"But imagine if he'd succeeded," Alix's face went white. "You children would be alone. Alone." She stared off into space, lost in thought. "The world is such a cold, cold place ..." She yawned.

"You are healing well now, thank goodness." He ran his hand down the cat's back as he spoke.

"Thanks to this wonderful tea. Thank you, Lexei; all of you, for getting it for me." She yawned again.

Lexei rose, kissed his mother's forehead and went to brew more tea. Standing in the kitchen, waiting for the pods to steep in hot water, he sighed, closing his eyes. Gypsy came out of the bedroom and jumped onto the counter, arching her back and rubbing against Lexei's arm. He absentmindedly ran his hand over the cat's back. The kitchen was quiet and still, and silence permeated the entire house. Lexei fished the pod out of the teapot and tossed it into the trash, then poured his mother a cup of tea, adding a quarter-cup of blood to the large mug.

Suddenly, Gypsy froze, a low growl sounding deep in her throat. Lexei froze as well. Gypsy's back arched, her hair standing on end, and she turned to face the locked front door. Lexei felt the hairs on the back of his neck lift straight up as he stared at the Gypsy, and then at the door. His heartbeat quickened, and his breaths came short and fast. After a moment of thought, he closed his eyes, concentrated, and his teeth grew out, claws appeared at the ends of his fingers, and huge black wings sprang out of his back, banging into the kitchen cupboards behind him.

At this sound, Gypsy jumped straight up, whirling to look behind her, and Lexei jumped as well. Then both swung back to stare at the front door again. Gypsy, on the ground now, walked stiff-legged around the counter to the hallway facing the front door, and hissed again. Lexei hissed along with her.

Wind and rain beat at the windows, and the lights flickered as the electricity threatened to go out. Excitement and energy charged down Lexei's back as he stared at the door. Gypsy spat and began growling once again, her tone rising and falling as she sounded her warning.

There was a thump on the door so loud it rattled on its hinges. Gypsy jumped and hissed. Lightning flashed and the electricity promptly went out.

"Oh, brother," mumbled Lexei, feeling foolish.

Gypsy disagreed and hissed again and again, growling deep in her throat.

"What are you so worked up about, you silly cat?" Lexei said out loud, working to dismiss the imaginary demons freaking them both out. "It's just a storm." He lit several candles, and the cheerful light flickered against the walls of the room.

He looked again at the door. "Of course, there was that thump." He thought for a minute as Gypsy continued to growl. "Probably just a tree branch blown down by the wind."

Another loud thump against the door made both vampire and cat jump a foot. Lexei hit his head on the wall, his wings banging against the ceiling. Feeling foolish now, Lexei grimaced. "Gypsy, I'm going to go look. You with me?"

The sleek black cat walked behind Lexei's legs and hissed again. "Confused? I don't blame you." Lexei took a deep breath, glanced back at the hallway to his mother's bedroom, and heard nothing. "She must have fallen asleep." Turning back to the front door, which stood mute and inscrutable, Lexei walked decisively forward, reached out, and grasped the doorknob. With one last look at Gypsy, he turned the knob and flung open the door.

Blowing rain hit Lexei's face, and lightning lit up the figure on the doormat momentarily. Lexei studied the man standing there, not believing what he saw.

Anna and Eric talked in low tones as they huddled close at Lestat's; between kisses, they gazed into each other's eyes, as they waited for the rain to subside. They held hands, fingers playing together in fondness and flirtation.

"Eric, thank you for all your help with Mama," Anna reached over and kissed Eric gently again, bringing her hand up to caress his cheek.

"Mmmm," Eric said, kissing her back. "It was my pleasure." They kissed some more, then, "Anna," Eric murmured.

"Mmm?" Anna said through the kiss, unwilling to take her lips from Eric's.

"Do you want to ..."

"Mmmm?

"Want to go back to my place? I think the rain's letting up a bit."

Anna smiled, nodding, and jumped up from the chair. Eric smiled, holding her hand, and they waved at Bob as they headed out the door.

The creature dozed on and off, waiting. Its eyes flew open as it sensed movement, and it watched as Anna and Eric emerged, laughing, from the coffee shop, arm in arm. Narrowing its eyes, it began to follow them, staying in the shadows, nearly invisible to the naked eye. If any bystanders happened to look directly at it, they would not have seen it. Only movement seen from the corner of the eye would have revealed anything, and then, only shadow and rain. But the creature was there. And it tracked the two lovers as they walked.

Eric held Anna close as they strolled, and the rain gradually diminished to a light patter the farther they walked. The streetlights shone in the wet street, and the traffic lights made a merry sight with reds, greens and yellows.

"Let's go through the park," Anna murmured, inhaling the clean, crisp air. "I love this smell." She closed her eyes and inhaled deeply again, smiling.

"Mmm, it is refreshing," Eric said, his arm around her, holding her close.

They ambled down the lane and up the path into the park, lost in each other.

Behind them, about fifty feet back, the pale creature darted from shadow to shadow, stalking them, tracking them the way a panther tracks a deer in the jungle. Deadly claws grasped the bushes and trees as it went, at one point almost alerting them to its presence.

Anna stopped and half turned, asking Eric, "Did you hear that?"

Backing off, it felt relieved when they entered the cover of the park, and it could take to the trees.

Eric and Anna wandered through the park, kissing and touching, until they found themselves in the remote clearing they had dubbed "our spot." Eric turned, and held Anna's face in his palms, gazing into her eyes with love and heat. Anna's face radiated the same feelings, and they were soon lost in each other, kissing passionately as they leaned against a tall tree.

Eric kissed Anna's neck, trailing kisses down and back, underneath her ear. Gasping and shivering with pleasure, Anna let her head fall back and to the side, to give Eric better access. She felt glorious shivers travel down her spine, and gasped. Eric's arms held her close, reaching around her back and holding her steady as her head dipped back. He curled over her, drunk with the heady sensations of loving her. Anna's breath became rougher as her excitement grew.

<hr/>

The creature approached, flitting from tree trunk to tree trunk, zeroing in on the couple kissing in the clearing. Pausing momentarily, it closed its eyes and inhaled deeply, smelling the pheromones pouring off the amorous couple as they kissed. It smelled vampire, and it wanted to kill Anna. Deep, passionate, vengeful hate filled its chest as it watched them. Anger swelled in the creature's heart until it felt blood rush into its head in a roar. Its breath quickened and its mouth opened, and drool dripped to the ground below, sizzling and burning the leaves and grass black where it touched.

It had waited over a million years for this moment, and it had been insane before the wait began. Its pale, splotched white face watched them, its eyes blood red with yellow irises, brows narrowing and sharp brown teeth clenching and grinding together in hate. It crept forward a few more steps.

Gathering itself, legs and haunches poised, it wriggled its body like a cat in anticipation, then sprang, mouth and claws opened and sharp, letting out a deafening scream as it launched itself through the air at the lovers.

It landed on Eric's back, it claws digging into his side and piercing to the bone, sticking into Eric's ribs like sharp knives. Its open mouth. filled with jagged teeth. clamped down simultaneously on Eric's shoulder, sinking in and locking in place.

Eric cried out and fell to the ground, Anna under him. Her eyes were close to the creature's face locked onto Eric's shoulder, and she focused on it, letting out a horrified scream when she realized what had attacked them.

The creature, latched onto Eric with teeth and claws, fell to the ground with him. Growling deep in its pale throat, it peered over Eric's shoulder as it bit, and saw Anna. Horror and revelation filled the creature's mind as it locked eyes with Anna, and ancient emotions of glee and heartache flooded its consciousness. Hearing her scream in horror, its mind cringed, and the last string of hope fled along with the last tiny shred of sanity it had left.

THE END AND THE BEGINNING

Lexei was sitting in the bedroom, chatting with the newcomer when he felt a psychic surge of fear and horror from his sister. "Mother!" His face blanched as he swung around in horror.

Alix had felt the same thing, and dropped the empty teacup beside her. Hurriedly, she scrambled out of bed and threw on her clothes, running out to join Lexei. They both ran up to the roof, the newcomer joining them. Wings out, they sprang into the air and flew faster than they ever had through the clouds and down through the trees, to the place where Anna's psychic scream still echoed.

Had anyone looked up in the split-second the vampires were overhead, they would have seen nothing more than three streaks of black, one larger than the rest, flying faster than a jet plane to the park.

They were there in seconds.

———————— >≈❄✦✦≈< ————————

Anna, awash with horror, struggled out from under Eric, who had lost consciousness, buffeted by the waves of fear that had emanated from the creature as it pierced his skin. Springing up, Anna released her vampire aura with such force that the trees around her blew backward several yards, as if a bomb had gone off. In an instant, she was a furious, deadly creature, a nightmare herself, something more deadly than the creature on Eric's back: She was an enraged female defending her mate.

Screaming a challenge, she reached for the thing locked onto her lover and pulled. The pain brought Eric back to consciousness, and he screamed again. The creature's claws and teeth ripped out of Eric, tearing open a dozen wounds in his sides and shoulder as the thing detached from him and rose up to meet this new challenge.

Anna hurriedly dragged Eric away from the pale creature and stood in front of him, barring its way, guarding Eric against further attack. Eric lay on the ground, bleeding, unable to speak because of the shock to his system.

There was a loud screeching as the three others arrived. They landed next to Anna, and all of them faced the creature, which crouched, panting on the ground before them.

"You have hunted us for the last time." The newcomer said. Anna's heart nearly stopped in shock as she glanced past her mother and brother and saw, standing taller than any of them, Nikolai Romanov, alive. There was a furious look on his face as he towered over the creature before them.

A garbled growl sounded, coming from the creature's mouth as it tried to speak. "Yyyyouuu ..." It rose up on two legs and screamed at them, blood spitting from its mouth. It stood as tall as Nikolai, pale splotched body mottled with scars from a hundred thousand battles it had fought through the millions of years it had lived, waiting, biding its time for this moment.

Pale, splotched wings, white and grey, tattered, rose above it as it drew itself to its full height. It was almost entirely covered with rough, ragged scar tissue from an ancient burn that had healed over, a gift from Zrandengthalull many millions of years ago. Eyes glowed yellow in blood-filled orbs as the creature that used to be Greg Ramsey hissed at them, baring its teeth and spraying diseased blood at them.

Nikolai was unimpressed by the creature before him, and rose up himself, taller and stronger, completely healed from the horrific wound Ramsey had inflicted upon him so many months ago. Strong wings spread out from Nikolai's back, blacker than the night, iridescent and shiny. Fury radiated from him like a physical force.

"You die tonight, Rasputin," Nikolai said, and jumped, launching himself at Rasputin as the pale monster who has once held an entire country under his spell lunged forward to meet him.

Screaming in challenge, ferocity in every atom of their being, Anna, Lexei and Alix jumped with Nikolai and attacked Rasputin as one.

As Nikolai and Rasputin came together, there was a fierce moment when the creature thought his old enemy would get the better of him, in a direct contrast to their battle so may months ago; but in those months, Rasputin had lived millions of years, surviving horrors that Nikolai could only have imagined, steeling himself, growing stronger. For such a one who had been flung backwards in time and trapped there, a victim of dragon fire and time, Nikolai was no match.

The crazed pale creature locked with Nikolai in battle and drove him backward. And still, Nikolai held his ground, his face furious, his anger giving him more strength than he thought possible. But the creature hung on, matching his enemy's fury with his own madness and rage.

The creature felt Anna smash full-force into his right side, biting down hard on its ribcage, tearing away chunks of its flesh as fast as she could. Blood and black gore ran freely from its side as Anna attacked over and over like a piranha, her claws hooked deep into Rasputin's flesh, hanging on tight as she attacked.

Lexei dove at Rasputin's head, and once on him, moved around to his back, attacking his enemy's wings. He tore at them with claws and fangs, ripping the huge pale flaps into shreds. Rasputin screamed in agony as Lexei dug his claws into the ancient vampire's shoulders and began pulling, intent on ripping the wings from his adversary's body. Blood began to pour from Rasputin's shoulders as the flesh parted. The creature screamed again as his exquisitely sensitive wings were torn away, and he felt the pain nearly overwhelmed him.

Alix dove at Rasputin's middle, hooked her claws on either side of its torso, and began biting at the creature's soft belly, intent on disemboweling the ancient monster. As the others attacked higher up, Alix stayed low, and, after a minute, was inside the creature. Digging with tooth and claw, she tore up Rasputin's insides, drawing out loops of fat, muscle and intestine with every swipe. Rasputin screamed again, his voice supersonic in the night air.

Their attack was weakening Rasputin, and the nightmarish creature began to thrash in panic. But it had not survived over millions of years since the dragon's attack for nothing. The pale, mottled vampire went into a berserk frenzy, its sanity gone, its mind frantic.

It began flinging its attackers off right and left. Pure rage channeled into ferocious power as the creature focused its desperation into a brutal surge of power in one last bid to kill its enemies. Anna fell off to the side with Lexei, but both jumped back onto the creature's back, screaming their own rage.

Nikolai, bitten repeatedly, kept attacking Rasputin alongside them.

After a while, the old tsar's arm was hanging nearly useless at his side, yet his attack grew more ferocious, more determined with each passing second. Alix sustained a deep blow to her back, and she stumbled momentarily before quickly healing; but she kept hold of Rasputin's torso, continuing her attack, the dead weight from her legs serving to pull her enemy down more.

The pale creature screamed again and again, fighting now for its life against the four enraged vampires it had hunted for over a century. And still it held its own against them, its strength incredible, its energy seemingly limitless.

Suddenly, Nikolai let go of Rasputin's body and grabbed his head, hooking his arms under the creature's jaws and ears. Lexei reached down and to the front and hooked his own arm around and under Nikolai's and around the front of Rasputin's neck, like a wrestler. Lexei wrapped his other arm across the creature's shoulders, bending its head down, forcing it against his other arm.

Anna and Alix dug their claws into Rasputin's shoulders and chest, trying to rip them from his head. Rasputin screamed and pulled at them with pale, wiry arms knotted with old, hard-as-steel muscles. He screamed again, tensing his neck and chest muscles, determined to hold on to his head out of sheer will and strength.

———————————◦>≈≈≈≈≈≈<◦———————————

At the edge of the clearing, Eric was regaining consciousness. He sat up, shaking his head softly, aching all over. His clothes were soaked with blood, and waves of pain rippled through his entire body. His eyes gradually focused on the incredible battle before him, and he gasped as he realized what was happening.

The vampires were knotted together on the ground, their struggle reduced to this single moment. The four of them somehow managed to hold Rasputin still, even as Rasputin, incredibly strong, fought against them and matched them, strength for strength. The Romanovs strained, digging their boots into the ground for purchase. Rasputin's head began to turn purple. Blood trickled down his neck as the skin threatened to split. But the creature's rage grew, and it held fast; and head and body did not part further.

———————————◦>≈≈≈≈≈≈<◦———————————

At the opposite edge of the clearing, drawn by the sound and stink of battle, another pair of eyes was watching. They belonged to a girl named Holly. She'd been living in the park for a month now, staying hidden from all who passed that way, observing, learning, and growing. She watched the battle with intelligent eyes now, cocking her head to the side, observing the impasse. She saw Eric wake up, and their eyes met over the huddle of fighting vampires.

Eric's eyes grew wide in surprise as he recognized the small vampire from the hillside outside his apartment.

They sat there unmoving, studying each other from across the small clearing. The vampires battling between them suddenly turned, tumbling to the side as the locked enemies tried in vain to grab any advantage.

Turning her attention back toward the battle, Holly watched as Eric crept toward the vampires, then reach out and take hold of Rasputin's feet. Pale and ghostly, the skin of the creature's feet and legs was scarred and wrinkled like melted wax, and the horned and ragged feet were sharp weapons in themselves. Eric grabbed above the creature's ankles, hooking his arms about its lower calves, then dug in his own boot heels and threw his weight back, adding his own strength to the fight.

Rasputin screamed again, weaker, voice muffled as Nikolai's and Lexei's arms held the monster's jaws closed. And still it hung on, its entire body tensed and strained, muscles bulging out, refusing to yield its head.

Holly crouched there, she recognized Rasputin as the creator of the thugs who had taken her life, and transformed her into a vampire. She cocked her head to the side as she watched them struggle, her mind working.

Then, she crept forward slowly, scuttling sideways, and reached out with one small hand. Her fangs were out, and her wings, and her sharp claws. She reached forward with her right hand, razor-sharp claw extended, and touched Rasputin's throat where it was exposed between the Romanov men's straining arms. Rasputin screamed once more, his eyes rolling with panic and fury, as Holly's claw pierced his throat.

She drew her finger across it, slicing an inch deep through tendon and muscle, providing the final breach the other vampires required to complete their intent. The slashed throat muscles, unable to hold the head on, ripped completely. The spine snapped. And Rasputin's head was pulled off with such force it was flung upward in a gentle arc, eyes opened wide in surprise as it landed in the trees behind Eric.

The vampires sprang apart, caught themselves from tumbling backward, and sat down hard. The creature's pale torso lay before them, twitching, blood pouring out of the neck in weaker and weaker spurts as Rasputin's heart finally stopped.

Rasputin's conscious mind felt the small, sharp claw pierce his neck and sever the muscles it found there, and his panic-filled heart beat even faster. As his neck tore, his mind howled one last time in agony. And as his head left his body, his eyes watched as the forest seemed to twirl before him.

His head flew high and gently turned as it made a parabolic arc through the air, and Rasputin, still aware, his mind in a total panic, felt it all. Landing among the ferns and trees a dozen feet from his body, he realized what had happened and looked over at the Romanovs. He focused on Anna, and his eyes drank in the final sight of she who had captured his heart so long ago. His mind was filled with pain, loss, and regret. The last emotion he felt as he died was sorrow.

The being that had been Grigori Rasputin felt its life fade and its soul leave the corpse it now recognized as unusable, shedding it like an old suit. It shot up into the sky, leaving the forest a hundred feet below it.

As it shed its old body, the insanity, the panic, the sorrow, the unrequited love it had endured for so long all left its mind, finally setting it free to ride the wind, to fly beyond the sky and beneath the sea. It looked out over the Seattle landscape as it rose in the air, nearly as high as the clouds.

It felt its mind fill with happiness and glee as its freed soul flew along the horizon, no longer encumbered by the trials of a bad life.

After a few minutes, all that remained were happiness and glee. Had it still possessed a mouth, it would have laughed in pure child-like joy.

FINALLY FREE

The vampires sat stunned in the clearing as Rasputin finally died. The head lay there, partially obscured by forest undergrowth, eyes wide in surprise as the six of them stared at it.

Although Rasputin's body had quickly bled out, his head remained alive for a few minutes longer. The head seemed to finally realize what had happened, its expression turning to deep sorrow.

The eyes fixated on Anna, and for a moment looked imploringly. Anna shivered as they watched, and Eric wrapped his arms around her and held her, and after a moment turning his head and shoulder to shielded her from the horror that was the fading consciousness of the head of Grigori Rasputin.

The jaw moved, trying to speak, but with no lungs to pump air through its vocal cords, it produced no sound. Its movements slowly became sluggish and lessened, until they stopped altogether. The eyes remained open, but glazed over. Muscles relaxed, the face went blank, and the head rolled slightly to the side, finally dead.

There was a space of a heartbeat or two as they all stared at it still, holding their breath.

Eric held Anna close to his chest, protectively, and vowed never to leave her side. A few feet away, Nikolai held Alix as well.

Suddenly, Lexei let out a choking sound as his heart abruptly constricted, and a wave of shock rippled through his system. His wings shrank back into his body with the sound of an electric zap, claws retracting into his fingers, fangs back into his mouth. He closed his eyes as this all occurred, paralyzed with the intensity of what was happening.

On the far side of the clearing, Holly watched Lexei.

Alix turned to her youngest child and held him as he fought the change, cradling his head in her arms, leaning close and kissing him. "Do not fight it, my darling. Let go."

Lexei groaned in pain, and Anna reached out and held his other side as Lexei fell back onto the ground. Nikolai reached around and put his palm on his son's torso, lending his love to him as the change ran through Lexei's body.

It took about three minutes, but seemed much longer. They knew it hurt. Lexei's hair stood on end on his scalp. His arms and legs shivered uncontrollably from the shock. He closed his eyes and tilted his head back in his mother's arms.

"What's happening?" Eric asked in a hushed tone. They didn't have time to answer him.

As Lexei finally relaxed, Anna, Alix and Holly began to go through the same violent change, falling to the ground, their bodies contorted in the pain of transformation. Nikolai held Alix close, and Eric held Anna, as they endured the same convulsions Lexei had just gone through.

Lexei saw Holly writhing in the grass, alone, groaning as her body shook with violent tremors, and he struggled to his feet, making his way over to her. Then, sitting beside her on the grass, he held her as she endured the change he'd just undergone.

Panic roared in Eric's ears as he held Anna, watching her and wondering what was happening. Tears filled his eyes as he watched her go through the agonizing metamorphosis, and his eyes briefly flashed to where Nikolai held Alix, and farther on to where Lexei held the little girl.

It's been said that it hurts more to watch a loved one go through pain, than to go through it yourself, and Eric was realizing how very true this was. His arms around Anna, he kissed her forehead as her eyes rolled back into her head. He waited, hoping it would be over soon, as it had been for Lexei.

After many minutes, Anna's spasms subsided, Alix fell quiet, and Holly stopped writhing. Their breathing became regular, and they opened their eyes. All was calm. For about 20 seconds. Then Nikolai began writhing, his head flung back. "Oh, God!" He cried. This time Alix held him, rubbing his back as the convulsions shook him.

When at last they subsided, he and the others stood quietly in the clearing. A light drizzle began to fall from the sky, and flickering magic rose from the clearing where so much had just happened. The Romanovs were grinning from ear to ear. Eric was kissing Anna. Lexei was speaking with Holly in quiet tones, both of them smiling. The clearing held only humans, no vampires.

✦✦✦✦✦

EPILOGUE

Later, the family would learn to laugh all the time, but for now it was just smiles as they all made their way out of the park and down to the town. They walked along, holding each other, feeling in a daze, everyone but Eric. He led the way, the others following with silly grins on their faces. Eric's wounds had almost completely healed as Rasputin had died, the magic reversing itself, but he was still very sore.

Eric started off toward home, but Anna had a different idea.

"Wait."

They all stopped and looked expectantly at her. Anna was looking farther on, a block away, where the twinkling purple lights of Lestat's coffee house winked at them. She looked around her at the other storefronts, their window all decorated for Christmas. In the distance, the lights of the college glistened.

"I want to drink a hot cocoa. I want to taste it without getting sick," Anna said softly. Smiling, Eric hugged her and led the family into the warm coffee shop, an island of light in the crisp, late-night air. The bell tinkled merrily as they all entered. Bob looked up and grinned at the procession, rubbing his hands in anticipation of some serious hot winter drink-making.

"Bob, six hot cocoas please, for me and my family," Eric ordered, smiling broadly.

"Wait." Lexei dug in his jacket pocket, hand emerging holding a wrinkled pod. "A cup of extra hot water," he gestured to the pod, "I need to make this into tea."

Eric looked grateful. His sides ached and the dragon's medicinal tea would really hit the spot. He smiled at Lexei, who put an arm around him.

The pod was soon steeping, and Eric sipped his first taste of the magic tea. "Mmm, this is wonderful."

"We can carry that, if you let me know the source," said Bob behind the counter.

"Um..." Eric smiled, "I don't think the source is available anymore."

Laughing, they all sat down in the corner booth and drank hot cocoa, some, for the first time in over a hundred years. They stayed a long time, enjoying the experience. Even Holly.

Lexei bent his head to hers, "You okay?"

"Yes," she said shyly. "More than okay. But please stay with me."

"I will, don't worry."

The next day, they were gathered in the living room of the Mercer Island home. Nikolai looked comfortable and warm, dressed in blue jeans and a warm sweater, his beard making him look like Saint Nicholas himself. Next to him sat Alix, her head on his shoulder.

Lexei and Holly sat on the other couch, and Eric and Anna sat cross-legged on the floor. A roaring fire crackled in the fireplace, and outside, the rain pounded on the windows, unable to get in. The warm glow of table lamps provided a cozy light for the family. Explanations were being exchanged.

"You know, you freaked Gypsy and me out when you showed up at the door last night," Lexei laughed, petting the cat on his lap. "The storm made the electricity go out just as you began knocking."

Nikolai laughed, "Sorry about that. It took forever to find you, you know. I wasn't even sure I had the right house. The vibes were faint."

"How *did* you find them, sir?" Eric asked.

"Please, son. Call me Nick," Nikolai smiled. "I know the magical signature my family sheds out, well, shed out until last night," his eyes twinkled. "But I was traveling from New York, and it is a long way to Seattle from New York. A lot of land to search."

"We came here trying to get as far away from Rasputin as possible," Alix said, smiling.

"And that was very smart, my sweet," Nick patted his wife's hand.

"They told me you were ... uh, well ..." Eric's voice trailed off.

"Dead?" Nick asked, eyebrow raised.

"Well, yes. Sir." Eric smiled.

"I was, nearly. When I found where Rasputin was holding my daughter," he winked at Anna, "and surprised him, and she got away, we fought. We fought a fight to the death."

"Father, I am so sorry I left you," Anna said.

"Now, now, Anya. I wanted you to get away. I needed for you to flee." Nick took a deep breath. "It would have gone much worse if you hadn't."

"I thought ... I heard ..." Anna trailed off.

"Oh, trust me, I heard it too. The sound of flesh ripping. It panicked me like nothing else." Nick looked off into space, haunted memories flickering before his eyes. Looking up again, he continued. "But Rasputin was clumsy. When he tried to rip my head from my body, he didn't quite succeed.

I hung on, and the left side of my neck muscles did not all rip. He was able to rip five out of the six arteries, but the last one, embedded in the muscles on my left side," here Nick bent his head and indicated the left side of his neck. "He didn't rip this last one."

"My god," Lexei said. Anna gasped and put her face in her hands, Eric's arm around her.

"Well, he fled. Blood was everywhere, and I was left lying on the floor in that room. For a long time. When I was finally able to drag myself from there, I hid in shadows and basements, and stayed as still and quiet as I could as my neck healed."

Eric's jaw had dropped open. Nick winked at him, smiling.

Lexei turned to Holly. "Tell us your story, Holly."

The shy girl smiled, and spoke quietly. "My friends and I were in an alley getting high, and three vampires attacked us. I think one was named Emil. I blacked out and woke up transformed. I was so confused. And hungry."

Alix, Lexei and Anna nodded to each other. "We've had dealings with that gang."

Eric sat forward, "Was that the bunch that attacked me in the graveyard?"

"Yes. They were Rasputin's thugs," Anna said.

"I hunted and learned as fast as I could," said Holly. "I was hiding in the park for the last week, and felt your presence last night, so I went to see."

Lexei turned to his mother and father. "Holly was a runaway. I think we should help her, after what's she's been through."

"That would make me happy," Eric smiled. Looking at Holly, he continued, "Young lady, you gave Jinx and me quite a start that night."

Holly smiled, ducking her head. "I was curious," she giggled.

"Well, wait until you walk in the front door – he'll be all over you I imagine," Eric said, watching her petting Gypsy. He sighed and groaned, shifting in his seat. His wounds still ached, though the tuber paste from Zrandengthalull had healed them almost completely in a few short hours. He turned to Anna and whispered. Smiling, she rose off the couch, pulling Eric after her.

Eric looked at Anna, feeling a surge of love as he studied her. He leaned over and softly kissed her rosy cheek, and smiling, they left on a lover's stroll.

⊷⊷⊷⋙⧉⧉⧉⋘⊶⊶⊶

ABOUT THE AUTHOR

Samaire Provost is a novelist and the founding editor of Black Raven Books. Her passion for creating stories is boundless. A writer by day and a reader by night, she is loath to discuss herself in the third person, but can be persuaded to do so from time to time. Owned by a cat named Tyrion, she can be found on Twitter here: @samaireherself

Made in the
USA
Columbia, SC